Mr. 365

Ruth Clampett

Mr. 365

Photography by David Johnston
Design Jada D'Lee

The gorgeous man on the cover is Christopher McDaniel

Betty, the delightful dog, was treated with love

and respect during the photo shoot.

Also by Ruth Clampett:

Animate Me

To Alex
My brilliant, badass, buttercup
My constant reminder
To live it large
'Cause this ain't no dress rehearsal

I love those times we tumble
Over each other's crazy thoughts
Laughing like loons

And the quiet moments
When you see me
As the person I one day hope to be
♥

Mr.
365

Chapter One

In the story meeting room at True Blue Entertainment's offices

"Okay, who has an idea? And not a crappy idea, I only want good ones," Rachel asks, clapping her hands together.

"Naturally," says Paul as he pulls on Lucy's ponytail.

She turns and swats at him. "Pay attention," she hisses. She sits up straight again and gives Rachel her full attention.

The bright L.A. sun pours in the large windows, making the muted colors of the standard office meeting room a little less dull.

"Do you ever worry that every kind of reality show has already been done?" Phillip asks philosophically as he leans back in his chair. "Dark thoughts like this keep me up at night, people." He pushes his glasses up on top of his head, sweeping his long bangs off his forehead. With his *Brave New World* T-shirt and jeans he looks like an ex-English teacher turned TV writer, which is exactly what he is.

"There's always a new idea," says Lucy, who ironically hasn't had a solid idea in two years. She's managed to hold onto her job by being a team player and eager to help with any project, even when it doesn't involve writing.

"We could mix ideas, like fat people who hoard, or people who lead secret lives online at night and coupon shop by day," Phillip suggests.

"Can I ask why the other meeting rooms at this highbrow studio have coffee and snacks and ours never does?" Paul gestures to the room's built-in hospitality bar with a Formica countertop, instead of the granite they had at his last job. He glances at the sofas and chairs in their sitting area.

It's all furniture pretending to be high design but actually falls short, not too dissimilar to how True Blue falls in the reality-show food chain. Still, it's a good gig and, best of all, it's close to his home in West Hollywood.

"Sorry to tell you this, Paul, but True Blue Entertainment isn't actually highbrow." Rachel lifts her Coffee Bean & Tea Leaf beverage she purchased on the way to work because she can't drink the swill they serve in the breakroom.

"You're right. It's lowbrow," Paul says in between coughs, "But it's a job."

Ignoring the digression, Phillip continues on. "What if we get a bunch of former child stars with fetishes to all live in a house together? I'm sure those messed up kids all have fetishes." Phillip's known for his weird ideas, several of which have made successful series.

"I know! How about people who have won the lottery and are addicted to porn," Lucy says enthusiastically.

"Reel it in, guys, reel it in." Rachel warns.

"What about extremists being interviewed by people who despise their particular type of extremism, only they don't know it?" asks Paul.

Rachel raises her eyebrows as if this idea is worth considering. "Do you mean something like Christiane Amanpour interviewing Honey Boo Boo's family?"

Paul nods excitedly. "Yes, not like you'd ever get Amanpour, but that's the general idea."

"Hmmm, could be interesting… And the subject would be unaware of the conflict?"

"Exactly."

"We'll look through our file of stories we passed on. With this new angle, they might be worth pursuing." Lucy studies the bookcase and pulls out a binder. She's only a few pages in when she points to a picture on a page. "What about that guy Will who celebrates Christmas 365 days a year?"

Rachel leans forward. "Oh, yeah, Steph in Procurement's second cousin. She said he gives gifts or does something Christmasy every day of the year. Part of his house is decorated for the holidays year round."

"He must be a complete nutcase." Paul observes.

"Or he hates setting that shit up and then taking it down, and does it for his wife. I know I sure do," says Phillip.

"Oh, it's way past that. It's not like some sloth-like ass who leaves their Christmas tree up until April because they're too lazy to deal with it. This is a guy who does this stuff intentionally." Lucy studies his bio. "And he's surprisingly good-looking."

Rachel examines the picture more closely. "He sure is, not like the lookers we usually get with this nut-bag crowd, that's for sure. That could add to the market appeal."

"Does he dress his children like elves?" Paul asks.

Lucy checks the spec sheet. "Steph said he's single." She rolls her eyes. "I'm not surprised. I don't know many women who'd put up with that."

Paul raises his hand. "I want to work on this one. I have some ideas for the interview."

Lucy shakes her head. "I don't know. You'll be too hard on the poor guy. He won't know what hit him."

"We'll get a compassionate producer. How about Sophia? She just moved over from our cooking shows. I remember when we talked she said she's a pushover for holiday stuff and loves sweet stories," says Rachel.

"This won't be so sweet when I'm done with it, but you may be right. Sophia can win him over so that he won't know what hit him. Since she's new to this format we can control her and how much she knows from the beginning," Paul adds.

"She told me at the Christmas party that she fancies herself to one day be a documentary filmmaker. I think she's in severe denial as to the purpose of reality TV in the big crock pot of entertainment." Lucy snickers.

"That's another reason why she's perfect for this. She'll be focused on making the footage meaningful and will convince this Will guy of her lofty ideas, while we focus on getting what we really need," Paul says with a grin.

"Good, good... one segment down," Rachel says, making notes in her book. "What else do you have in that binder, Lucy? We need two more segment ideas, and I'm not bringing lunch in until we've got them nailed."

Chapter Two
Sophia

Feeling energized, I tap my pen on the tabletop as the phone rings. After years of working on cooking shows, it's exciting to work on something different and less predictable. My stomach flip flops when I think about all I have to learn producing human-interest stories but I'm hopeful it's a step closer to my documentary roots than shows on braised broccoli and nacho cheese delights.

When we talked about working together, the writer/director Paul assured me Will Saunders was delighted to be part of the show, but I want to find out for myself. I've been fooled before. People in this industry will do anything, absolutely anything for ratings and getting a show sold.

"Hello?"

"Hi there, is this William Saunders?"

"Yes," he replies.

"I'm Sophia Worthy and I'm a producer for True Blue Entertainment. I want to talk to you about being part of our reality show on people with interesting hobbies."

He lets out a frustrated huff. "Did you get my information from my overly ambitious cousin, Steph? Because I'm *really* not interested in being on a show. I've told her this."

He's not interested? That's certainly an annoying turn of events, but I'm not giving up so easily.

"Really, Mr. Saunders? Can I call you Will?"

"Sure, most people do."

"Okay, Will… if you don't mind my asking, why aren't you interested?"

"Well, Steph tried to talk me into it. She said it would be a way to promote my work with kids... but I doubt it."

"Yes, my notes show that you allow your house to be used for fundraisers and tours to gather hundreds of toys for Toys for Tots. I read you also let teachers bring underprivileged kids through in December."

"Yes."

"And you give gifts throughout the year to the homeless."

"I do, but..." He sounds uncomfortable with how much I know.

I jump right in. "Well, Steph's right. People often underestimate the benefits this type of exposure can bring to their endeavors."

"But Sophia... I can call you that, right?"

"Of course."

"I enjoy what I do, but I really don't want to be judged for it from the world in general. I have enough trouble from my neighbors."

"I can understand that." This guy sounds sharper than I expected, so I decide to try another tactic. "But what if you weren't allowed to do this anymore? I learned about the trouble with your neighbors, the Hoffmeyers, and how they're trying to stop you."

"So you already know about crazy Fred and his looney family?" He sounds impressed but still uncomfortable with the invasiveness of my research. "I wish they'd move back to the trailer park, but for now their life's ambition is to make me suffer for wanting to give some kids a happier holiday."

"Have you considered that we could make Fred look really bad and help raise public awareness of your work?"

He considers the idea. "You really think that would work?"

"You'd be amazed what this type of positive exposure can do." I cross my fingers and hope I'm right.

"Okay. But how can I be assured it will be positive? These shows portray someone like me as a nutty goof for entertainment."

"That isn't our intention," I say, hoping he can hear the sincerity in my voice.

"How do I know that?"

"You'll just have to trust me."

"You want me to trust *you*? I don't even know you."

"But you could," I say politely. "I'll tell you what, I see you live on the east side of Windsor Square. I'm not far from there. Let's meet for coffee tomorrow and just talk about it."

"I don't know."

"Please, Will?" I ask softly as I turn on the charm, hoping his resolve crumbles. "Please?"

"Okay," he says with a quiet laugh.

Over the last few years I've come to the conclusion that being a producer is akin to being a magician without a top hat and magic wand. Somehow you have to take an idea and actualize it, convincing your team, and most critically a potential subject like Will, that magic is possible. We can pull the rabbit out of our hat while making something out of what at times can be a misfit jumble. With each new project I imagine something grand. Maybe Will's story will be a standout—that something grand that changes my course and bolsters my career.

I say goodbye to Will, and hang up satisfied. Victory is within my reach.

As I open the door to the King's Road café, I catch my reflection in the full-length mirror leaning against the entry wall. I stop for a moment to check myself. As I straighten my belt, I twist sideways noting that the Pilates classes I've been doing have paid off. My legs look especially long, and my curves are toned the way I like them.

I smooth my long auburn hair down and check my lipstick. People tell me I'm pretty with my large green eyes, full lips and fair skin but I just think I grew into my looks. When I was younger all I wanted was straight blonde hair and a dark tan but that would never be. I shrug and turn from the mirror before walking further into the café to find Will.

I try to imagine what Will's personality will be like. I figure he's an oddball, perhaps with eccentric tendencies. I shouldn't judge him too quickly on his outward appearance. Just because he really, *really* loves Christmas doesn't mean he has to be a total freak. He may not be as strange as I imagine.

I scan the café and notice several people sitting alone. Unfortunately, the photo Lucy sent over was rather fuzzy, so I can't be sure I'll recognize

Will. I spot an effeminate middle-aged man wearing a bow tie and reading a magazine. I grin. That must be my guy.

I approach his table with a big smile on my face. "Will?"

He looks up, confused.

"Hi, I'm Sophia."

He tips his head and closes his magazine. "I'm sorry—"

"Excuse me," a young dark-haired guy a few tables away calls out. "Are you Sophia?"

I glance over to see that the guy calling out to me is a serious looker. I have trouble hiding my shock. There's just no way this is Will. I look back at bow-tie guy and then over at the gorgeous hunk, confused.

He taps his chest. "Sophia, it's me, Will."

My cheeks burning, I apologize to bow-tie guy for disturbing him. He shrugs and returns to his design magazine. As I walk to Will's table he's appraising me with his striking eyes and it makes me blush.

I'm glad I wore something flattering. My fitted blue dress accents my figure while the tailoring and fabric give it a professional look. I try not to ogle him as he stands to greet me, his hand extended.

"Hi, Sophia, I'm Will."

I smile as we shake hands. "So I've gathered. It's great to meet you, Will. Thanks for coming." My head's spinning with confusion. This can't be the Christmas guy. Not only is he handsome, but there's a spark in his dark blue eyes that indicates he's the furthest thing from goofy. *Seriously.* If they lined up the most appealing guys in his age group on a reality show contest, he would win the grand supreme title.

I glance around the café to make sure there are no hidden cameras. I wouldn't put it past my team to put me on one of those reality shows where they do fake setups to humiliate the subject. I approach my chair when I see no sign of impropriety.

He studies me as he pulls my chair out. I'd love to know what he's thinking since my instincts tell me it's good.

After we smile at each other, he glances at the café counter. "What can I get you?"

"Iced tea would be great. Passion-flavored tea is my favorite, if they have it, but please, let me take care of this. I asked you to meet me." I pull out my wallet.

He holds up his hand to stop me. "This is my treat."

As he approaches the counter, I get my bearings, still not convinced this isn't a mistake. This handsome and rugged man is the Christmas guy from the file? It just can't be. The girl behind the counter is shamelessly flirting with him as he lingers at the sweets case.

He's tall with broad shoulders and a solid build. His worn jeans hang low on his hips. *Is that a tattoo peeking out under his shirt sleeve? Good lord.* I'm all fired up, and I fan myself while his back is turned toward me.

As he moves back to our table, the light from the window casts his face in perfectly balanced planes and structure and reminds me of a marble bust I once studied in the Uffizi Museum in Florence. The ease with which he carries himself and his natural grace add to the effect. I imagine in another place and time he could have modeled for Horst or Irving Penn, classic photographers, who would've photographed him in black and white, all elegance, highlight, and shadows. The fact that he does charity work makes him a gentleman in my eyes, despite his outward appearance. I'm most definitely intrigued.

When he rejoins me he hands me the iced tea, and then rests a little box embellished with the shop's label on the table and slowly slides it over to me.

"What's this?"

"A little something for you. I saw them and thought you might like them." His eyes are bright. "Go on now. Open it."

I smile, realizing I've just received my first gift from the Christmas guy. I carefully lift the lid. Three little French macaroons are nestled in wax paper, each a different color.

He watches me expectantly. "The pink one is strawberry, the yellow lemon, and the orange one passion fruit."

"How did you know I loved macaroons?" I ask.

"Just a guess. They're kind of fancy… like you."

"Fancy? I'm not fancy!" I laugh.

He shrugs. "If you say so." But he grins as if he knows better.

"Which should we try first?" I ask.

"Oh, they're all for you."

I lift the passion fruit carefully out of the box and nibble on the edge. "Mmm, it's so good," I say, closing my eyes. When I open them, he's watching me so I slowly run my tongue across my bottom lip, catching the stray crumbs.

I'm flirting with him and I really should know better since technically I'm working.

"What?"

"You're different than I expected," he says.

"Really? How? And don't say fancy."

"Softer, prettier." He tilts his head to the side. "You seem all right."

"You sound surprised about that. What did you expect, an Amazonian woman with a cross bow prepared to hunt you down?"

He laughs. "No but that's a great image. My limited experience with the media is that they're rough around the edges"—his expression hardens—"and very pushy."

"I'm sorry that's been your experience. I'm not like that," I say softly.

"I sensed that when we talked. It's the only reason I agreed to meet you. I had a feeling. I mean you were a little pushy, but not too much."

I laugh and he grins.

"Well as long as I wasn't *too* pushy! Besides, if you keep spoiling me with macaroons I may very well lose my edge completely."

I hold out the yellow macaroon to him. "Why don't you try this? It's heavenly."

"No, no… they're for you. Besides, I'm good with my coffee."

"Okay, but you're missing out," I say, taking another bite.

"Not really. It's sweeter watching you enjoy it," he says with a quiet smile.

"You aren't quite what I expected either," I admit.

"How so? Wait… If you researched me, you saw the *Larchmont Chronicle* article. I bet you thought I'd be wearing the Christmas tree sweater, right?"

"Yeah, how did you know?"

"That woman pushed me unrelentingly until I agreed to wear it for one photo. I did it just to shut her up. Of course that's the photo they used for the story. I'll never be that stupid again."

"Did the sweater really light up?"

"Yeah, it had a battery pack and everything. You could make the lights blink together like a strobe light or sporadically. It was idiotic. I'm still mad for agreeing to wear that thing but the story was just for our local paper. I thought what's the harm, but I forgot that everything lives forever on Google."

I smile. "Yes, it does."

"So I was right… you assumed I was a super freak."

"Not a super freak… just passionate about your interests." I stretch the truth to keep from hurting his feelings. I like this guy and have a strong desire to win him over.

"Well I can't argue with that. I'm most definitely passionate about my interests."

"And because I think you're interesting, I'm sure other people would find you interesting too," I say.

"I don't care who besides you in this equation finds me interesting." He gives me a coy look.

No one besides me? Is he flirting too? I try to narrow my focus, or I'll never convince him.

"We all have our things, Will, our stories, our passions that make each of us unique. Yours is especially unique, and I'd love to have the chance to tell it to the world."

"Careful, you are making reality TV sound too good to be true."

"I don't know about that. Why can't the good stuff be true? I was a documentary film major in college. There's such a challenge in documentaries to portray the subject accurately, with dignity, and be entertaining in a compelling way. I carry those ideals into my TV work."

"I bet though in your current field you are more the exception than the rule."

I shrug. "Maybe. I can only be accountable for my own work. I went to a retrospective of Haskell Wexler's work last weekend. Are you familiar with him?"

Will shakes his head.

"He's one of most highly regarded documentary filmmakers in history. There's so much truth and beauty in his work it takes my breath away."

He folds his arms over his chest and smiles. Perhaps he came into this meeting thinking I was a pleasant but tacky producer. Hopefully I've convinced him I'm anything but, and I push some more.

"Will, wouldn't it be great to show on film the beauty and soul of your holiday masterpiece? People would love your story and why you do what you do."

"Really," he says as if he doesn't believe me. "You're not just charming me?"

"Yes, I promise. I'd truly love to understand more of what motivates you."

He lifts his coffee nestled between his two hands. I sense he's not going to spill out his secrets if I bat my eyelashes. No, he's going to be a challenging nut to crack, but truly understanding our subjects is one of my strengths.

Whoever Will appears to be isn't at all what I expected. I've never been more curious to figure someone out. He's a puzzle of perfect pieces that don't fit together.

He finally speaks up. "So this is going to sound corny, but I think you may understand. There's something out there… a kind of magic or whatever… it's different things for different people, maybe a great movie or concert, but whatever it is can distract you from the rough stuff in life. So, if it's there… why wouldn't we surround ourselves with it if we could? Why wouldn't we want it always around?"

Is this guy for real? I sense this idea is true for some part of him, but there's much more to what he does than he's admitting. I'm more determined than ever to figure out why.

"Do you understand?" he asks, looking tentative but hopeful.

"I do," I say and he relaxes.

I take a long sip of tea, and I wonder what kind of hardship could've been in Will's life to inspire him to want every day to be Christmas. What's he hiding? It pulls at my heart, and I find strength in his expression. Whatever it is or was, he appears to have a handle on it. *Not every reality show candidate has to be broken, do they?*

"What are you thinking?" Will asks.

"I appreciate your motivation," I say thoughtfully even if it's only part of my reaction to what he shared.

He chuckles. "Well that right there puts you way ahead of the crowd."

I nibble off the edge of the macaroon before asking, "So, will you show me your house? Steph said you've already started setting up the front rooms for this holiday season."

"Yeah, I like to spread out the setting up and tearing down. I enjoy it more that way."

He studies me for a minute and then smiles. "So, you want to come by just to see it? I'm not promising anything. Are you okay with that?"

"Okay… just to see it. I'll share a secret with you."

He leans forward, a playful smile on his face. "Yes?"

"I'm a Christmas junkie. Honestly. I've collected ornaments and Santa figurines since I was twelve. I think I was an elf in a past life." I blush with the admission. "I have a storage unit because I don't have enough room in my apartment for all of it."

He leans all the way back in his chair and takes a deep breath. Something in his eyes gives me hope that I'll have a chance to work with him.

"I promise, Sophia, you won't be disappointed."

Chapter Three

"Oh my!" My mouth drops open and I'm filled with childlike wonder as Will leads me into his house. "I mean wow!" Clearly the file didn't do it justice. The other extreme holiday people are lightweights compared to Will. *What's up with this guy?*

He laughs. He must be used to big reactions by now, and by his big grin I can see that my response delights him. He nods slowly as he surveys the room. "Well, I guess you could say that I don't do anything halfway."

"No, you don't. I knew the moment I saw the enchanting architecture outside that it would be special inside too, but this is over the top!" I scan the foyer of the house. Between the high-coved ceiling, elaborately carved woodwork and cascading strands of twinkle lights, I know this isn't the average home.

The huge Christmas tree in the entryway is covered with miniature tin toys and vintage figures. It's like Willy Wonka put on Christmas. "Is this the kids' tree I read about? Do you still hand out ornaments to the kids after their visit?"

He laughs. "Yeah, great idea right? Until they fight over which ornament they get."

"No, really?" I ask, horrified. Why would this guy want to deal with a bunch of annoying rude kids?

He shakes his head. "Kids can be ruthless. I once saw a little boy so pissed off that his friend got the last Batman ornament he snapped the head off his friend's ornament and threw it in the bushes."

"So much for holiday spirit."

"It's okay. The good kids always outnumber the mean ones. I was kind of a jerk when I was little, so I get it."

I point up to the dome. "And what are all those wrapped gifts hanging from the ceiling? Are they floating? How's that happening?"

"They're suspended on a very fine filament that washes out in the theatrical lighting."

"Tricky." He's super high tech. I'm impressed.

He grins. "Are you ready for more?"

I instinctively grab onto his arm and lean into him. "Yes, please."

He pulls me closer.

"Where are you taking me?" I ask with a flirty smile.

"You'll see." He guides me forward, leading me into his living room—the winter wonderland.

"Wow!" Other than a path of hardwood floor cutting through the room, the entire room is white with silver accents. White flocked trees are scattered throughout the room and covered with white twinkly lights and silver ornaments. Projections of clouds slowly drifting across the ceiling and snow lightly falling down the wall create an effect that is ethereal, almost heavenly.

"This is stunning. You let kids into this room?" I ask, studying the very white carpet. I have to imagine he has to replace this rug frequently.

"They're only allowed to stand on the hardwood floor when they tour. It's easier if they aren't touching everything. We had a kid hide under a tree once, and when the group leader finally realized he was missing and found him, he refused to come out. We changed the rules after that."

"Oh, my." These kids sound worse by the minute. I can't imagine having the patience. *What is he, some kind of saint?*

"So, no hiding under the tree, okay? I've got my eye on you." He teases.

I give him a sideways glance and coy smile. "I bet you do."

"What's this?" I ask, walking toward a long table against one of the walls. A collection of snow globes are arranged on the table, and they're all snowing as if they each were just shaken. "How are they continually snowing like that?"

He grins mischievously. "Trade secret. I'm a scenic guy at a studio, mainly building sets, and I work with a lot of lighting and special effects guys. We have all kinds of tricks up our sleeves." He leads me to the couch and when we sit down, I take it all in.

"My file says you work at Burbank Central Studio?" I ask.

"Yeah, I'm sure you can blame this house being over the top on that. My grandparents were big on Christmas but this really all started on a grand scale after I worked on a film set during a Christmas themed shoot. It was an independent film and they ran out of money. So instead of some of my pay, they gave me a lot of the scenery and special effects stuff. Plus the guys I work with are always coming up with new ideas, and they find new effects and props. We help each other. One of them does a huge haunted house every Halloween and I help him with that."

I take a fresh look at the room, realizing it all makes sense now. The rooms have a movie set feel, cleverly staged and dramatic. It goes well beyond regular decorating; this house is a stage for his ideas.

"It's interesting you're a scenic craftsman. I would've never guessed until I saw the house." I'm intrigued.

"You sound surprised. What did you imagine I did?" he asks.

"Well, you don't fit the builder types I've hired, for sure."

"And that would be?"

I fidget for a moment, as he watches me.

"I don't know." I blush as I look down. "Rather forgettable. Not"—I wave at his worn jeans and fitted T-shirt—"hunky."

He grins victoriously. "Hunky? You think I'm hunky?"

"Well, for a builder kind of guy."

"I see, so there's a qualifier."

I shake my head.

"What?" he asks.

"I'm in such trouble." I say, thinking out loud as I twist a strand of hair around my finger.

"Really? And why's that?"

"Because I'm being so inappropriate. I'm supposed to be convincing you to be on the show, not—"

"Flirting with me?"

"Oh, God," I whisper. "I'm that obvious?" Of course he's right, but who wants to be reminded that they have no subtlety. I'm supposed to be a professional, after all, not some girl at a bar.

"I'm pretty sure," he says as he stands and extends his hand to me with a wink. "Please don't stop on my account. I like it. Here, let me show you more."

I smooth my slacks nervously and take his hand as I stand. "By all means, show me more."

As we enter the next room he has a faraway look in his eyes. He tucks his hands in his back pockets and smiles. "Here we have *under the sea*." The walls of this room are an iridescent aqua with a glittery tree of the same color covered with ornaments of mermaids, seashells and sea horses. "This room stays decorated year round."

"Ooooo! I love this!" I exclaim, a little confused. Maybe he's gay after all. I mean glitter and mermaids? I love it, but what kind of guy does this?

Will nods. "Most girls love this room. It's genetic or something. The girls I've met think the deep sea is romantic and swoony. If you've ever been scuba diving, you'd know that isn't the case. It's amazing but nothing like this."

"So then, what inspired you to do a romantic under-the-sea theme?"

"Well it started out much differently. When I was, little my older brother and I used to play deep-sea diver games, looking for sunken treasure. He got the idea from a book he read."

I point to a small treasure chest at the base of the tree spilling over with gold coins. "So, that explains the treasure chest."

"Yes, and when I first themed this room it was much more boy oriented. I even had some sea creature models I got from the special effect guys. My brother would have loved that."

I note the use of past tense. Was this room done in his memory?

"Then later, I had a girlfriend who loved mermaids. I think she believed she was a mermaid in a past life. She's the one who girlified the room with all the glitter and girl stuff. Andrew would not have been amused," he says, shaking his head. "He had a No Girls Allowed sign on his bedroom door."

Hmm... girlfriend. He must not be gay after all. Trying to figure this guy out is wearing me out. I decide not to ask him more about his brother right now.

"So, what's this room anyway? Was it the dining room?" I ask, changing the direction of the conversation.

"Yes, but I eat in the kitchen. I'm not really one for dinner parties or anything. Speaking of which, do you want to see the kitchen? I have to warn you though, Romeo's in there. I'm not sure if he can be around you."

My eyes get wide. "Around me? I think I'm pretty easy to get along with." I try to imagine what type of person couldn't tolerate me.

"It's not that. Well, you'll understand." He approaches the Dutch door into his kitchen. The bottom panel is closed, and something is frantically scratching it.

I grin with relief. "Romeo's a dog. I love dogs! What are you worried about? Does he bite or something?"

"Not exactly. He's not a biter. He has other issues." Will slowly pulls open the half door. "Sophia, meet Romeo."

He's really cute and looks like a mutt terrier similar to Tramp from the Disney movie, *Lady and the Tramp*. I lean down to let the little dog sniff my hand, but he dodges it, goes straight for my leg, and humps it wildly. How annoying. I shake my leg, but he's steadfast.

"Whoa, that was some kind of record!" Will exclaims while peeling Romeo off my leg. "He usually takes a couple of minutes or so to start up, so I wasn't prepared to head him off at the pass. Sorry about that. I guess you're especially appealing, and not just to the human species."

"Lucky me!"

He turns to Romeo. "Dude, you have no class. You didn't even buy her a drink first."

"Very funny, a drink? You think I'm *that* easy," I say with my hands on my hips.

"I didn't mean *that*, just that if *he* were human that's what *he* would've tried with a woman as beautiful as you. What can I say about the little guy… he's insatiable. You should see him at the dog park."

I make a note of his compliment before saying, "No thanks, I can already imagine."

"That's how he gets his name. He loves the women."

"I can see that. He's got quite the winning personality."

"He sure does." Will laughs, sets Romeo outside the kitchen, and closes the door.

"Why don't you do your reality show about little dude instead? He loves being in front of a camera."

"We'll leave the dogs humping to Animal Planet, thanks." I look at my watch. "Oh no! I'm late!"

"Something wrong?" he asks.

"Yes, I was supposed to be back at the production offices for a meeting already."

His eyes lose their gleam and the corners of his mouth turn down. "Okay. Let me walk you out."

By the time he gets Romeo back into the kitchen and we get to his front door, I'm disappointed to be leaving.

"I didn't get to see everything, did I?"

He shakes his head and smiles. "Nope."

I lightly touch his arm, and that small gesture sparks something in his expression. "I'd like to come back. Could I?"

"Just to see the house, or me too." He narrows his eyes playfully.

"Well, I'd see you if I were going to see your house, wouldn't I?"

"That's not what I mean. I don't care about the show, but I'd like to see you again."

"Really?" I ask, blushing.

"Most definitely." The intensity in his expression is unnerving. "Come for dinner tomorrow night."

I look up, surprised at his directness. "I could bring takeout," I say, knowing full well I shouldn't agree to something so date-like.

What is wrong with me? Do I have no resistance to a handsome man who's trying to charm me? Am I forgetting he's over the top with this Christmas stuff and not too dissimilar from the obsessive hoarders that the guy in the office next to me works with?

He flashes the killer smile again, and my resistance sags like an un-plugged inflatable yard Santa.

"Actually, I'd love to cook for you. I'm pretty good, and you won't have to bring anything." He tilts his head and smiles. "Say yes."

I pause, looking in his eyes, and then at the tall tree covered in tiny lights in the foyer. *Damn, you crazy irresistible Christmas hunk.*

"Say yes," he repeats softly.

"And you promise we can talk about the show?" I ask, not completely off my game.

He holds up his two fingers pressed together. "Boy Scouts honor." He steps to the tree in the foyer, apparently looking for something. He pulls out a vintage ornament of Glinda the Good Witch from *the Wizard of Oz*. He returns and slips the ornament into my bag.

"Hey, why'd you do that?"

"She's the good witch. She'll make sure you make your way back here... back here to me." He grins.

I rest my hand on my purse, wondering what other wizardry treats Will has in mind.

Back at the office I slide into the meeting without drawing too much attention to myself. Luckily it started late so I didn't miss much. Afterward I corner Rachel and ask if we can talk for a minute in her office.

"So what's up?" Rachel hands me a bottle of water and eases into the chair next to the couch. "How's the project developing? Have you met with the Christmas guy yet?"

"Yes, as a matter of fact that's what I want to talk to you about. This guy's a puzzle, and I'm not sure how to handle it."

"A puzzle?"

"For one thing, he's got a hard-edged look, in a tough guy sexy way. That shot we had of him in the light-up Christmas sweater was very misleading. He's actually hip... he has at least one tattoo that I know of."

"Really?"

"And he's way too good-looking."

"And he's single? Maybe I should come to your next meeting," Rachel adds.

"Really?" I ask, hiding the apprehension in my voice. I'd forgotten Rachel's single status.

Rachel shrugs. "There are worse things than a gorgeous, hip guy who overdoes the holidays. My last boyfriend made me leave him catalogue pages with items circled for gift ideas."

"How romantic," I say, wrinkling my nose.

"Exactly."

I think of attractive Rachel meeting Will, and I'm surprised how quickly jealousy flares up inside me. "No, coming to our next meeting isn't necessary. Besides he's not boyfriend material. He has to be twisted inside just to do all this crazy stuff. Right? I just want your advice on how to convince him to do the show when he's wary of our intentions."

"It's like dating a new guy; you have to flatter, romance, and seduce him until he wants to do the things you want him to. If he gets distracted enough, he may forget his trepidation. Try building up his ego. Tell him women will be falling all over him."

I resent such a ridiculous strategy. *Besides, would this even work with Will?* Nothing in his behavior suggests he's that kind of guy. Even though we'd just met, I was the only one he wanted to impress.

Maybe I've grown tired of the men I've met lately who never know what they want, or what they're sure of. Will is certain of everything, including his reaction to me. As much as I hate to admit it, I find this incredibly appealing.

I'm suddenly protective of this man who doesn't realize how odd he is with his obsession. "But he thinks we'll make fun of him… make him look the fool."

Rachel shrugs disinterestedly. "Well, then it's your job to make him think we aren't doing that."

"And we aren't, right?"

"No, of course not." Rachel checks her watch and stands. "Hey I just realized I have a meeting with Don. I have to get going, but you know what you need to do, right?"

I sigh and say what Rachel expects to hear. "Flatter, romance and seduce."

"That a girl," Rachel says. "If anyone can do it, it's you."

Chapter Four

When he answers the door, I hold up the ornament dusted with fine glitter.

He grins. "I told you Glinda would get you back to me." He pulls the door open wider. "Come in, come in."

I hand him a bottle of wine. "I was going to bring sparkling water, since this is work related."

"But?"

"That just seemed goofy. So, I brought wine instead. Red okay?"

He takes the bottle. "Perfect. I've got Romeo in the backyard so the kitchen's safe. Come keep me company while I finish up."

I step toward the towering tree in the foyer and pause to hang Glinda on the tree. When I step away, Will rests his hand on my lower back and guides me to the kitchen. I pull a stool up to the center island while he opens and pours the wine.

"How was your day?" he asks.

"Good. I powered through all the boring chores and errands so I'd have plenty of time for fun."

"Sounds good. Do you live alone?"

"Yes." *He doesn't drag his feet, does he?* I imagine where this is leading.

"No boyfriend?"

Well he's certainly direct. "Nope, not right now."

He smiles like a Cheshire cat.

"How about you? Girlfriend?"

"Nope, not right now." He looks me right in the eye, and it's unnerving.

There's a charged pause as I think about the fact that he's single too. We both take a sip of our wine. I glance up at the elaborate molding running along the circumference of the ceiling and the antique light fixtures with their warm glow of light.

"Before I came in, I was marveling at this house. I have a particular passion for architecture. There aren't a lot of gingerbread Victorian's in L.A. How did you ever find this place?"

He lifts his glass in a silent toast. "It was my grandparents. They left it to me."

"Wow, that's amazing. What an incredible house to inherit."

"When I was a boy, I'd spend a month here during the summer, and Gramps and I spent most of our time in his workshop or around the house repairing something. He was always showing me how to fix things. An old place like this requires constant attention. Now I think he was teaching me, knowing one day it would be mine."

"Well, I bet they'd be proud of how you've kept it up."

"I hope so," he admits.

I take a whiff of the spices in the air. "So, what are we having for dinner?"

"Penne with vodka sauce," he says as he stirs the pot. "It's one of my favorites, so I hope you like it. There's salad and grilled chicken as well."

A man who can cook. Even though I shouldn't crush on a potential subject, the odds are not looking good for my restraint. Then I remember the promise I made after I broke up with the last "interesting" but crazy boyfriend. *No more crazies!*

Finished, I push my plate aside. "That was delicious, Will. Thank you."

"Glad you enjoyed it."

"So what's next?" I say, trying to sound focused. I'm not much of a drinker and the second glass of wine has gotten to me a little.

"Whatever you want."

I lean back in my chair. "What's your favorite room?"

"I like them all. But I do have a particular love for the family room since the train set is in there. It's still being set up, but I can show you what's been done so far."

MR. 365

"I'd like that." I notice he's much less affected from the wine than I am. Of course he's tall and muscular, so much bigger than me.

Taking me by the hand, he leads me down the hall and swings open an elaborately carved oak door.

"The main track is set up, let me show you." He picks up the remote control, dims the lights, and presses a series of buttons. A miniature village lights up, complete with street lamps and an ice skating rink. The skating figurines cut circle-eights across the faux icy surface of the rink.

"Wow! This is amazing!" I marvel at the intricate detail of the houses and sculpted people.

He grins. "And only half of it is set up. Steph and her friends take care of the village stuff. I stick with the trains. Speaking of trains, you ready?"

"All aboard!" I say, laughing.

The expression on his face makes him look like a little kid, which is both disturbing and amusing. I remember a segment of a show about grown men with model train hobbies. There are even shops around L.A. that cater to them. They must have coined the term *man-child* for people like Will and these guys.

He pushes another switch on the remote and then another. I hear the flurry of model trains moving around their tracks before they actually come into view.

"Who designed all this?" I ask, amazed at the intricate detail and planning that must've been involved.

"I did," he says proudly, pointing toward the right corner of the room. "My grandfather collected model trains. Some of the cars on that table in the corner belonged to him."

"And you put all this together every year?" I ask.

"Well, I have friends that help with the trains too. But I like doing this stuff. It keeps me out of trouble."

I try to imagine what type of trouble he's referring to.

He shrugs. "I have a lot of pent-up energy and was kind of wild when I was young."

"So, all of this keeps you distracted from your natural inclinations." His bad-boy looks and tattoo make more sense now.

"Yeah, it does."

"Seems like a healthy way to stay distracted. Good for you I say."

29

I examine the setup along the back wall and can feel his gaze as I move away from him.

"Well, I can still get distracted."

I look over my shoulder and smile before focusing on the table again to study the village setup. "My older sister, Emily, has a few of these houses, but nothing like this. She'd love to see what you've done here."

"You're welcome to bring her over."

"Thank you. I wish I could, but Emily and my family live in Portland. Sadly the only way she'll see this room is if you do the show." I flash a bright smile.

He makes a face. "You're smooth."

"Thank you. I'd love to work with you."

"Yeah?" he asks, walking toward me. For a moment I imagine he's going to step close enough to kiss me, but he stops short and just studies me. It unnerves and confuses me how much I wish he'd kiss me. *What's wrong with me?* It must be the wine.

The pause starts to get uncomfortable.

"I'd like a little more wine, you?" he asks, turning toward the hallway.

Am I going to be smart about this or reckless? I spin the roulette wheel in my head and blink as I wait for the ball to land. I catch myself nodding before I make up my mind. *Oh my.* Reckless it is.

"Yes, thanks."

He returns a minute later with an open bottle and clean wine stems. He settles on the couch and pours two glasses.

I sit down and accept the glass, reminding myself to take it slow.

"So tell me more about your family," Will says.

"My dad's a project manager for a distribution company and my mom teaches art at the local high school."

"And they're still married?"

"Yes. They'll always be married. They're like peanut butter and jelly, meant to be together."

Will smiles.

"Besides Emily, I have an older brother, Tim, who's married and a pilot, no kids yet. Then there's Nick, the youngest. He's the most talented but kind of a lost soul. He's still figuring things out."

Will nods with a silent acknowledgment.

My heart hurts thinking about Nick's recent failed stint in rehab. I don't share that with Will, even though part of me thinks he may understand.

I lean back on the soft cushions of the couch and close my eyes for a moment to regroup. When I open them the twinkling lights of the little village and the moving train lift my spirits.

I turn toward Will who appears to be deep in thought. "What about your family?"

Will takes a deep breath and a long sip of wine. I wait patiently.

"My story's a lot less pretty. Things were good when I was little. We were your average family, but then my older brother died in an accident when I was six, and everything fell apart."

For a moment I try to imagine what life would have been like if Emily or Tim had died young, and I feel a surge of sympathy. It's one of those moments where someone gives you a peek inside their window and you realize their inside is even more dark and jumbled than you imagined.

I touch his forearm lightly. "I'm sorry, Will."

"Yeah, it was rough."

His tone suggests it was worse than rough.

"And your parents?"

"We don't talk. They blamed me for what happened, so it's complicated."

They blamed him? My stomach curls into a tight ball. How does a small child survive such judgment? Maybe this Christmas fantasy has new meaning. Perhaps one survives by *not* growing up.

"What about your grandparents? Did you spend a lot of time with them when you were young?" I ask, wondering how they must have felt. I hope someone was nice to this emotionally abandoned little boy.

"Well as I said earlier, I used to spend some of my summers with them after the accident when my parents just couldn't deal. By the time I hit my teens, things were even worse with my parents. So they asked if I wanted to live with them, but I was too far gone and too wrapped up with the wrong people at that point to find my way out."

"So, is that what you referred to as being in trouble?"

"Yeah." He doesn't elaborate. He looks down where my hand still rests on his forearm, and he slides his hand into mine. His hand is warm and strong, and I want to comfort him.

He gazes at me as he slowly rubs his thumb over the top of my hand. "I like having you here. It just feels really nice," he says quietly.

I press my fingers into his palm. "You're really something."

"You are, too."

We sit together holding hands for several minutes, both of us lost in thought. As his thumb traces circles lightly over my hand, I wonder what he really wants from me. I also wonder what I'm willing to give.

I turn back to the Christmas village, and try to remember my place. Why am I compelled to get closer to him when I know it's just going to confuse things for both of us?

"It's getting late. I better go," I finally say, feeling cautious.

"Are you sure you can't stay a little longer?"

I give him a gentle smile. "Yeah, I better not."

"I understand. I want to make sure you're okay to drive. Do you want some coffee or something?" he asks as we stand.

"Yes, that'd probably be a good idea."

As we head down the hall, I stop in my tracks. "We really need to talk about the show. We keep avoiding the main reason I'm here."

"Do we?" He grins as he looks above my head.

"What?" I follow his gaze. "Mistletoe!" I gasp and then laugh, pushing him on the shoulder. "You're so smooth!"

"It's the Christmas house, Sophia. What did you expect? Besides I didn't make you stop and stand under it. You can always step away and break the spell."

I don't take a step, but put my hands on my hips and tilt my head instead. The curious part of me is overstepping the logical side. *Will he really try to kiss me?*

"I think *you* planned this." He teases.

"You're trying to divert me."

"And you're still standing under it." He steps in close and gently combs his fingers through my hair until he's holding the back of my head. I'm stunned with how smooth he is as he slowly pulls me toward him. "A little diversion is nothing compared to what you're doing to me."

When our lips meet, his kiss is soft and gentle at first, but within moments he wraps me up in a passionate kiss. He moves his hand across my back as he kisses my neck.

"Sophia," he whispers in a low voice. "What am I going to do with you?"

I blink rapidly as he holds me. For a moment I'm not sure if I can stand. There's no feeling in my legs since all the feelings have moved to places they shouldn't be. My thundering heart and red cheeks are a clear sign that my libido just got a swift slap in the face. I've never been so awake, yet I'm floating in a hormone-induced stupor.

Holy hell! This Christmas guy can kiss. Really kiss. That kiss should be eligible for a gold medal in the first kiss Olympics.

His hand glides lower on my back and pulls me closer.

I don't know whether to run for the hills or kiss him again. I seriously need to get a grip, snap to it, and remember why I'm there. I take a deep breath and get my bearings.

"Well for starters, you could shoot a TV show with me," I say, playfully tracing my finger along his bicep and down his arm. My move has the intended effect, and the spell is broken.

He gently pushes me back until we're face-to-face. "Is that it then? The only way I'll see you again is if I agree to do a show I don't want to do?"

I'm losing him for the show and make a halfhearted attempt to bring him back.

"But it would be fun shooting together, don't you think? And think of all the people who will discover the amazing visual experience you've created here in this house."

His smile fades and he steps away. "Yes, it would be fun to spend more time with you, but honestly, it's the rest of the attention I don't care about."

"Are you sure?" I ask, searching his expression for any indication of uncertainty.

He takes my hand. "I'm sure. So, if that's the condition, we'll have to say good-bye."

I look down for a long moment. I remember my favorite documentary teacher in school telling us that your work is meaningless if you can't look through your lens and find the complete truth in your subject. My reply surprises even me and I look up. "I can't believe I'm going to say this since it contradicts my job responsibility on this project, but I admire you for staying true to yourself."

He squeezes my hand and smiles. "Thanks, Sophia." He lightly brushes his fingers through my hair, lingering on the ends before letting go. "And you're sure you don't want to see me again?" The hope in his eyes breaks me.

I'm feeling wild and reckless, despite knowing that I'll probably end up in therapy over this. My intrigue with this man is allowing me to look past his Christmas craziness. "I don't care if I lose this gig as a result of it. I *would* really like to see you again."

"Now you're talking!" he says, smiling and stepping closer.

I nod, my lips pressed together with determination.

He puts his hands on my waist. "Can I tell you how appealing it is that you're defending me? So, you'll let me take you out on a real date?"

"I'd love that," I say as I wonder what lusty, love struck cyborg has invaded my body.

He pulls me into his arms and kisses me again. I consider slowing him down, but pull him closer instead.

Suddenly a howl and scratching noise come from the other side of the back door.

"Romeo," Will says with an eye roll.

"Sounds like he wants some attention."

"I'm sure you're right."

"Why don't you check on him, and I'll start the coffee," I say, glad for a moment to search for my lost sanity.

"Okay, There's milk in the fridge if you like it light. I'm not sure I have any sugar but you're so sweet I bet you take yours without it."

That was so corny, but he's so happy I can't even roll my eyes. Instead I tease him. "Aw, you keep at it mister, and I may never leave."

My cell phone rings as I'm slipping into bed two hours later. Will's name comes up on the caller ID.

"Hey," I say softly.

"I've been thinking about you," he says.

"I've been thinking about you too."

"Good thoughts?"

"Very good thoughts."

"Any naughty ones?"

"Hmmm, is this going to be *that* kind of phone call?" I ask.

He clears his throat. "Actually, I called for another reason. Are you really going to lose this gig if I don't do the show?"

"Hey, I don't want you to worry about that. I thought we'd worked through this," I say, testing him.

"But I really need to know. Will you?"

"Probably. You were the focus of the show. But don't stress about that. I've got some other potential things lined up. I'm fine, really."

"I was thinking after you left. You gave up trying to get me on the show because it was more important to be with me and have me be happy."

"Yes, and that *is* how I feel."

"That really means something. So, you know what? I'm going to do the damn show. I'm doing it for you. And the bonus is we'll get to see each other, right?"

"Yes! Are you sure, really sure? We'll have to hold off on dating until the shoot is over." I'm so happy and relieved. Maybe it's all going to work out.

"I'm sure," he says resolutely. "And we can still go out and talk about the project."

"Sure," I say, liking his style. "We're going to have so much fun!"

"Promise?"

"I promise. So, I'll call you tomorrow to schedule the next meeting."

"And can we still go out on Saturday? Like I said, it doesn't have to be a date."

"Yes, I can't wait! Hey, Will?" I hope he hears the smile in my voice.

"Yes?"

"Thank you."

Chapter Five

I grin when my team and I pull up to Will's place. I've been looking forward to their reaction.

The Victorian gem is a confection of intricately shingled turrets, wrap around porches, picture windows, and elaborate woodwork with spindles and arches. There's even an assortment of different weather vanes on the roof. My favorite part, however, is the color—periwinkle with cream and celadon green accents. It's like something you'd find in an upscale neighborhood of San Francisco, not Los Angeles. On this street of Spanish haciendas and regency revivals, this grand old lady of a house stands out rather dramatically.

"Wow! What a beauty!" Aaron exclaims. He pulls out his still camera and takes some shots as we approach the vast front porch with intricately carved railings.

"Can you imagine when it's covered with Christmas lights," says Lindsey. "When does he do the front yard, Sophia?"

"The neighbors got an injunction from the city that prevents him from starting until the week before Thanksgiving, so you're going to have to work that out so we can set up mid-October according to the schedule."

"Okay. I've already started the process." Lindsey makes notes in her pad. She looks up and down the street. "I have to say, I can't blame the neighbors. The crowds he gets when he does his thing at Christmas must be really annoying. I sure as hell wouldn't want to live next to it."

"Me neither," adds Aaron.

I shrug. "I hadn't really thought about it that way, but I suppose you're right. But we're on Will's side now, right?" I say, making sure they're clear.

"Of course," Lindsey says, smiling.

We ring the bell and when Will pulls open the front door, Aaron and Lindsey are as stunned by Will's appearance as I was the first time we met. He shakes everyone's hands, and when he turns to lead us inside, Lindsey mouths *"Whoa!"* with a stunned, wide-eyed expression.

I grin and nod.

Once inside, Will takes a minute to explain the towering Christmas tree in the foyer as Lindsey frantically takes notes. Aaron circles the room, looking through the camera and shooting stills of different angles.

"We may have some lighting issues in here. We'll have to control the light so that the tree lights and twinkle lights all over the room stand out," Aaron says.

I nod. "Whatever it takes to capture the holiday feeling, Aaron."

Will smiles as he watches me.

"What?" I ask.

"Nothing. I just like your professional mode."

"Whatever." I nudge him in the shoulder as we head into the living room.

"Holy hell, this is gorgeous." Lindsey gasps with delight when we head into the living room.

"Interesting way of putting it." Will teases, and Lindsey's cheeks burn bright pink.

"Everything's white, and look at these projections on the ceiling and walls," Aaron says in despair. "This is a technical nightmare."

"I'm sure you'll figure it out," I say.

Luckily Aaron is much happier in the *under the sea* room.

"He has a light meter built into his forehead," I whisper to Will.

He looks over at Aaron, then turns back to me and nods, smiling. "Hey, before I forget, I wanted to let you know that I saw Hank today."

"Hank?" I ask.

"Yes, Hank is the homeless guy I'm friends with. I thought you may be interested in meeting him. I've always thought he'd make a meaningful subject if you guys ever do anything to help the homeless."

"I'd like to meet him," I say, wondering if there's a way to tie Hank into the show.

"Great. I'll set it up."

Lindsey looks over at us talking. I wonder what she's thinking. She's always telling me I have an easygoing personality, so wouldn't it be natural for me to get along with our subject?

After Aaron gets his stills, Will shows him the other rooms and explains how they'll be decorated.

"Anything upstairs?" Lindsey asks.

"The master bedroom is themed, but I don't want anything shot up there," Will replies before winking at me and smiling.

"Just as well," says Aaron. "We have more than enough down here, and I sure as hell don't want the guys carrying all the equipment up there if we don't have to."

"So, I think we have everything, Sophia," Lindsey says as she checks through the list I gave her one last time.

"Good, and you've checked on the permits?"

"Yeah, we're taking care of that tomorrow," says Lindsey.

"I really want your assurance I won't have trouble with the neighbors. They aren't at all fans of my Christmas stuff," Will explains.

"Yes, Sophia has told us, so we've already contacted them and offered compensation for the inconvenience. I'm sure we'll work something out," Lindsey says confidently.

"I hope so. If not, this shoot could end up qualifying for a very different kind of reality show," replies Will.

We all say our good-byes, and as Will opens the front door, he turns to me.

"Sophia, did you drive separately? I wanted to ask you about a few other things."

I smile to myself, knowing he's up to something. "Actually no, we all drove together."

"Take your time. I want to get more shots of the exterior anyway," says Aaron.

"And I can make some calls in the car while we wait," Lindsey adds.

As soon as they step out onto the porch, Will closes the door.

"So, what did you—"

Before I can say another word he pulls me close, presses me against the front door, and kisses me.

Stunned, I still for a few seconds, but then I run my fingers through his hair and pull him in for another kiss. I press my whole body up against him with wanton abandon.

Good lord, here we go...

"Wow," I whisper when we finally part. "Where did that come from?"

"I only lay in bed and thought about doing that all night. I couldn't let you leave without having you in my arms again at least once."

"You know what?" I ask with a sly smile. "I felt the same." *Should it trouble me that I mean these words?* My conscience kicks in and compels me to speak up. "But didn't we agree no dating until after the shoot?"

"So that means no kissing too?" he asks, feigning innocence.

"I suppose that could be negotiated." I slip off my high horse.

He gives me *the* look. "Because I've got to tell you, Ms. Producer, you're quite the kisser."

"As you are, Mr. Holiday Guy."

"And although this is going to sound a lot more forward than I intend it to," he continues.

"Yes?" My curiosity piqued.

"Well, after the shoot, if *you* ever want to explore the upstairs, including the master bedroom—my bedroom—I'd be more than happy to show it to you, and you alone."

I kiss him again but extra slow as I wonder why seeing his bedroom is suddenly a priority in my mind. I've become a shameless hussy. I'm considering getting wild with a grown man who plays with trains. I gaze into his deep blue eyes, which might as well be quicksand for the way they pull me under his spell. "Yes, me alone. I'd like that."

He grins. "Good, I'm glad we got that clarified. So how many hours is it until Saturday night?"

I quickly calculate in my head while he gently runs his fingertips up and down the bare skin of my arm.

"Sixty-one."

"Ooo, you're good," he says as he kisses my cheek.

"And bad." I tease.

"Just the way I like it."

"Sophia, wait!" Steph yells as she hurries down the hall toward the reception area of True Blue Studios.

"Hey, Steph," I say when she reaches me. I study her in a new light, realizing that there's a family resemblance between her and Will in their coloring and build.

"How! How did you ever get Will to agree?" Steph practically yells.

"Agree?" I'm momentarily confused.

"Yeah," Steph says. "To do the holiday show. He just kept telling me no whenever I asked!"

I fold my arms over my chest and jut my hip out to one side. "Really. That's not what your notes said or what the studio told me."

Steph looks sheepish. "Hey, can we go outside for a minute?"

"Okay." I follow her out to the landing in front of the building. "Well?"

"Tell me what they said when they gave you the job."

"That Will was on board. That he was happy to participate. But after meeting him and now talking to you, that assessment couldn't have been further from the truth. Am I right?"

Steph holds up her arms in surrender. "Yeah, all right. Guilty as charged."

"Why'd you do it? It put both Will and me in a really awkward position."

"I was terrified I was about to get laid off. They kept telling me I wasn't bringing in enough subjects. So I may have stretched the truth on a few of them."

"And you actually used a relative to cover your ass. You knew he absolutely didn't want to do it. That's pretty low, Steph."

Guilt floods her expression as he presses her hands over her face. "I know, I know. I hoped they'd never contact him. It was so wrong but I was desperate. I was about to get thrown out of my apartment for back rent, and if I lost my new job I was five steps away from turning tricks on Sunset Boulevard."

"Oh, for God's sake, could you be a little more dramatic?" I say, exasperated.

"Okay, maybe not quite that bad, but close. But you said he agreed so it's okay after all. How'd you get him to do it?" Steph's face brightens.

"Well, I think Will kind of likes me." I can feel my cheeks heating up.

"So, you used that to your advantage?" Steph asks, trying to make the point that I manipulated him too.

"No, no! We talked about a lot of stuff but in the end he said he wanted to help me."

"That's so sweet. I swear Will can be the nicest guy. My Dad told me some stories about Will from when he was a teenager. I still have trouble believing them."

"What kind of stories," I ask, twisting a lock of hair between my fingers.

"I guess he was kind of wild and had anger issues. Even got into serious trouble and spent time in juvie."

"He did? That seems so unlike him now."

I think about the man I've spent time with, who loves Christmas and helps the homeless and underprivileged kids. I just can't imagine he was ever that troubled and wild. "So how does a kid go from that kind of life to being Mr. Holiday?"

"It's because of his grandparents. His grandpa Joe, my grandfather's brother, took him in and straightened him out when he hit bottom."

"Hit bottom?"

"That's what I heard. He ended up living on the streets. His grandparents took him in and worked hard to get him straightened out."

"Wow. He's lucky he had them."

"I'll say, and his grandma Della loved Christmas. Joe would do the lighting and rig stuff up, but Della was the one who decorated. After Joe passed, Will stepped in and helped her."

I'm tempted to ask more about Will's family, but I'm not sure I should. Steph continues to talk about his house and how helping with the holiday setup every year has helped them grow closer.

Warmth floods my heart for both Will and his grandparents, who clearly saved him. The fact that Will has carried on their traditions makes the story that more poignant. I wonder if Paul would be interested in using this angle in the story. But I realize that it would be too personal for Will, so I push the idea out of my mind.

"Anyway," Steph says, interrupting my thoughts. "I'm just so glad you two hit it off. This is weird to say about my second cousin, but isn't he gorgeous?"

I grin. "Most definitely."

"And you're his type. He likes strong women that are feminine and kind… but also classy."

"Really?"

"Yeah, probably everything he missed from his mom. Well listen, I've got to get back to work but I'm so glad we talked. It's a big weight off my chest."

"I'm glad we talked too. And although what you did was wrong, I'm glad you did it."

"Right, 'cause if I hadn't, you'd never have met him." Steph's grin is a little smug.

"Exactly," I say as Steph opens the door to head back inside.

"Well, if things work out and there's ever a wedding, I want an invite." Steph teases and rushes off before I can assure her not to hold her breath.

Chapter Six

Early Friday I get ready for our not-really-a-date date, taking my time with everything from putting on makeup to styling my hair in soft curls. As I slip on my dress I think about how much I'm looking forward to seeing Will again. Despite my reservations, the pull to get closer to him is overwhelming.

Will had mentioned taking me to a place on Robertson for dinner. My stomach's so fluttery I really don't care where we go. I probably won't be able to eat much anyway. I'm so nervous because I've gone off track with my work ethics and I'm not sure I have the fortitude to get back on. This guy, as crazy as his world is, does something to me.

The buzzer for the main door downstairs goes off.

"Will?"

"You didn't tell me you live in one of the coolest apartments in L.A.!"

I grin, not surprised that he loves the vintage art deco design and elegant lines of the old building. Judging from the love he puts into his house, he must appreciate classic architecture. "I'll buzz you in—apartment 6D—so just come on up."

When I open the door, he pauses for a moment and stares. Finally he steps forward and kisses my cheek.

"Hi, beautiful." He's clean-shaven and wearing a sport jacket with his jeans. He definitely looks good... too good.

"Hi, handsome." I pull the door open wider. "Would you like to come in?"

"Just for a minute so we can make our reservation." He walks into the living room.

"So how did you know my building? Have you been here before?"

"A year or so before my grandmother died, I brought her here to visit her old friend May. She'd been a wardrobe person for years on the Warner Brothers lot. Even in her old age she had so much style. Her whole apartment was vintage deco furniture."

"Wow. I'm not sure she still lives here."

"Probably not, she was pretty old back then. But I'll never forget her or her place. Yours is pretty great too." He steps over to the large windows. "Look at your view."

"Thanks, but my place and view can't compare to your amazing house."

"But what about all the Christmas stuff? You really don't mind it?"

"No I don't." It's not really a fib since I do enjoy it. I just don't mention that the fact that he devotes so much time to orchestrate all of it makes me worry about him personally.

"You're not just saying that?"

"No I'm not just saying that because of the shoot. I'm just happy when I'm in your house. I get that excited hopeful feeling I had when I was a kid." I *am* happy in his house, but I wouldn't feel the same if it was someone else. It's Will who makes me happy when I'm there.

He looks really pleased with my answer. He turns to peruse some of my framed art. "I like these pen and ink sketches. I used to do those when I was younger."

"Really? I imagine they require a lot of patience."

"Which is why I think I did them. It forced me to slow down and focus, not just be angry at the world all the time."

"Sounds rough. Were you really like that?"

"Yeah, when I was a teen. Now I draw schematics for the holiday stuff." He laughs softly. "It's a little more upbeat." He glances down at his watch. "But hey, we better get going."

I like that he has a sense of humor about himself. "Sure, let's go."

During the ride down the elevator there's an awkward silence between us. He drums his fingers against the elevator wall.

"What?" I ask.

He smiles. "I guess I'm nervous. I've really been looking forward to this."

If he only knew. I step closer and nudge shoulders with him. "Me too."

He smiles and squeezes my hand just as the door opens.

When we arrive at Chaya Brassiere I realize that Will must have wanted to make a good impression. I've heard great things about this place, but even with the wonderful ambience, his face is the only thing I can focus on.

After our food arrives Will asks me about my work. "So did you ever think you'd end up in reality TV when you went to school?"

"Hardly. I wanted to do documentaries. I had this fantasy of working for someone like Joe Berlinger or Bruce Sinosky and working on films like their great *Paradise Lost.* I guess I was a big dreamer. In the end I just couldn't figure out how to make documentaries and pay my rent and student loans."

"From what I know, it seems like documentaries would be much more meaningful work to you, but I understand having to pay the bills. And this is an expensive city to live in."

"It sure is. Unfortunately I couldn't stay in Portland with my family and work in the film business the way I wanted to. At least I'm learning a lot about production. And I've made some connections. So hopefully one day…" I pause, feeling determined as I think about my goals.

"You'll get there," he says confidently, offering me a bite of his tiramisu.

I lean forward as he brushes the overflowing spoon against my lips. When I part my lips he eases the spoon inside my mouth. I roll my eyes and sigh before responding.

"So how can you be so sure I'll get what I want?"

"I just have a feeling that you're not the kind of woman who settles for less."

I fold my arms across my chest and tilt my head as I appraise him. I wonder if he sees the fire in my eyes. "I never settle."

On the drive back to my place, and while stopped at a red light we notice several homeless people gathered at the front of a public park. It reminds me of our recent conversation involving the homeless man he wants me to meet.

When the light turns green and he continues driving, I turn to Will. "Will you tell me more about Hank?"

He nods. "I've known him a few years. It's tenuous at times. He can disappear for weeks at a time, and like anyone on the street he has a hard time trusting people, but there's something about him. I'd like to think of him as a friend, as much as you can, considering the circumstances. He reminds me in many ways of a middle-aged version of my grandfather."

"With being homeless, where does he sleep at night?"

"The last I knew it was in a park not too far from my house. There's heavy tree cover and shrubs along part of the perimeter. A small group of homeless people have set up camp in the section near the freeway, where people can't see them from the park or street."

We both remain silent all the way back to my apartment. I stare out my window and remember how one of my classmates had made a short film about an older woman who was homeless. She was friends with a group of runaways who lived on the street, too. It was artfully done and very moving.

Finally Will breaks the silence. "You got quiet. What are you thinking about?"

"I'm just remembering a film about a homeless woman a classmate of mind had made. It's heartbreaking to wonder what kind of life that must be."

Stopped at another light, he studies me. "It's a rough one. Believe me."

"You sound like you—"

"Yeah, I've lived on the street. It wasn't that long—about nine months when I was a teen—but it was long enough. Believe me. No one should have to suffer the indignity that comes along with that. It messed up my head for a long time."

I sit stunned. Coming from Will it sounds even darker than Steph's explanation of his past. He lived on the streets for months? Will's childhood is sounding worse and worse. *Can I handle knowing exactly how bad it was?*

Will shakes his head and looks upset. "I shouldn't have told you about that."

I press my hands together. "Don't say that. Please don't regret it. I want to know all about you."

"I feel the same about you," he says quietly.

Will's mood remains serious, but when I reach out to hold his hand, his expression softens. I continue to stare out the window as he drives. I can barely sort out the crazy array of emotions surging through me.

Will parks in front of my place and walks around to open my door. When I get out, he rests his hand on my shoulder and gazes down at me. "Thank you for asking about Hank and wanting to listen to my story. It means a lot to me."

"Of course," I say.

"It's not pretty, but Hank's situation and what I went through is a reality that's part of the world we live in."

I look into his eyes and find pain there. The mood is so much more somber than earlier in our non-date.

He gazes me intently before continuing, "And it's a part of my life and experience, so I'm kind of glad you know that now."

At my front door he brushes his fingers along my jaw, cups my chin with his hand, and kisses me gently.

I don't ask him in, nor does he ask. Instead we kiss sweetly as I settle into his arms. When we part my expression's happy.

"What?" he asks, smiling.

"I like hanging out with you."

He sighs and hugs me tight. "And me with you."

He kisses me again and then pulls away from me with a long sigh. "I better get going. I've got to get up bright and early to get the house ready for this shoot thing that's happening next week."

"Is that so?" I tease.

"Yup. I've got this crush on this pushy producer I'm working with, so I've gotta keep her happy."

I swoon at the word *crush*. *This man*, I sigh. In this moment he's almost perfect even with his imperfections.

"Then, you'd better get a good night's sleep. Those producers can get sooo demanding."

"But there are advantages to this plan. You know what comes with good sleep?" He asks, running his hand firmly down my back and stopping just below my waist.

"What?" I ask as I close my eyes and imagine him stretched out across a bed—preferably naked, or perhaps just with a thin sheet draped over him.

"Dreams," he whispers in my ear, before easing me against him. "And I'll be dreaming about you close to me like this."

My resolve to be good almost crumbles with our final kiss, but he steps away and waits as I let myself inside. Just before I close the door, he rests his hand across on the wooden surface for a moment before whispering, "Sweet dreams, Sophia."

Chapter Seven

The next morning I wake up and wonder what I'm going to do about Will. Clearly I'm doing a number on myself when a date that was supposed to be work related was romantic. I brush my fingers over my lips when I remember our kisses and the way he held me when he whispered good night.

How can a man be so amazing and hard to figure out at the same time? The only thing I know for sure is that despite my reserve about his extreme obsession with Christmas, I'm crazy about this guy. I resolve to try harder to stay low key until we are done with the shoot, but the closer we get the harder it will be for me to stay professional during production.

My phone rings just after lunch. Anxiously hoping it's him, I dig through my purse to find it.

"Hi, Sophia," he says, his voice a combination of creamy dreamy and sexy smooth.

I immediately let go of all my reservations as I melt into my armchair.

"Hey, how's it going?" I ask.

"Pretty good. Steph brought over a bunch of Christmas-loving sorority sisters, and among other things, they've transformed the kitchen and breakfast room into Santa's workshop. Romeo was in heaven when they showed up. I finally had to lock him outside."

"There are a bunch of sorority girls decorating your house?" I ask, sounding uneasy and wondering what "other things" he's referring to.

"Yes. Frankly, I'd be screwed without them with the first day of shooting next week. A few of them are coming back tomorrow. My friend,

Jeremy, came by to help, but he's acting like Romeo and trying to hook up rather than doing any meaningful work."

There's radio silence for a moment as I come to terms with the disturbing visuals in my head. A scene with a bevy of scantily clad co-eds fawning over Will as they primp his fantastical home unfolds in my mind. I squirm with discomfort.

"I think I'll come help tomorrow too."

"You don't have to," he says.

"Don't you want me to?" *Is there a reason he doesn't want me there?*

"It's not that..."

"So, what is it?"

"Maybe, I want to *wow* you when you see it finished next week?"

"I bet all those sorority girls want to *wow* you too," I say, my voice edgier than usual.

"Are you jealous?" he asks, amused.

"Should I be?"

"Sophia?"

"Hmm?"

"You're already under my skin, woman. You're all I see, all I think about." He pauses for a moment and then adds, "Don't you realize what you're doing to me?"

"Of course I do," I say, my voice low and sweet. "Because you're doing the same thing to me."

"Yeah?"

"Yes, and mark my words, I'm coming over tomorrow. I'm going to have those girls understand they can finish their work and go on their way. I'm the one who stays."

"Promise?" I can almost hear his smile in his words.

"Girl Scout's honor."

The group plans a later start the next day, so Will invites me to breakfast at Dupars with the plan to meet Hank afterward. It's astounding to watch Will polish off bacon, eggs, and a stack of pancakes before I've barely started my half order of French toast. The man can eat.

Afterward we drive around the streets where Will typically finds Hank. Not far from Western and Third Street, Will pulls his truck over.

An older man with a kind face approaches us. Hank's expression brightens as he gets close to Will's window.

"Hey Will, I was hoping I'd see you today." He glances at me and smiles timidly.

"Yeah, Hank. I wanted you to meet Sophia. She's a TV producer, and I'm working with her on a show about my Christmas house."

"Nice to meet you, Miss Sophia," Hank says, bowing his head.

"Nice to meet you too, Hank," I reply.

"So, Hank, I've got a job for you," Will says.

"Anything."

"We need to set up the yard early this year for this show. We have to do it this Thursday morning around nine. You guys up for it? I'll pay you like always and pick up lunch."

"Sure. Five guys again?" Hank asks.

"Yeah, and you can supervise on the ground and be the only one handling the lights, okay? I'll be doing the ones on the roof."

"Sounds good," Hank says, standing up straighter and squaring his shoulders. He looks like a guy ready to work.

Will picks up a little box from Dupars and hands it to him through the window. "We got you something at breakfast."

Hank brushes off his hands before he accepts the box. I note the effort Hank has put into taking care of himself despite his situation. His clothes are clean and somehow he's shaved and his short hair is combed. From a distance you wouldn't even suspect he's homeless.

"Is this what I think it is?" Hank asks, smiling.

"Your favorite—blueberry. Fresh out of the oven too."

Hank opens the box and sniffs the muffin. A huge grin spreads across his face. Tucked next to the muffin is a folded ten dollar bill.

"Thanks so much, Will. Hey, let me do your windows. They could use a shine." Hank offers.

"Nah, man, I've got to get Sophia home and then back to the house. Besides, you should eat that muffin warm." He nods to the McDonald's to their right. "Head over to Mickey D's and get that coffee you like."

"I think I will. It's good to meet you, Miss Sophia."

"Likewise, Hank," I answer, smiling.

He holds up his box. "Bless you, Will."

Will nods. "Take it easy, Hank. We'll see you soon."

As we continue toward my apartment, I think about Will's conversation with Hank.

"And they help you every year?" I ask, curious how Will has developed relationships with Hank and his friends.

"Yeah," Will says.

"How did Hank came to live on the street? He seems like the kind of man who would have family to help him out."

"Well, Hank worked in maintenance for years at Boeing before they shut down and his life started sliding downhill. When I first met him he was living in subsidized housing after not being able to find work, losing his home, and being flattened by a mountain of medical bills after his wife died. But he hated that subsidized place, got into a big fight with his neighbor, and was thrown out."

"He doesn't have any family left to help him? I ask, feeling overwhelmed by his situation.

"He has a daughter and she keeps arranging shelters and stuff for him, but he says he likes it better on his own than being there. Meanwhile she lives in New York City and wants him to come live with her."

"Why doesn't he do that?"

"I guess she has a roommate and they share a tiny apartment. On top of that, Hank says he can't handle New York."

"How awful. That's such a sad story."

"There's a lot of stories out there on the streets that are much more complicated than people think. It's not just drug addicts, the mentally ill, or lazy people."

His comment plants an idea in my mind for my own documentary short film project. Maybe I could get Aaron and some of the guys on board. For a fleeting moment I envision it all in my mind and wonder if meeting Will might lead to a greater purpose in my life.

The next day, it's just past noon when I approach Will's front door and ring the bell.

He pulls open the door with a smile. "My afternoon just got a whole lot better. Did you finish your work at home?"

"Yes. Sorry, it took longer than I thought but look what I brought for you." I hold out a platter of cupcakes I baked yesterday for the occasion.

"For me?" he asks, grinning.

I scrunch my nose. "And those *girls* in there helping you."

He takes the platter in his right hand as he gives me a one-armed hug with the other. I curl up against him and tilt my face up for a kiss.

"You're a sweetheart. Thank you."

"You're welcome," It feels so good to be close to him, to have his lips pressed against mine. "I've been looking forward to that," I whisper.

"Me too. You have great timing. You're saving me," he says, leading me into the house.

I arch my brow. "From what exactly?"

"An eager helper. Her name is Liza, and she just asked if I was interested in renting her a room. She said she'd cook for me."

"Oh, really? By all means, I'd *love* to meet her."

He grins even wider. "This should be interesting."

Once inside, Will sets the cupcakes in the kitchen. I'm impressed by the transformation of this room into Santa's Sweet Shop. There are large glass apothecary jars full of colorful candies lined up against the back of the counters and elaborate gingerbread houses on every surface. There are even lights shaped like little peppermints lining the windows.

Room by room, Will shows me the rest of the house, checks the progress, and introduces me to everyone. We come across a couple unpacking ornaments in the sunroom. The guy notices Will's holding my hand as we approach. Will introduces us.

"This is Jeremy and Susi."

Jeremy speaks up before Will can finish. "You must be Sophia," he says, shaking my hand.

I'm pleased Jeremy knows who I am. "Great to meet you both."

From the looks of it Jeremy has taken an interest in Susi, and the feeling seems mutual.

"Hey, Will. Do you know that Susi drives a vintage Mustang she rebuilt with her dad?"

Susi beams with pride.

"I didn't. How cool."

We learn that Susi has a passion for performance cars and vintage pinups, which explains her extra short shorts and Betty Page hairdo. According to Will, that also pretty much makes her Jeremy's dream girl.

She smiles at me. "Are you here to help too? There's still so much to do." She turns to Will. "I hope you can get it done in time for the TV people."

"Well, Sophia's the producer of the show, so I bet he'll make sure it gets done in time," Jeremy says, laughing.

Will wraps his hand around my waist and pulls me closer into his side. "She's a taskmaster for sure, but I bet she'll be a good helper."

"I am, and I baked cupcakes for everyone. They're in the kitchen if you want one."

"Let's go." Jeremy nods to Susi and they head out.

"Come meet my wannabe roommate." Will teases as he takes my hand and leads me to the den.

"Hey, Liza, this is Sophia," Will says as we step into the room.

I notice Liza smile when she sees Will until she realizes he's holding my hand. Her eyes narrow ever so slightly as the edges of her mouth turn down.

"Hello," I say, smiling.

"Are you a friend of Will's?" Liza asks boldly.

"I guess you could say that. Are we friends?" I ask Will.

"Special friends," he says, squeezing my hand.

I step closer to Liza. "Can you show me what you're doing? I'm going to help too."

Liza looks like she's going to protest but then thinks twice about it. She stands and smooths down her T-shirt. "Actually I think I better go. I have a final to study for, and I really wasn't in the mood for pizza anyway."

"Okay. Thanks so much for all your help," Will says politely.

"Sure."

I smile. "And before you leave, I brought some cupcakes, so take one with you on your way out. They're in the kitchen."

Once she's gone I turn to Will. "Should I feel guilty? We crushed that poor girl's dreams."

"I'm sure she'll survive. Besides, she couldn't have been too heartbroken. She didn't even put up a fight."

"What a slacker. I'd fight for you."

"I think you just did. It was a little subtle for my taste—no hair pulling or anything."

"I'm classy!" I say, laughing. "So, tell me, Mr. Saunders, how many other pretty young girls do I need to chase off tonight before I have you all to myself?"

"A few. Just a few."

I sweep my arm toward the door. "Well, go on then, lead the way."

"Where's our designated driver?" Susi asks.

The kitchen is littered with beer bottles and empty pizza boxes.

"I'm here," Steph answers as she enters the kitchen. "You guys ready to go?"

Susi grabs onto Jeremy. "Can he come too?"

He pulls her onto his lap, looking hopeful. "You want me to come to your place?"

"Yes. A thousand times, yes," Susi whispers.

"She's an English major. She always quotes Jane Austen books when she's tipsy." Steph explains.

"Is it true you're going to be on one of the style channels? I want to make sure and watch it." Susi asks Will.

"Not me, the house."

Steph glances at me, surprised, before focusing on Will. "You know you're going to be on it too, right?" she asks.

I realize Steph's nervousness is unsettling Will.

She turns back to me. "Sophia, you did explain all of that to him, didn't you?"

Before I can answer, Will jumps in.

"Well, we haven't gone over too many specifics. Maybe I'm a little casual about everything. It's like another day at the studio for me."

"Just remember it's different when it's not *your* office. At the end of the day you can't just walk away like it's someone else's place," Steph retorts.

"He'll be fine, Steph," I tell her, feeling irritated.

Will frowns. "What are you saying, Steph? And aren't you the one who suggested me for this show?"

She pulls out her car keys and looks down. "Forget I said anything. I'm sure everything will be fine."

Will walks everyone to the door, hands them each a small gift wrapped box and thanks them profusely for all their help. When the door finally shuts, he leans against it and sighs.

"As grateful as I am for the help, I swear I thought they'd never leave."

"I didn't either," I reply from just inside the entryway.

We stare at each other for a few long seconds.

"I want a cupcake." I announce. He follows me as I return to the kitchen.

I bend over the kitchen counter to consider my options when he steps up close and wraps his arms around my waist from behind.

I pluck a cupcake from the platter and slowly, gently, remove the paper wrapper with intricately folded edges. When the cupcake's bottom is naked, I lift it to my mouth, open wide, and take a bite full of frosting and soft cake. He rests his chin on my shoulder and sighs. I lick my lips slowly, making a production of it.

"I want some," he says, with a sexy sounding longing in his voice.

"Some of this?" I hold up the plump cupcake tauntingly.

"Yes, that. Share with me?"

"I'd love to." I turn in his arms and slowly run my hand up his forearm and over his shoulder before pressing the cupcake against his lips. "Take a bite."

He sinks his teeth into the sweet moist pillow of confection, and his eyes roll back with pleasure.

I smile and skim my tongue over his lips, drawing up the spare crumbs and frosting.

"You like it?" I ask breathlessly.

"So much." He pulls me close, pressing us together tight enough so I feel his body's reaction to me and our undeniable chemistry. He slides his hands to my hips, lifts me onto the island counter, and kisses me.

"Sophia." He moans as our lips meet. When he caresses my thigh, his hand catches a box on the counter next to me. He pulls away and looks around the room.

"What's the matter?" I ask.

He sweeps his arm across the kitchen. "It's a mess in here. If I get to kiss you like this it has to be someplace fitting, like under the stars."

"Well, let's go somewhere else," I say. "We could go in the living room and make-out in the winter wonderland. You could take me into the sunroom and kiss me under the canopy of twinkly lights. Where do you want us to be?"

"Do you really want to know?" he asks, with a sexy sigh.

"Yes," I whisper.

He kisses my forehead, my neck and along my shoulder. His fingertips press into the flesh of my hips suggestively.

"I can't deny it, Sophia. I want you in my bed," he whispers.

"Oh, oh my." I moan as he kisses my breasts through my sweater and his hand works up my leg. I focus on the sensation and try not to pay attention to the warning light flashing in my head.

"Maybe this is too soon. What do you want?" He strokes my thigh and kisses me again.

"I want you too," I whisper against his lips, but then pull back. "But yeah, it's too soon." I search his face for his reaction and give him a shy smile.

He pulls back and takes a deep breath. "That's okay, we'll wait. It'll be worth the wait."

I nod slowly as he steps back. He runs his fingers through his hair and grabs a bottle of water off the counter. He offers me a sip before chugging half the bottle. The tension in the room is thick.

"We weren't even going to date until after the shooting." I remind him.

He closes his eyes and nods. "Yeah, believe me, I know that in here," he says, pointing to his head. "But don't so much understand it here." He points to his heart, looking disappointed.

"Maybe I shouldn't have come over this afternoon."

He lets out a frustrated sigh. "Maybe not. Honestly, Sophia, you're sending me mixed signals and it's screwing with me."

"I am?" I ask, not sure why I'm asking when I know he's right.

"Yes, you are. I mean, what was with the cupcake show a minute ago? That was cupcake porn. You knew what you were doing."

My stomach starts to sink. He's on to me and my internal flip-flop. I bite my lip as my mind spins, trying to decide what to do.

"What do you want from me, Sophia... besides being on your show?" His expression is pained.

Did it hurt him to ask that? He's made it clear that he always hoped there was more behind my interest in him than just work.

I decide to be honest. "Look, Will. I am wildly attracted to you. I have been from the moment we met, and at times I can hardly restrain my emotions."

He's fights back a smile, but his expression drops with my next words.

"But as far as getting involved, well, let's just say we're pretty different. I'm not convinced it could work."

"Different?" He studies me for a moment. "It's because of what I do here, isn't it?" He gestures to the house.

"That's part of it." I admit.

"I see." He shakes his head and slips his hands in the pockets of his jeans.

"What?"

He clears his throat before looking at me so intently it makes me uneasy. "Look, rightly or wrongly, I live what is in my heart. If I feel it, I do it… two hundred percent. That's just who I am. You're flawed too, Sophia, but I look past that. I still want you so much."

My entire body tenses. "Flawed?"

He shrugs. "I'm starting to wonder if you're afraid of what you really want. It's like you're living on the surface, when I know you're capable of so much more depth. You're attracted to me, but you won't let me into your heart. You want to make documentary films full of humanity and truth, yet you're working in fake, reality TV. You want to travel the world, but you don't seem to have much of a personal life at home. Do you ever worry that it's kind of superficial?"

"Is that what you think?" I feel as if I've been kicked in all my tender spots.

"Maybe, but I believe you want more. Together we can help each other be more."

It's all too much to process. "I think it's time for me to go," I say, wanting to cry.

He studies me and then helps me off the counter. We're silent as we walk to the front door. I keep my head down to hide the tears.

He pulls me into his embrace and cradles the back of my head against his shoulder. His comfort almost breaks me, and I barely control the shudder in my sigh. He pulls back and brushes the tears off my cheeks.

"Why are you crying?" His voice is soft and gentle. "I didn't mean to hurt you."

I meet his gaze, and his eyes search mine with a worried intensity. Taking a deep breath, I gather my courage. "You think I'm shallow? I can't believe you said that...You are important to me, and I do care about you."

"Oh, baby," he says with a sigh as he pulls me into his arms and hugs me. This time I'm the one who presses my lips to his. He reacts instinctively, not holding back, and every emotion roars through us as we cling onto each other.

When we part after our kiss, he whispers in my ear. "I want you, but I need you to want me, in here," he says, placing his palm over my heart. "Let's lighten up with the deep thoughts and get through the shoot. Then we can figure it out. Okay?"

I nod. "Okay."

He walks me to my car and seals the deal with one of his special Will kisses—the panty-dropping one. He's ensuring I'll lay in bed tonight with the heat of his kiss still burning my lips as I slide my hand between my legs and imagine all the things he would have done to me if I'd followed him to his bed.

I did the right thing, but there's part of me that wishes I'd been brave enough to let him in.

Chapter Eight

The next afternoon at work I focus on making sure everything is ready for the shoot at Will's tomorrow. I stop by Lindsey's cubical.

"So we're set for tomorrow, right?" I ask Lindsey.

"Yeah, I got Will's final sign-offs at lunch. He was in an interesting mood, by the way. He asked about you."

"And is everything else set?" I say, ignoring her comment.

"Aaron's almost done with the schedule. I got sign-offs from all the neighbors except for the Hoffmeyers. I'm heading over there in a minute to go over the schedule and compensation *again* for the hundredth time." She rolls her eyes. "They're a wacky bunch. You'd think we were drilling for oil in their backyard. I think they're trying to get rich from this."

"Like that old TV show, *The Beverly Hillbillies.*" I laugh despite my concern.

Lindsey blinks. "I've never heard of that one, but I bet those hillbillies were a lot more charming than this motley bunch."

My apprehension starts setting in. "Really? I hope they don't cause more trouble."

"Me too. I'll call you after the meeting if they don't sign."

I head to Paul's office next.

"Hey, Paul. Do we need to go over anything for tomorrow?"

He looks up from his computer and pushes away from his desk.

"I think we're set. How's the guy"—he pauses and glances at his notes— "Will. How's Will feeling about this?"

"I *think* he's okay with everything."

Paul furrows his brow. "Okay? Not happy? Not great? You know we want this to be an upbeat show."

"I do. He was slow to come on board, and he's not an attention seeker despite what he does."

"What? That's different. Most of our subjects are attention whores. So why'd he agree?"

I pause, wondering how to answer his question. I'm not willing to share that my influence is a lot of why Will is doing the show, or how we're involved personally. Judging on how Paul seems, it could backfire later.

"He agreed, wanting to bring more support to his cause," I say.

"*Really.*" His response drips with skepticism. "Aaron mentioned this Will fellow is *very* taken with you."

My cheeks redden. "We do get along well." My mind replays our kiss last night and the fantasies that resulted later, including my favorite—me on his sleigh bed with my legs wrapped around him as he thrusts into me so completely I can barely breathe.

Oh, my God! I squeeze my thighs together. I can almost imagine the fullness of him inside of me as I squirm.

"Get along? Well, I'm sure you're completely professional, right?"

"Of course I've been professional," I respond yet my mind wanders again to the other fantasy of me slowly taking off Will's clothes and kissing every part of him. The idea of it almost makes me moan out loud. I must be losing my mind. I need to get out of here before I say something I shouldn't.

"True," he says, studying me as if he's looking for a crack in my barely contained composure.

"I've got another meeting. Let me know if you want to go over things after Aaron finishes the schedule," I say, trying to control the nervousness in my voice.

"Will do," he says as I dart out to the hallway.

That evening Will and I agree to have dinner to go over the shoot and what he can anticipate. I keep catching myself nervously fiddling with my silverware as we talk.

We're almost through with our meal when Will takes my hand in his. "Hey, what's up?" he asks as he places his other hand on my bouncing knee. "You keep asking how I feel about tomorrow, but what about you? Are you okay with everything?"

I sigh. "I'm tense, I guess."

"Why?" His eyebrows knit together as he studies me.

His concerned expression makes me realize I should've put up a better front for his sake. "Don't worry. I'm fine. I get like this before every shoot."

He waves down the waiter and gives him his credit card before leaning toward me. "I don't believe you, Sophia. I don't think you get this nervous before every shoot. You're a pro."

I smile warmly at him. "I *am* a pro," I say.

"That's more like it." He takes my hand and squeezes it. "Besides I think I know what's really bothering you about tomorrow."

"You do?" I ask, mildly amused. "I can't wait to hear what it is since you've never been on a shoot with me."

"I think you're nervous because I'm going to be there and I have all kinds of ways to distract you." He winks playfully and lightly runs the tip of his index finger up my inner arm.

I grin, charmed that he's lightening the mood. "And you're so hot, so hunky that I can't even see straight in your presence." I take a big sigh and pretend swoon with my hand on my forehead.

"Exactly. So I'm going to turn down my sexy dial tomorrow," he teases.

"Is that even possible? Your sexy is off the charts. I'm pretty sure there's no taming it."

"As is yours." He shrugs. "I guess we're doomed."

"Yes, doomed." I agree. "You see, I had a conversation with the writer and director of the show. He questioned my relationship with you." I duck my head, my cheeks glowing pink with my admission. "I guess Lindsey said something about how familiar we were. I've never been in this situation before."

"I imagine our chemistry was hard to hide," he says.

I look up and lean in on my elbows, grinning. "Chemistry indeed. I can't believe the effect we've had on each other in such a short time. Have you noticed we can't keep our hands off each other?" I shake my head as if it's a bad thing.

He grins. "Yeah, I really like all the touching."

I laugh. "Believe me, I do too, but we have to stop until the shoot is over. Or at least when we're around other people."

"True, but it's organic. I don't even think about it."

"My neither, that's the problem."

"I can't help that I'm so drawn to you. I feel like a kite in the wind, and you're slowly pulling me in," Will says.

"Is that a good thing?" I ask.

He smiles. "Yeah, as long as you don't let go of the string."

We sit silently for a minute taking it all in. Suddenly I realize that Will is clenching and unclenching his fists, over and over, his eyes looking far away in thought.

"Hey, you. What's up? Has your kite flown into the dark clouds?" I whisper.

He squints and he presses his lips together. "This is really going to happen, isn't it? Can I change my mind and back out?"

His question stuns me. "Is that what you want to do?"

He nods, scowling a bit and looking off to the side.

"Oh, no." I moan, lifting my hands to my face in horror.

"Don't worry, Sophia. I said I *want* to back out. I didn't say I would. I agreed to do it, and I follow through with my promises."

I let out a loud exhale. "Well, thank you for that. Damn, you scared the hell out of me for a moment."

"Sorry. I promise I'll pull through. I'll just grit my teeth and bear it, no matter how tortured I am," he says sheepishly.

"I promise I won't let it be torture."

"Okay. What's the worst that can happen, right?" he says, lifting his hands up like he's reasoning with himself.

"Exactly, and by next year we'll be like, 'so how'd we meet again?' All of this stress will be a distant memory."

"Yeah." He grins.

"And maybe I'll be working on documentaries."

"And maybe we can take a trip somewhere exotic. I haven't really traveled much."

Feeling great, I lift my water glass in a toast. "So, here's to our big adventure."

I have a thought as he walks me to my car. "Remember what you said last night about keeping things light? Why can't we just decide to have fun working together?"

"Really? It will be fun?"

I wink at him. "I'll make it fun. You'll be my Mr. Christmas."

"Is this going to involve me wearing a Santa hat and no clothes at some point?" His teasing has a hopeful edge.

"No, but I've been a *really* good girl this year," I say, biting my lip and batting my eyelashes.

"How good?" His smile turns into a grin.

"Really good, except when I was *bad*, of course. I can't help it—you make me want to be really naughty."

"That works for me. You can be naughty with me any ol' time."

"Hmmm," I moan while I tap my finger on my chin like I'm thinking up lots of naughty plans.

Will looks properly seduced with his hooded eyes and sexy smile. "Okay then, so what do you want from Mr. Christmas?"

"I want to jingle his bells."

Will laughs. "Anything else?"

"And ride his sleigh."

"Really?" He grins like a Cheshire cat as he leans against my car and pulls me into his arms.

I press my body against him and glide my hands up his chest, while he runs his fingers up and down my back.

"So if I'm Mr. Christmas, who are you?" he asks.

I moan as he kisses my neck. "Who do you want me to be? And don't say an elf."

"No," he says as he gently bites my earlobe and whispers in my ear. "How about my girl... Ms. Christmas?"

I lean back and look him in the eyes. "Yeah?" I say, my heart fluttering. "I'd like that."

He smiles and gets a playful look in his eyes. "And one day I'll take you for that hot ride on my sleigh."

"Are you flirting back, Mr. Christmas? 'Cause that was saucy. You've got mad skills."

He leans down to kiss me good-bye. "Oh beautiful, when it comes to my mad skills—you haven't seen anything yet."

Chapter Nine

The next morning the production truck from True Blue Entertainment pulls in front of Will's house. The sun's still so low in the sky that it shimmers over the wet grass and casts long shadows from the production team as they unload equipment. Will watches from the front window with an apprehensive look on his face.

The studio group gathers on his front sidewalk, and I lead them up the walkway. Almost everyone has a steaming travel mug of coffee and a backpack.

Will steps away from the window and opens the front door. He looks at me first with a small smile, then scans the group. "Good morning."

"Hi, Will. It's the big day! We're all here and raring to go. Are you ready?" I ask.

He shrugs. "I guess so."

I'm impressed with his polite and neutral countenance. You'd never know that he had me pressed against my car last night.

He notices Paul, who's studying him intently. "We haven't met. You must be Paul."

Paul shakes Will's hand. "Yes. Good to meet you and thanks for participating on our show. From the stills Aaron showed me, you're really going to wow our audience with your amazing Christmas house."

"Thanks." Will steps back so everyone can enter.

Aaron and the equipment guys swarm in like it's their place. Tarps are spread across the floor and one of the smaller guys starts moving things to the edge of the room.

"So they won't get damaged," he says when Will's eyes get wide.

Lindsey grabs his arm. "Hey, Will, while they set up let's go to the kitchen and go over the schedule and some details."

He seems a bit dazed as he leads us down the hall. "I've got coffee going," he says when we're all gathered around the island.

"So can we walk Will through what's going to happen today?" I say to the group.

Lindsey sets her pad of notes and scheduling on the counter. "Sure. Right now the guys are getting long shots and details in the foyer and living room." She turns to Paul. "We may have some budget kickbacks 'cause we had to do some supplemental lighting I hadn't budgeted for."

Paul groans and rolls his eyes back. "You can bet we'll get shit for that."

"Anyway." I push them to get back on track.

Lindsey shakes her head and looks at her watch. "Will, we should be ready to do some shots with you by eleven. Why don't you sit for makeup at ten-thirty?"

She turns to Gia sitting at the end of the counter. "This is a good spot, don't you think?"

"Yeah, good light." Gia turns to Will. "I'm Gia, by the way. And don't worry. I'll make you look great." She gives him a wink.

Turning back to Lindsey, Gia asks, "What about wardrobe?"

"Right. Look what I found. It's perfect." Lindsey lifts up a shopping bag and pulls out two T-shirts. She holds up a green one with a large cartoony reindeer on the front. "We were going to do this, but then I found this one." She holds up a deep red T-shirt.

"Mr. Christmas!" Paul exclaims, reading the caption on the front of the shirt. "That's perfect!"

Will blinks repeatedly before looking over at me.

I shake my head frantically with my hands up like I didn't know anything about this.

"Can you iron both just in case?" Lindsey says to Gia.

Gia nods and gathers the shirts and works them onto hangers.

"Those aren't for me, are they?" Will asks, his "what the fuck" look still firmly in place.

"Sure they are. Aren't they awesome," Paul says happily.

"Sophia tells me you're the one interviewing me on camera. So, are you wearing one?" Will asks Paul.

"Ah, that would be no," he says, laughing.

"Good, then I'm not wearing one either. This is the first I've heard of it anyway. I'm just going to wear my own clothes."

Paul's face gets a little red as he considers what to say to Will. Finally he turns away and walks toward the hallway.

"Sophia, you work this out," he says as he passes me.

Later when the group takes a break to check on the work up front, Will heads to the backyard. I watch from the window as he stomps across the wet grass and away from the house. I follow him out.

He looks wary as I approach. "What was that about?" He doesn't even try to hide his anger.

"I swear, Will, I didn't know about the shirts... and I sure as hell didn't know about Mr. Christmas."

Will gazes off into the distance and shakes his head. "I don't feel good about any of this. You said they weren't going to make me look like a fool."

"Please don't be upset. I'll say you won't do the shirts. It'll be fine, I promise."

"Sophia, don't make me promises you can't or won't keep."

"I wouldn't do that," I say softly, my eyes glazing over with the realization that this has damaged his hard-won trust in me.

He glares toward the house and squints. Then he turns toward the back of the yard. "Follow me," he says gruffly.

I rush after him to the back corner of the yard and come to a stop behind a towering shrub. He turns to me and grinds his boot heel into the hard soil.

"Will?" I ask, trying to control the concern in my voice.

"I need to know something." He jams his hands in his pockets.

"I'll tell you whatever I can."

"Sophia." His eyes are so intense it's as if he's looking straight through me.

"Yes?" I whisper, fear bubbling up in me about whatever dark thing he's apparently thinking.

"For this shoot... to get me to do this"—he pauses and looks down—"did you play me?"

"What?" I say, now fighting back tears. "How can you ask that?"

"I need the truth."

"I'm telling you the truth. I did *not* play you." I drop my chin and close my eyes. "I wouldn't do that to you," I whisper.

When I finally look up at him he's watching me intently.

"I swear Will."

He studies me and then looks away.

I step closer to him and put my hand on his forearm. "Will?"

He lifts his chin and looks up at the sky. "Sophia, when we first met you asked me to trust you and I decided I would. But since then some of your actions have made me wonder if I made the right decision. I'm just hoping I didn't make a mistake."

I curl over and press my hands above my chest like I'm trying to protect my heart. It's as if his words slapped me and I can still feel the sting. "How can you say that after all of our talks? Don't you know how important it's been to me to earn your trust? Why would I jeopardize it like that?"

He shrugs, and looks off into the distance.

I step even closer until we're almost chest to chest. "Last night you told me I could be your girl. I may not have had all the struggles you've had in life, but I've been hurt too. My heart is on the line here as well. But I believe in you. I believe in the possibility of us."

He watches me and I can see there's a battle raging in his eyes.

"Don't let this shoot mess it all up." I turn to walk back inside the house.

Before I can take more than one step, he grabs hold of my arm. "Come here," he says softly.

I step into his embrace, and he holds me tight. "I'm sorry, Sophia. I just got really freaked out."

"I know," I whisper, my lips against his shoulder.

"I'm falling for you, woman, and I don't do that easily."

"No?" I ask, feeling a mix of haunted and hopeful.

"But you....You just do something to me."

I take his face in my hands. "Will, can't you see what you do to me? I think I started falling for you from the moment I saw you in the cafe."

"Yeah?" A smile breaks across his face as his hands take hold of my hips.

"Hell, yes! I'm standing in the shrubs... with a client... on a shoot... pouring out my heart... not caring that I may lose this job. You're making me crazy. Can you please just kiss me so we can forget about everything for a minute?"

His lips are on mine so fast I don't have time to breathe. It's an amped-up kiss fueled with unguarded passion and edged with fear. He groans and lifts me up. Then he slowly slides me back down against him.

I sigh when we part. "Look at what we have. Please, don't give up on me."

He nods looking determined. "I'm gonna try because I want to trust you."

We fall into another kiss.

"Yeow!" I say, jumping back and shaking my leg. "I think this has become a threesome."

"Dude! What the fuck. Get off my girl!" He pulls Romeo, who is frantically getting it on with my leg, off me and holds him down while I step away. "How'd you get out, you horny bastard?"

I glance over my shoulder. "I better get back in there anyway. Let me go in ahead of you. Okay?"

He doesn't look completely convinced but still looks me intently. "Yeah, okay."

For most of the morning Will stays in the yard, hanging with Romeo. Maybe it's easier for him to be away from whatever the hell is happening in the house. At ten-thirty, Lindsey calls him into the house to sit for Gia, and I join them.

He stands next to me and waves his hands as he talks. "I don't wear makeup, so thanks but no thanks."

"It's not like that, Will," Gia explains patiently. "I make sure you'll look like you don't have makeup on. The thing is, video washes people out and any shine on your face becomes a beam of light. So actually what I'm going to do will make you look natural."

"Trust Gia," I tell him.

Will raises his eyebrows skeptically. "I've got to admit," he says, "I've spent all these years on the lot and didn't pay attention to the makeup and wardrobe crews. It's a completely different world than my set and scenic people."

"It is." Gia agrees.

"So let me get this straight. You put makeup on me to make me look natural on camera?"

She nods. "That's right."

I smile at him, realizing that he's coming around.

"So that's like how they have a writer write the reality show to make it seem real."

She laughs and gives a knowing smile. "You're better off not having these deep thoughts, Will. This is La-La Land after all."

"And I work in the business, but this reality show stuff is new to me," he says.

"*Reality* is a concept. It's open for interpretation, isn't it?" She challenges.

I roll my eyes, but the idea stings that reality shows are rarely real regardless of what I hope them to be.

When Gia's finished, Will remembers the list he made of the children's charities and shelters he supports, along with the schools that have visited the house during the holidays. He goes to grab it and returns.

Lindsey and I are in the hallway going over the schedule. I turn and smile as he approaches.

He hands a page to each of us once he has our full attention. "So here's the list of the charities the proceeds from the house tours and benefits go to. Sophia said that they could be listed and mentioned in the special."

Lindsey casually accepts the paper and tucks it partway down the stack of papers on her clipboard. "Sure Will," she says, giving him a warm smile before turning back to continue her discussion with me.

I touch her arm. "Lindsey, this is important. Okay? We need to make sure that happens."

Lindsey tips her head but nods. "Okay, Sophia, I'll see what I can do."

I nod to Will. "I'll make sure it happens."

He walks away with a huff. I step away from Lindsey and follow him as he heads up front. He dodges all the open equipment cases and steps over the cords snaking all over the floors. I imagine it's unsettling to have his furniture shifted around and all the lights they've brought in. It must not feel like his house.

Aaron looks up from where he's hunched over the camera and notices us. "Hey, guys. How you doing, Will?"

Will shrugs. "Okay, I guess. You getting what you need?"

"Yeah, it took a while to get the balance of lighting right, but I think we've got it now."

"Good," Will says.

"And we're almost ready for you. You ready for us?" he says with a laugh. "You look uncomfortable, but I bet you'll come off great on camera. And Paul's a kick. He'll make it fun."

"Listen to Aaron," I say.

"Okay," Will says, trying to give him an unforced smile. "I'll take your word for it."

When we wander back out to the hall we, run into Paul.

"Good, I was about to go find you," Paul says, slapping Will on the back. "So we thought we'd start with you welcoming us in the front door. If you're ready we can do a run through?"

"Let's get it over with," Will says.

Paul motions to Lindsey and me to join them, and we head out to the front porch.

Paul turns to Will. "Okay, this is really straight forward—the opening shot. When we say action we're going to have you open the front door and then say your line. Then you'll step back and open the door wider like you're letting us in. The cameraman will actually do a tracking shot going through the door."

Will nods.

"I'll show you the walk through." Paul steps inside and closes the door.

A second later Lindsey yells, "Action!"

Paul pulls the door open with a huge grin on his face. "Hi, I'm Will Sander, and—"

"Saunders," Will says.

"What?" asks Paul, barely restraining an eye roll.

"Saunders, my last name is Saunders."

"Right. Well, you get the idea. Let's start over."

"Action!" Lindsey shouts.

Paul swings the door open. "Hi, I'm Will Saunders and welcome to my magical Christmas wonderland!" He steps back and does a dramatic arm sweep, then waits several beats, pretending to watch the imaginary cameraman entering the house.

"Cut!" Lindsey yells to end the scene.

"Magical Christmas wonderland?" Will's face twists in disbelief. "You've got to be kidding. That's so corny."

Will looks over, and I cringe a little.

"Is he always this literal?" Lindsey whispers.

"Corny? Corny?" Paul asks, the edges of his ears turning red. "We're talking about a house full of Christmas decorations, are we not?"

"Paul," I say with a warning tone.

"Where's his shirt, Sophia? I thought we had an understanding."

"He's not wearing the shirt, Paul," I say firmly.

Will folds his arms over his chest and shakes his head.

Paul presses his lips together and glares. "We'll discuss this later," he says to me in a low voice.

He motions to Will. "We need to get going. Come on, you do this now."

Will reluctantly steps inside the door and closes it.

"Action!"

He opens the door and stares straight ahead at a tree in the front yard then starts speaking in a monotone voice. "Hi, I'm Will Saunders and welcome to my home." His movements are robotic as he pulls the door open further and counts to four before looking back at the threesome.

"Cut," Lindsey says with a weak voice.

"Sorry, Will. No can do. We need more energy or it will fall completely flat on camera. Flat as a dead fish," Paul says.

"I'm flat as a dead fish?" Will says, amused at the idea of it.

"No, no." I jump in. "He just means to use a little more energy so it appears like you actually want us to come in."

"And how about sticking to the script while you're at it," Paul adds.

"We throw that word around, but I'm not saying *magical* on camera. That's misleading. There's no actual magic," says Will.

"You're right, Lindsey," Paul says, turning toward her. "He's not Mr. Christmas, he's Mr. Literal. We've got him on the wrong show."

"Paul," I say, sounding more threatening this time.

"Okay, take out *magical,* but say the rest as I wrote it."

I step close to Will. "Is it really a big deal to say it's a Christmas wonderland? It is, you know?" I smile, hoping he'll cooperate.

He thinks about it for a moment. "Okay, I'll do it."

"Thanks." I turn back to Lindsey and Paul and nod. Aaron steps outside with his camera and sets up for the sequence.

Three takes later, Paul decides to move on since Will was at least smiling on the third attempt.

We break for lunch and as soon as the union's allotted time is over, everyone jumps back into the shoot. The first scene of the afternoon is shot in the foyer with Will explaining the massive kid's tree laden with vintage character and toy ornaments.

Paul doesn't even have to direct Will for this sequence because when he asks questions on camera, Will gets energized talking about the kids and their reaction to the tree and their experience of visiting the house.

When Aaron takes a minute to adjust the camera, I overhear Paul say to Lindsey, "Thank God. Mr. Christmas actually has a personality."

As the camera rolls, I smile as I listen. For a moment it occurs to me that I'm getting a peek into Will's heart, a flash of something fundamental to his makeup. Perhaps his Christmas house allows him to relive his childhood the way he wished it had been.

One thing is for sure. His past holds many answers to his personality, his strength, and his carefully constructed shield of defense. Hopefully I will have enough pieces of his puzzle to link together and give me insight to all the mysteries that define him. Maybe that will set my concerns about his eccentricities at rest.

They do a second take for a safety backup, but we really don't need it. Will was electric and engaging the first time.

I approach him when the set breaks and rest my hand on his arm. "That was great, Will," I say, giving him a big smile.

"You think so?" he asks, his eyes wide.

"I do. Your enthusiasm was palpable. It made me wish I was a kid touring this house at Christmas."

"It's weird. Easy—maybe because I was talking about the kids."

"Well, whatever it was, it really worked."

"I know they edit it down to sound bites, but hopefully they'll leave enough for people to understand what this means to the kids that visit."

"We will." I assure him.

Will's visibly less wound up when we head to the living room for the next scene.

Even Paul looks more optimistic as they start the next setup. "So, Will," he says. "This room is amazing… truly a winter wonderland. Can you tell us how you made the transition from a guy who likes decorating for the holidays, to someone intent on taking Christmas theming to a whole new level… because that's what you've done here."

"Thanks, but I can't take all the credit. My grandparents had a passion for Christmas and really started this tradition of decorating. They bought this house in nineteen fifty-five, and every year they made their holidays bigger and bigger. I inherited that passion from them."

"So it's in the genes," Paul says, smiling.

"Yeah, it is. But naturally during their time, the décor and theming was a lot more basic. My grandmother was a crafter and made a lot of the decorations. Now as every year passes, stuff gets more elaborate with lots of new ideas."

"So true!" adds Paul enthusiastically. "Look at the snowing effect you have projected on the ceiling and walls. That's amazing."

"Thank you. But a lot of credit goes to my studio friends I work with. Some are special effects experts, and they've devoted many hours to taking this house to an entirely different level of technology and spectacle."

"There's a lot of female touches too. Who do you credit that for?"

"Some of my past girlfriends contributed too. Everyone who gets close to me somehow touches this project."

"How great. You have to tell me, Will. You're single and good-looking. How do girls react when you bring them home and see what you've created here?"

"They seem to like it," he answers modestly but with a smile.

Lindsey chuckles and elbows me. "Wow, look at him go," she whispers.

"Yeah, he's downright chatty," I whisper back, unsettled.

Paul rubs his hands together with delight. "See folks, he doesn't kiss and tell, but we know the truth." He speaks directly to the camera. "Now we know Will's real motivation with all this… this place is a chick magnet! Am I right?"

Will looks shifts from one foot to the other but he laughs. "Well, I wouldn't say that, but as I said, women do like the house, yes."

"And I bet you don't have any problem getting dates," Paul continues.

"Well, no. Not really," Will answers with a smile.

My stomach lurches.

"So you bring 'em here and ka-ching! You score," Paul says.

Will laughs. "When I'm lucky." A second later he turns and points to their left in an attempt to distract him. "Paul, did you check out the snow globe collection?"

I silently step back from the set until I'm out of the tight circle of the sound and cameramen. As soon as I'm clear, I head for the kitchen. I pace back and forth for a minute, then pull open the back door and wander across the lawn. His words, *when I'm lucky*, keep echoing in my head. Was he joking?

I'm only a few paces in when Romeo charges toward me from the back of the yard. This time I'm prepared. I stop in my tracks and turn to face the pint-sized beast. When he's a few yards away, I throw out my arm powerfully with my hand up.

"Stop! Don't even think about it, you little horndog, or you'll regret it!"

Romeo skids to a stop, apparently stunned by my outburst.

I'm still not sure he'll be stopped so easily. "I'm not kidding, you little wild man!" I yell. I sound like a crazy person, but a woman can only take so much, and I'm at the end of my rope.

Romeo takes a tentative step forward as if testing me.

I shake my finger dramatically. "I'm not messing around, Romeo. Stay away from me!"

I realize that I'm raging, gasping for breath as I glare at him. The good news is my outburst is apparently effective. Romeo tucks his tail between his legs and cowers away.

I spot a picnic table in the back of the garden and I march over and sit down, ignoring the dirt on the bench. I lean on my elbows and wish I were anywhere but here.

I allow myself to embrace my moping. I was feeling hopeful about what was developing between Will and me. Now all I can hear are asshole Paul's inappropriate questions painting Will as a lady's man repeating in my head. Suddenly, I'm just one more in a long line of women that have been charmed by Will and his house. *Magical indeed.*

Was that stuff he said about not dating anyone for a while, true? He never painted himself as a monk, but certainly he hasn't portrayed himself as a ladies man either... until he suggested it on camera for the world to see. It angers me to think he accused me of playing him earlier and now I'm wondering if *Will the Womanizer* has been playing me.

I stew for a minute but find my resolve and straighten. I'm at work on an important shoot, for God's sake. I need to get my act together.

I'm glad I learned about this side of Will now, before we'd gone too far. Paul actually did me a favor. I stand and brush the dirt off the back of my slacks. I pull back my shoulders, and as I march back to the house, I renew my all-consuming focus on work.

As I reach the back porch I see Roger, the sound guy, watching me.

"Hey, what are you doing out here, Roger?"

He squints at me and takes a long drag from his cigarette, then slowly blows out the smoke. "I could ask the same, Sophia. As my Aunt Beth used to say, it looks like you have a bee in your bonnet."

I stop in my tracks and wonder who else saw me pacing in the back-yard or yelling at Romeo. It's just another kick in the pants and a remind-er to put my work face on and soldier through the day. I clear my throat and smile. "I'm fine, just taking a break."

"Uh-huh," he says, not sounding the slightest bit convinced.

"So, why are you out here?"

"Some days I can only take Paul in small doses. That poor guy in there—Christmas dude—doesn't know what hit him, and that shit gets to me sometimes. These people have no idea what they're getting them-selves into when they sign up for these shows."

"Will? I ask.

"Yeah, he seems like an all right guy, but Paul is toying with him. I'm not sure why yet, but I'll figure it out."

"I'm starting to wonder if Paul always has an agenda."

"I have some theories about this setup."

"Come on, Roger, share." I press.

"Maybe Paul has the hots for the dude and is pissed he doesn't pitch for Paul's team."

My eyes go wide. "Oh, geez, you can't be serious," I say. *Great, one more thing to feel awkward about on this shoot.*

"Sorry." He lifts his hands up in defense. "I just call 'em as I see 'em, and that guy is definitely straight. If you don't mind me saying so, I think that dude fancies you."

I absentmindedly bite on my thumbnail and try not to look too curious. "Yeah? What makes you think that?"

"You walked out during the last setup."

I swallow nervously. "Yeah, what about it?"

"He was doing fine, and then he lost his focus when he saw you walk away. I thought he was going to go after you, but Paul pulled all the stops to keep him focused where he needed to be."

The back door suddenly swings open, and Will steps outside.

He gives me a relieved smile but when he spies Roger, his demeanor changes. He nods to Roger before turning to me. "Hey, Sophia. You got a minute? I wanted to check with you about something."

Roger smiles quietly and snubs out his cigarette. "Think I'll head back inside."

"Talk to you later, Roger," I say with a wave before turning to Will. "What's up?"

Will steps closer and slides his hands in his pockets. "Well, I was just thinking about our lunch today."

Lunch? That's a little random. I eye him, bewildered. "What about our lunch?"

"Well, there was so much food left over."

I realize where this is going. "And…"

Will gives me a hopeful smile. "Do you think we could donate it to a shelter? I could make some calls."

Oh, Will. It's hard to be angry with him when he shows this side of himself.

"I'll check with Lindsey, but I can't imagine why not. I'll go find her."

Will grins. "That's great, thanks." I'm almost past him when he turns and touches my arm.

"Hey, is everything okay?"

"Sure," I reply, giving him a blank expression.

"I noticed you left in the middle of the shot in the living room."

I'm embarrassed but I'm not willing to get into it now. *He's our subject,* I remind myself. I need to keep him upbeat and focused for the shoot.

"Bathroom. Sorry if it distracted you."

He takes a deep breath and relaxes his shoulders. "No worries, I just wanted to make sure you were okay."

"I think it's going really well, don't you? You're getting comfortable in front of the camera."

He rubs his chin. "Well, I wouldn't say comfortable… but it's gone from excruciating to tolerable."

I laugh. "That's progress indeed."

"Besides, I know Paul goes on and on with me, but in the end they're just going to use a few sound bites, right?"

"Probably."

"So, how bad can it possibly be?"

I nod. "It'll be fine. All right, let me go find Lindsey to make arrangements for the leftover food before the next setup starts."

"Thanks, Sophia."

There's something in his parting smile that breaks me a little. He looks so genuinely happy. It's that kind of feeling that narrows one's vision to only the bright and shiny things. Under a bluer sky, the dirty fingerprints of disappointment fade away.

But the fingerprints are there, and I am covered with them as I open the back door and step into the house.

"Oh jeez, he's really something. Is he for real?" Lindsey asks.

"What do you mean?" I ask, trying not to sound too curious.

"It's just not every day you find a guy his age, who looks like *that*"— she fans herself dramatically— "and is all about helping people. I mean what the hell is wrong with him?"

I shake my head. "You're so cynical, Lindsey. Can't he just be a good guy?"

Lindsey rolls her eyes. "Yeah, right. It's not like he's Amish or something and living in Dutch country. This is L.A. That would make him as rare in this town as a well-intentioned studio mom."

"Oh, that's a good one!" I laugh.

"Besides, maybe it's like what Paul was getting at on the last take—he does it to charm the ladies. If so, it's working. He was so distracting, I don't even remember what I ate for lunch."

I keep a fake smile plastered on my face. "Well, tell all, Lindsey. Was he flirting with you?"

"I wish! Nah, he's quite the subtle one if that was flirting. But you can bet I was. Alas, he was oblivious to my charms."

I fight the relief bubbling up inside of me. "His loss then. I'm going to go check in with Paul. Do you want to tell Will about the food for the shelter?"

"I'd be happy to," she says with a smile.

<hr />

"So, for this last take I want to talk to you about your favorite Christmas gift ever," Paul explains to Will.

Paul, Will, and I are in the sitting area of the living room while Aaron, Terry, and Roy get set up. With Paul's question I see a glint of pain in Will's eyes before he looks down.

Twenty minutes later the camera's rolling and Paul puts his spin on the subject. "So Will, I remember my all-time favorite Christmas gift when I was a kid. It still makes me giddy just thinking about it."

Will goes with it like a pro. "What was it, Paul?"

"A Super 8 camera and a toy clapper board so I could make my own movies. For weeks after, every time my family heard the clapper snap shut and me yell *action* they ran and hid."

"That's great."

"So what was your favorite gift ever? When did Santa thrill you the most?"

Will's smile turns wistful. "Actually it wasn't from Santa. It was a bike I had wanted for almost two years: a bright red racing bike. With our situation, it was out of reach, but one Christmas I got it from my parents. I was beside myself."

"Nice. Nothing like making a kid's dream come true," says Paul, nodding.

Paul turns to the camera and points. "So, all you viewers at home, what was your favorite Christmas present? Log onto our website and let us know!"

When Aaron gestures and Lindsey yells *cut*, Paul jumps off the couch. "Okay, that wraps it up for today. Good job, Will. We got some good stuff."

"Thanks."

Lindsey steps into the circle. "Hey, powwow. There's been a development."

"What's up?" I ask.

"We just got a confirmation. That big Pacific Northwest storm is heading this way. We knew there was a chance of rain this week, but now it's confirmed. We're going to have to reschedule Friday's exterior shoot."

"Crap, I really wanted to wrap this up this week," says Paul.

"I'm sure we all did," I say.

Will rubs his chin. "I should probably reschedule the yard setup on Thursday."

"Definitely. They say the storm will hit late morning Thursday, and it's supposed to be a big one. I've looked at the schedules. We could probably make it work a week from this Thursday. Would that work for you, Will?"

"I think so. We're still on hiatus on my show," Will replies.

"Good," says Lindsey. "So tomorrow will be the last of the interiors. We'll be covering the kitchen, family room and the *under the sea* room, so it's another big day."

"Yes, thank you everyone," I add. "See you bright and early tomorrow."

Will wilts a little, but hopefully he knows that having made it this far it's just a matter of soldiering on.

"Oh! Don't forget the author that will be joining us," Paul says.

"Author?" Will asks. He glances at me but I'm surprised as well.

"I thought we didn't have time for her, Paul?" I ask.

"Well, now that we've expanded this idea into a series of specials, she has a unique way of pulling it together. George agreed to it."

I fold my arms over my chest and fall silent. *Can this day be over yet?*

"So, what does this woman write about?" Will asks.

"Helena Marche… I guess you could say she writes about people with interesting hobbies," Paul replies.

"Okay," I say. "I've got to head out. Lindsey, do you mind checking everything when the guys are ready to go. I've got some things I need to take care of."

"Sure, Sophia." She doesn't look sorry at all to be the last one to leave Will after the shoot.

"Thanks. I'm going to grab my stuff, and I'll see you all tomorrow."

I head to the kitchen, and as I gather my backpack and coffee mug, I sense someone behind me. I turn and can't decide if I'm happy or sad to see Will with big doe eyes staring at me from the doorway.

"You're going?" he asks quietly. "I thought—"

One of the crew passes behind Will, so I motion for him not to say anything.

"Let's talk outside for a minute," he says moving to the back door.

I follow him outside. This is a conversation I'd prefer to avoid.

He sits on the top step of the deck and pats the space next to him.

I feel a mix of emotions as I sink down on the step. I wish I could pull him apart like a Russian nesting doll, one after the other—the charmer, the wounded child, the holiday over-doer—getting smaller and smaller until I got to the last doll. Will's true self. Maybe then I would have the right words.

"So, you're leaving now?"

I take a deep breath. "Yeah."

"I thought… well, I hoped you'd stay. Can't you?"

I look down. "I'm just really tired, so I think it would be good to rest at home and catch up with some work."

"Oh, I understand," he says quietly.

We watch Romeo head toward us, but instead of his usual enthusiasm, he approaches warily. When he's a few feet away, he stops and sinks down to the ground just to the right of Will.

"Hey, what's up, dude? You all right?" Will turns to me. "Romeo appears to be over you."

"You know how it is with guys like him. You never hold their interest for long."

Will shrugs. "Still, it's strange. He's normally not so fickle. He may flirt a lot, but when he makes his mind up about someone, that's it."

Romeo's woeful eyes are just too much. Between disappointing Will and his little man, I feel guilty.

"Okay. I admit it. We had a conflict earlier, Romeo and I. Words were exchanged, spirits may have been broken."

Will lifts his eyebrows. "Ah, so you let him down hard."

"I guess you could say that."

He holds out his hand, "Come here, boy." Romeo comes right to Will, who lifts him up into his lap. Romeo turns and licks Will's jaw. Will scratches him behind his ears.

"So she broke your heart? I'm sorry, dude. The road to love can be a rocky one."

You aren't kidding, I think.

The more I watch the two boys together, the more it softens my unsteady heart. I extend my hand to Romeo as an offering of peace. He sniffs it tentatively and gives it a tiny lick. I scoot closer and rub the sweet spot on his chest, and he swoons.

"See that little kiss you just gave her, Romeo? Sometimes that's all it takes. Just be classy and kind. Women like that," Will tells his little friend encouragingly.

We sit quietly for a moment, loving up Romeo before I take a deep breath and stand.

I nod toward the house. "I better get going before…"

Will nods. "Okay. And you're sure you're all right? I just haven't seen you like this before."

I force myself to smile. "Yeah, I'm fine." *Well not really, but I will be… eventually,* I think.

"I'll see you in the morning," I say and walk to the back door. I take one last look. His back is to me as he and Romeo look out over the yard. His energy has changed as if I just pulled him down to where the light isn't quite as bright and nothing is extraordinary.

Something occurs to me as I work my way through the house. Infatuation is magic with fireworks exploding in your heart in brilliant snaps and sparkles. But when the show is over, the sky is empty and darker than it was before.

Chapter Ten

My apartment feels emptier than usual. I wander around trying to figure out how to fill my time so I don't miss the idea of Will. I jump when the door buzzer goes off. I'm not expecting anyone, so I'm wary as I approach the intercom.

"Hello?"

"Hey, Sophia, it's Will. Can I come up for a minute?"

"Will?" I let out a long sigh. *What's he doing here?*

"Yeah, the guy from the shoot today." He teases but sounds nervous.

I laugh softly, but it sounds sad. "What's up? Why are you here?"

"Because. I. Want. To. See. You."

There's a long pause. "But I'm in sweats, I look terrible... I wasn't expecting anyone." I fire off, trying to persuade him to not come up.

His tone becomes determined. "And I have the biggest bunch of flowers here. So, if you don't let me up, I'll have to leave them here and some drunk coming home from a night at the clubs will get them instead of you."

Thus commences another long pause as I try to decide what to do. Can I turn him away? I should since he probably considers me easy and just a flavor of the week. That would show him.

"I don't—"

"Sophia, I'm here on your doorstep, with a bunch of flowers and a troubled heart. Are you really going to turn me away? Really?"

I let out a big sigh of defeat and press the buzzer extra long.

I'm standing in the open frame of my door when he gets off the elevator and walks down the hall. My hair's pulled back in a severe ponytail and with my face sans make-up, I'm paler than ever. I'm sure my face resembles the moon on a hazy night, round and hopeless.

I focus on the flowers as he approaches. He holds them up as an offering. They're the biggest bunch of Gerber daisies I've ever seen in one arrangement. It's a big smile, a riot of color. The hot orange, yellow and pinks are explosions of happy, challenging every shade of gray I feel inside.

"For you." He happily pushes them a little closer to me. He squares his shoulders back and looks proud with himself that he thought to bring them.

"What's the occasion?" I ask giving him a small smile.

"I wanted to cheer you up. You seemed kind of down when you left today."

"Thank you. That's really sweet," I say, taking the flowers and opening the door wider. "Do you want to come in for a minute?"

His expression falls. Is he disappointed that I'm setting this up as a short visit?

He nods and follows me into the kitchen where I pull out a large vase and put the flowers in water.

"I was just having some tea. You want some?"

"No, thanks."

I want to say something, but instead I just hold onto the edge of the kitchen counter as if to steady myself.

"I'm really here because I needed to talk to you," he explains.

"Okay," I say, carrying the vase out to the living room and setting the flowers on the coffee table. I settle down on the couch and he does the same. "What do you want to talk about?"

He twists his hands together. "This afternoon, I started talking to Stu as he packed up the lights."

"I'm sure you got an earful," I say, rolling my eyes.

"Yeah, apparently he was impressed about what a stud I am."

"Yeah, a real lady-killer," I say, chagrined.

"He was under the impression that I had a line of babes to choose from."

"I think everyone is under that impression now."

"Including you?" he asks.

I nod and avert my eyes.

Will leans forward, his elbows pressed into his knees. "I swear that's not the way I am. I want to see that footage because I would never portray myself that way. I just can't believe it was that bad."

"It was very enlightening," I say softly.

He turns toward me, and I look away. I'm frowning and I can't even pretend to be okay about all of this. I imagine his confidence—that he can convince me he isn't a stud, is melting like ice on a hot sidewalk.

"Paul was the one portraying that image of me," he argues.

"But you didn't disagree. What else am I to think when you're okay with being perceived that way on national television?"

His hands curl into fists and he presses them down on his knees. "No. That's not it."

"And I'm normally so much more careful when I date. After we met I just jumped in with both feet. I mean look how close I came to sleeping with you and we've had, what… a few dates and meetings? I don't normally do that. There's so much I don't know about you," I say.

"What do you want to know? I'll tell you anything."

"After today, I think I know all I need to know."

"Damn, I knew this shit would backfire on me! This is exactly why I didn't want to do this show, and I did it for you… to be with you. And now look at us."

"Yeah, now look at us." I rest my face in my hands.

A heavy silence falls between us, and I wonder if I should just ask him to leave. Maybe I wasn't meant to be his girl. It's so early on in our dating to have these kinds of problems.

He scans my living room and my stuff.

What's he doing? I've tried to portray a quirky elegance with my place. Besides the piles of books stacked everywhere, I have artfully framed pen and ink sketches on the walls. He'd noticed them during the last visit, and is interested in them again. He scans a vintage Parisian travel poster hanging just above old oversized wooden letters of varying shapes leaning up on the mantle. They spell out the word *inspire*. Just next to it he studies a small abstract sculpture. He points to the display.

"I like that," he says quietly.

I scrutinize the sculpture, trying to understand why he'd bring it up just now. Is he trying to distract me?

"The sculpture? It's by an Italian artist. I bought it when I was in Florence," I explain.

"Wow, that's cool. So when were you in Florence?"

I look up, thinking. "Just over two years ago?"

"Who'd you go with?"

I let out a big sigh. "My boyfriend at the time. His name was Marco."

"Was he Italian?"

"Indeed, he was."

"I see," says Will, falling silent.

"So, you've had boyfriends in the past?"

I give him an exasperated look. "Yes, I have. But not an assembly line of them."

"No, of course not. I would never have thought that of you." He looks back at the mantle. "And where did you get those letters?"

I smile at the memory. "There was this guy in Covent Garden who inherited all of this vintage lettering stuff from his family. It was so cool. I wanted to buy his whole collection."

"Covent Garden in London?" he asks.

"Yes, I spent a lovely afternoon there," I reply.

"Who'd you go there with?"

I fold my arms over my chest. "I know what you're getting at, Will. Yes, I've had boyfriends in the past. Not that many, but I have fallen in love before."

"You have lived," he says as if it's the most natural thing in the world.

I sigh. "Yes, I have."

"As have I. It's not like we're sixteen."

I put my hands on my hips. "You're twisting this around."

"I don't think the past should hold us back. What matters is us now."

There's truth in what he's said, and I give him a slight nod.

He points to the letters on the mantle. "It's a great word... *inspire*. It fits you. It fits us."

"Really?"

"Yes, because you've inspired me. Completely, from the bottom of my feet to the ends of my hair."

I laugh. "The ends of your hair?"

He combs his fingers across his scalp. "Yeah, and I've got a lot of hair." He smiles and when I smile back he scoots closer to me on the couch. I don't move away so he scoots a little closer.

"Can I put my arm around you?"

"I'm not sure." I chew on my bottom lip, silently cursing the thousands of invisible threads pulling my heart toward his.

"Please?" I think he's trying not to sound like he's begging.

"Maybe," I whisper.

I scoot a little closer, and he slides his arm over my shoulder. I soften just the tiniest bit, realizing that having him close feels so right.

He tips his head down to my ear and whispers, "There's no assembly line, Sophia. I'm not a ladies' man. Can't you tell I want to be *your* man?"

I press my face into his shoulder. "I'd like to believe that. This is just a tough subject for me. I've had my heart completely broken by a lothario."

"I'm sorry." He kisses the top of my head.

"And I jumped in too fast with you. I'm always drawn to creative men who are different, and you're a stand-out for sure."

He smiles. "Creative and *different*, huh? How bad can that be?"

"It's great until they decide to get creative and different with someone else."

"I'm not like that, Sophia. And if you want to slow things down until you're sure of what I'm about, I'm okay with that. I'll wait for you."

"We were already waiting." I point out.

"But I'll wait even longer," he adds.

"You will, huh?" I'm not ready to believe him yet.

He takes my hand. "As long as it takes."

I'm silent as I think about the fragile, shimmering bubble of trust with a lover, all transparency and rainbow reflections until it suddenly pops. But in all fairness to Will, it's not right to deny him any chance because of what happened with Paul during the shoot.

"Can I stay a while more and just hold you?" he asks. Maybe he can tell that my anti-Will stance is softening.

"Nothing else?" I know how easily he could seduce me.

"Nope. Not even if you twist my arm." He teases.

I nod and curl into him, and gradually we each keep shifting until we're stretched out and almost spooning on my long, wide couch.

He wraps his arm around my waist, tying us together like a Christmas present.

"I feel so much better already," he whispers in my ear.

I rub my hand over his arm lightly. "Me too. Can I ask you something?"

"Sure, anything."

"During the shoot today you mentioned your favorite Christmas present ever was a bike your parents got you."

"I did."

"You told me they didn't celebrate Christmas. Did they celebrate that Christmas? Is that why the bike was such a special gift?"

Will sighs and pulls away just far enough to rub his hand roughly over his face.

"What?"

"I only told Paul half of that story… the good half. The second half isn't nearly as nice."

I take a hold of his arm and pull him close again. "I'd like to hear about it if you want to tell me."

"I've never told anyone the entire story of what happened that night."

I stroke his arm and wait.

He clears his throat. "It was the Christmas when I was nine, and I kept begging my parents to let us celebrate Christmas again. My persistence was making them crazy, so they let me go to my grandparents to get out of their way. On Christmas Eve, Grandpa Joe called me to the living room after dinner, and when I got there, the bike I'd wanted forever was parked right in front of the tree."

"Aw, that's so great."

"I lost it for a while, yelling and jumping up and down. When I finally calmed down, I asked Grandpa why Santa came early. He smiled and gave me a card to read."

"It was from your parents," I say softly.

"Yeah. It said that even though they have a hard time showing it, they were proud of me and loved me. That card meant the world to me, Sophia. It meant more to me than the bike."

"So, what's the sad part? Were they supposed to show up too?"

"Not exactly, although it got me hoping they would and we were going to be okay again. Late that night I couldn't sleep. Between Santa coming and getting that card from my parents, I was just too amped-up.

I snuck out of my room, even though I wasn't supposed to go downstairs, because I wanted to read the card again."

"I'm getting a bad feeling." I shiver in his arms.

He nods. "When I got to the living room, I heard Grandma and Grandpa talking in the kitchen, so I snuck up to the door to listen."

"They didn't know you were there?"

He shakes his head.

"What did you overhear?"

"Long story short, I learned that my parents had nothing to do with the bike or the card."

My expression falls. "No. Why would they lie about it?"

"I guess my grandparents were so upset Mom and Dad had emotionally abandoned me, they felt this gift would give me some comfort. They had been worried that with the way things were, I would turn into a wild and angry kid."

"Oh God, how awful."

"I was so upset when I found out," he says, his voice still heavy. "I've never been so disappointed in my life."

I stay silent, but turn around so I'm facing him and take his hand.

"The worst part is when they heard me in the living room ripping up the card, they realized I'd overheard everything. They were devastated. I'm not sure they ever got over their guilt."

I gently stroke his face to comfort him. "They meant well, but that was not a good idea."

"No, it wasn't. False hope is like a disease that eats away at you until you have no faith left."

"And that was your best Christmas gift ever?" I ask, bewildered.

"Well, it was for about five hours. And if I hadn't snuck downstairs, it probably still would be."

"That's incredibly sad. It's pretty remarkable, considering your upbringing, that you turned out as well as you did," I say softly.

"I'm still working on it. I guess you could say I'm a work in progress."

This time he runs his fingertips down my cheek and over my lips. He watches me intently as he does and I really wish he would kiss me, but he doesn't.

"So what was your favorite Christmas present ever?" he finally asks.

I think for a moment before I give him a warm smile. "It was a doll-house, an intricately hand-crafted dollhouse. It was from Santa and my parents told me that it was especially made in his workshop."

"How cute." Will grins as he rests his hand on my hip.

"Years later I found out that Dad and Mom made it from a kit they put together late at night. It took them several weeks to finish it, working on it in the garage after we'd gone to bed. Being the third of four kids, I got a lot of hand-me-downs, not just clothes but toys too. So having something so unique and made just for me was extra special."

"I envy your childhood."

"I was lucky." I roll over to my back and gaze at the mantle. I take his hand in mine and press it down high on my chest, above my heart. "You inspire me, Will. You took a devastating childhood and decided not to let it define your life. Instead you've created something extraordinary that's positive and makes people happy."

"I suppose, but you make it sound like I had a master plan, and it was completely altruistic. But it wasn't, especially in the beginning. It started by me trying to gain back what I'd lost, or even more so, what I never had."

"That's understandable. But now it isn't all about you, is it? I'd say not by a long shot."

He nods. "Yeah, I have to admit you're right."

"So, with that established ... what in the world inspires you about me?"

"You may guess that I'm inspired by your beauty, that you're sexy and smart. Perhaps you think I admire how hard you work... that you're good at what you do."

"But?" I ask, tensing up. I can tell he's going another direction and I hope it's one I feel good about.

"You inspire me because you're grateful for what you have, that you admit your flaws but still love yourself. You inspire me because you do want to be more than who you are now even though you're already amazing."

"I don't want to be shallow in any way. I do want to be more," I whisper, my breath catching as I remember our conversation from several days ago.

"And you will be. I know you will."

"You truly think so?" I ask, sounding hopeful.

He nods. "Yes. And maybe I understand it because I feel the same."

I turn and gaze at him. "And I believe you will be more too."

He smiles. "My dreams are always tucked just inside the edges of my mind. Careers and all that are important, but one day I want to be a great dad and the kind of man a woman like you would be proud to be married to. I may not be there yet, but I want to be one day. When I am, then I'll prove that I'm stronger than my fucked up childhood... that I have it in me to hang in there even when things get tough, that I can be what a real man should be."

What a real man should be? For a moment I forget how to breathe.

This time I'm the one stunned by the fireball of passion that explodes, showering me with thoughts of rolling on top of Will and kissing him until he can't think straight. It takes every bit of restraint I can manage just to lay there like a living mannequin. He runs his fingertips down my neck and over my shoulder like a human navigation system. His wonderful wandering fingers head south and glide over my hip and down to circle my knee. My legs instinctively part as his hand heads northbound again, gliding up the edge of my inner thigh.

"You okay?" he whispers, leaning close.

I shake my head. "No, I'm not okay."

"Join the club," he says, pressing the evidence of his lack of composure against my hip. "I want to keep my promise, so I think I need to go." He sits up, the frustration evident in his tight expression as he drags his fingers through his hair. "But rest assured, you have no idea how much I want to stay."

I am speechless. Would it really be so bad if we messed around tonight? I shake my head, disappointed with my lack of composure. He's doing this for me.

He scoots off the edge of the couch and sways as he stands, as if his legs are unsteady. "Thanks for this," he says, gesturing to the couch.

I nod. "Thanks for coming by. I feel worlds better than I did before."

"Me too."

I get off the couch and step into his open arms.

He holds me tight. "See you tomorrow."

"Yeah, bright and early."

Chapter Eleven

The next morning the equipment truck pulls up as scheduled. I hope Will has a better understanding of what to expect so he's not so nervous. He steps just outside the open door to greet us.

Aaron bounds up to Will first, holding an extra large coffee from the local coffee house. He doesn't even say hello as he gets right into work mode while the rest of us wait to get on the porch and in the house. "So, Will, we're going to start in the family room. I want to get all those train shots nailed first. Will you be available to show us how the system works?"

Will yawns and nods. "I could use some of what you're drinking."

Aaron laughs. "It's rocket fuel, man, I couldn't function in the morning without it."

Lindsey files up next and gives Will a big smile. She's closely followed by Stu, Terry, and the rest of the team. I slip by third to last, and Will's face lights up like I blasted his morning open, bringing the sunshine with me.

"Morning, Will," I say, all Doris Day demure.

"Morning, Sophia," he says, his expression smug like we belong to a secret club.

"Coffee?" I ask.

"Sorry, I haven't started it yet. I've had other stuff on my mind." He grins and raises his eyebrows.

I blush and look down. "Well, let me do it." I turn and head down the hallway.

"By all means. My house is yours," he says quietly as I pass.

Will waits a minute to head to the kitchen, and when he arrives, Paul, Lindsey and I are all in a powwow. He grabs a mug and approaches the coffeemaker.

"She's getting here just after lunch?" Paul asks.

"Yeah, she couldn't come this morning, she had some kind of early presentation. But I've gone over it with the guys, and we can make it work. It's not a problem," Lindsey says.

"What's all this about?" Will interrupts.

"Hey, Will," Paul says with a big smile. "Ready for another day of fun?"

For a moment I fear Will is going to punch Paul in the face, probably from yesterday's stud portrayal. But just as quickly the expression fades.

"I wouldn't call it fun, but I'm ready for whatever it's going to be."

"We were just talking about Helena. Remember, she's the writer that's coming today to ask you some questions on camera? George, our boss, decided that we should use her to tie the series of shows together."

"It won't take long." Lindsey assures him.

"Okay, I guess," Will responds.

We head to the family room to watch the guys set up. When they're finally ready, Will fires up the trains and turns on the ice skating rink and miniature ski lift. What a delight it is to hear the little boy come out of every one of those gruff tech guys.

"I had a train set when I was a kid," Stu says.

"I always wanted one," Terry replies.

"I'd spend hours in the basement changing the layouts. Then to keep things interesting I was always setting my sister's dolls on the track and crashing into them."

"Nice," says Aaron, laughing.

Stu turns to Will. "So you do all this shit, and you really don't have any kids?"

"Nope, not yet."

"But you get all those inner-city kids to visit, right?" Terry asks.

Will nods.

"So, you're like a fucking saint," Stu announces.

"Yeah, and did you hear about all his homeless stuff?" Terry adds, shaking his head.

"Are you for real? Or are you one of those closet assholes who tries to make up for it by being all generous and self-righteous in public?" Stu asks, half teasing.

"Stu!" I yell. "Don't be such an ass. Are you forgetting he's our subject?"

"I thought it was a fair question, and he's like one of the guys now," he says grumbling.

"I really don't think Will's a closet asshole." I fight back a laugh.

"Thanks, Sophia. Listen to your producer, Stu. She's a smart lady, Will says without taking his eyes off me.

Out of the corner of my eye, I see Stu grin and nudge Terry. With a toss of his head, he motions to Will. Terry snorts and whispers something to Stu, who tries unsuccessfully to cover his laughter with a cough.

I make a silent note to myself to be more careful.

The guys get to work and I step over to the village setup. I kneel down and survey it now that all the characters are in place.

"This is so great. Oh no, Will—two of the ice skaters have face planted on the ice." I point at the apparent disaster on the plastic ice rink.

Will comes over and kneels down so our thighs are pressed against each other, then puts the little skaters upright and positions them over the magnetized track so that they can continue skating. The girl skaters in their fur-trimmed jackets continue their figure eights and turn as if they never missed a beat.

"That's better," Will says.

Meanwhile my leg is on fire feeling him this close again. After he left my apartment last night I had the rest of evening to think about him pressed against me and the alternate ways the night could've proceeded if he hadn't left. The burn is moving through my body and making my heart thunder. I subtly press my thigh back against his

"So how are you feeling this morning?" he asks quietly.

"Really good. Although I didn't sleep much. I was really distracted after you left." I smile.

He grins back. "Me too."

A quick peek at the guys assures me everyone is focused on their work. My cheeks color when I turn to Will. "Remind me to tell you about the dream I had last night."

"Was I in it?" He teases.

"Let's just say you were the star," I whisper and then boldly trail my hand up his thigh.

"Tell me more," he says with a deep breath.

I lean closer and press my breast against his arm. "You were naked through most of it."

He swallows thickly. "Good, good, but more importantly... were you?"

My fingers tighten high on his thigh. "Oh yeah, completely."

"Sophia," he whispers, his eyes wide as he looks at my hand precariously close to the danger zone. "What are you doing?"

"Hey, Will. Can you show us something on this remote control?" Aaron asks.

I yank my hand away and stand. *Good God, what am I doing?* "I'm sorry," I whisper.

Will stands and stretches his legs. "Be right there, Aaron."

He leans in. "Don't be sorry. Don't ever be sorry for that." He winks and joins Aaron and the guys.

I leave the room to get my bearings. *Geez Sophia, what was that about? Last night you agreed to slow down and this morning you're all over him? Get a grip, girl.*

Paul's picking through the box of doughnuts when I walk into the kitchen.

"Hey, Sophia, how's it going?"

"You tell me, Paul."

He gives me a devilish grin. "I think it's going splendidly. We got some good stuff yesterday."

"Why did you portray Will as a manwhore in that last segment?"

"Ha, manwhore! I like that. If the shoe fits, honey."

"That's my point, I don't think it does."

"Come on, you have to admit he was completely flat earlier. I think that Q and A was by far the most entertaining. Besides, the viewers will love it. Mr. Christmas isn't some geekazoid who wears holiday sweaters his grannie knitted him. No, he's a stud who seduces women right under his well hung mistletoe."

I blanch, wondering if True Blue has a secret camera in the house that caught us under the mistletoe. I need to snap out of it and refocus.

"Paul, do I need to remind you the demographics for these shows are seventy percent middle-aged women, and they do not find manwhores appealing in the least."

Paul rolls his eyes. "Sure they do! Besides, me thinks you're a wee bit jealous, Ms. Sophia."

"What in the hell are you talking about?" I'm fuming.

"You think I didn't notice you ogling his ass yesterday… and other body parts as well? You've got the hots for him," he says smugly.

"Was that me or you doing the ogling?" I ask, trying to deflect his accusation.

"Well, it's a given I'm going to ogle him. I wouldn't be a self-respecting gay man if I didn't, but I would guess you, my dear, are normally all work and no play."

Lindsey joins us as she flips through her schedule and long list of notes. "They're taking too long with the trains. They're like a bunch of little boys in there. I knew we should've shot that last."

"Hey, Lindsey," Paul says, interrupting her rambling. "What did you think of the last segment yesterday where I brought out the inner stud in Will?"

"I thought it was hot," she says, smacking her lips.

"Ugh." I groan.

"Come on, Sophia. He's a total stud muffin. The ladies are gonna love that because they'll think they have a chance. It's sexual desire meets aspirational fantasies. That's a home run for sure," Lindsey says.

"Exactly," says Paul. "And who are we to tell them they're delusional. They can eat their pint of ice cream in front of their wide screen TVs and imagine climbing Will's tree."

"Okay, enough!" I yell and turn to walk out of the kitchen.

"Someone's got it bad," Paul says to Lindsey as I pass behind him.

"Well she can get in line behind me. I get him first."

I linger closer to the set for the next segment in the *under the sea* room.

Once the camera starts rolling, Paul heads right into the forbidden forest. "So is it true the mermaids in this room were inspired by a girl-friend who thought she'd been a mermaid?"

Will looks off camera and nods to me. "That's true."

"So, a lot of people think mermaids are sexy. Could you shed some light on that?"

What the hell!

"Uh…I thought this was a Christmas special."

"All I'll say, viewers, is I imagine Will has some great stories."

"Um, Paul," Will says nervously.

Paul looks directly into the camera. "So listen up, female viewers. Will may be a little shy, but I bet he knows how to make dreams come true."

Will's face turns red and the veins on his neck and forehead bulge.

I finally snap to attention. "Cut!" I call out.

"Why did you call cut, Sophia?" Aaron asks.

I step in and pull Paul aside. "I called cut because this demeans and objectifies our subject. I can't allow this type of direction for the interview to continue."

Paul points to Will and mouths the words *stud muffin*. He looks as if he wants to cackle with glee.

Lindsey grabs my arm and asks me to step outside for a minute.

"We'll be back in a minute," she says to the crew.

Once Lindsey has me alone, she turns to me.

"What. Are. You. Doing?"

"Protecting the subject," I say with a huff.

"Hey, girl, can you step off your high horse one minute so we can get real here?"

"What do you mean?" I ask.

"Well, first of all, why are you being so irritable and saying Paul's not being 'professional and appropriate' with the subject while you keep touching Will? This morning, every time I turned around, you were rubbing his arm or stroking his cheek. I mean, what the fuck! And you're giving Paul shit for teasing him when you know most of this shit won't be used. He's just trying to get the energy going."

"But it's so *wrong*. He's doing this on camera, and it's humiliating Will."

"Can we just call a spade a spade girl and get on with things."

I fold my arms over my chest angrily. "What are you alluding to?"

"You want to fuck him, and you don't want anyone else *fucking* with him."

"What?" I bark.

97

"Oh, just own it and stop being a special buttercup. I want to fuck him too. So does Gia, for that matter."

"That's great, just great," I say.

"But bottom line is none of that matters. What matters is that we have to get this show done, and it has to be top priority."

"This is so completely out of line." I retort so convincingly that I almost believe it myself. "Have you forgotten that I'm the producer of this shoot?"

"Whatever. Live in denial land all you want. I'm sure it's a bright and happy place. But meanwhile I need you to take a break, walk away, and get your bearings. We can't afford anymore drama delays today."

Paul strolls into the kitchen. "Break time!" he calls out cheerfully.

Lindsey glances at her watch. "It's not time for a break."

"Well, Will just blew up and told me he was going to kick my ass, so Aaron took him for a little drive to cool him off. So yeah, it's break time."

"Fabulous!" Lindsey says, exasperated. "Let me go get things back on track. Why don't you take a break and cool off too, Sophia."

I glare at Lindsey as I head out the back door.

When I step onto the porch, Romeo peeks out from his doghouse. I'm too stressed to let the dog get to me too, so I smile. He steps outside the doghouse and sits down to watch me. I'm encouraged that he isn't charging over to hump my leg. Maybe our relationship has possibilities. I sit down on the step and hold my hand out to him.

"Here, boy."

He stays seated and keeps eyeing me.

"Are you playing hard to get now?" I ask, laughing.

As soon as he hears me laugh he stands and trots over, stopping just in front of me.

"Good boy."

He steps closer and gives my leg a little lick.

"Ah, so we're friends now. I'm glad." I scratch him behind the ear and he licks my leg again.

"Perhaps you've just been misunderstood. Maybe all you wanted was to be loved."

He steps closer, and I run my hand down his back in long strokes. "Thanks, Romeo. I feel better already."

The rest of the morning everyone tries to play nice. I decide to put on my big girl panties and make my best effort to get along.

I'm especially relieved that Will is in good spirits after his time with Aaron.

"You okay?" I ask as the filming moves to the kitchen for setup scene shots.

"Yeah, Aaron got me to relax about everything. He explained how Paul likes to be provocative to get things going, but it's harmless. Once the sound bites are pulled, the rest is trashed."

"Good," I reply, not sure I completely agree with Aaron, but glad Will is okay.

"I've decided just to chill and have a good attitude. It's really the only way I can get through this without beating the crap out of Paul."

"Me too." I laugh.

"I like how fiery you are though," he says, grinning.

"What can I say? You bring it out of me."

Stu has a question for Will, and when he steps away, Lindsey joins me. "So, Will's fine now. I think everything's back on track."

"Yeah, I agree."

"And I'm sorry if I was out of line earlier," Lindsey says. "You go ahead and touch Will all you want. He doesn't mind, so why should I say anything about it."

I laugh. "Well, thanks for the permission but I really shouldn't."

Chill out. You're always professional. So what that you have a crush on this subject? The shoot will be over soon, and then it's back to the oddballs and dweebs. Have fun with it while you can." Lindsey adds.

"Ah, thanks, I guess," I reply, feeling awkward.

"And believe me. I'd touch him too if I thought he wanted me to."

Despite all of my initial good intentions, I slip further as the morning goes on, taking Lindsey's playful permission too much to heart. I'm an out of control octopus with swirling arms and grabby tentacles. If I could, I'd just latch myself onto Will and ride him around the house all day.

I roll my eyes at myself as that vivid picture pops into my mind.

Paul continues to tease, but Will now responds by giving it back. The whole atmosphere is charged and unpredictable. My stomach churns hoping we can make it through the day in one piece. By lunchtime I halfheartedly pick up a sandwich just as Lindsey grabs Will to be her lunch buddy.

Okay, so that's how this is going to go, I think.

When I sit down next to Stu, he starts in. "So you and Will the stud, huh?" He wiggles his eyebrows suggestively.

I look down and take a deep breath.

"You've gotta move faster, girl. Lindsey ain't goin' down without a fight."

I silently get up and push in my chair. As I turn to move away, Stu makes a face.

"Ah, come on, Sophia. Where's your sense of humor?"

"I don't know, Stu. I'll let you know when I find it," I snap before heading into the house.

"Oooo," Terry adds as I storm off.

From two tables over Will watches me leave, but Lindsey distracts him by asking him a question.

Ten minutes later Will finds me sitting on the steps of the deck and Romeo curled up at my feet. I feel completely deflated.

"I've been looking for you. I noticed you left lunch without eating."

"I've lost my appetite. Paul and Lindsey are intent on riling me up and now the others are joining in. They're all so pleased that you come off like a stud muffin." I make air quotes with my fingers as I say it. "And along with that they're saying all of us females are acting like your rabid followers. It's infuriating me."

"What exactly is *your* definition of a stud muffin?" asks Will, teasing.

How to explain stud muffin. "Well, a stud is a really good-looking guy who plays the field, right? And we like to eat tasty muffins. So I've always assumed it's a guy so hot you want to gain his attention and then consume him."

"Do you think I'm one of those? 'Cause I could be *your* stud muffin," he says jokingly with a smile.

I've got one eye closed and my face scrunched up. "Do you really think that's helping?"

"What? You've got me amped-up with how touchy feely you've been this morning. Don't get me wrong, I love it, but I suspect it only supports Paul's theory. Besides I've vowed not to be bothered by Paul's shenanigans," he says.

"Do you think I objectify you?"

"No, I think you just like to touch me. A lot."

"Oh God. I'm out of control." I moan.

"Why are you feeling bad? Do you have any idea how much I want to touch you? But I made you a promise and I'm trying to stick to it."

I lean forward, my face in my hands. "And I'm not making it easy for you, am I?"

"No, you aren't," he says, laughing. "The irony is part of me is thrilled that you want to be close to me, and the other part of me wants to drag you somewhere private and touch you *everywhere*." His eyes are closed as he says the last word, as if he's picturing it all in his mind.

"Everywhere?" I whisper, pressing my thighs together.

"Oh, yeah," he says, his eyes still closed.

"I'm curious. If we did make that choice—to be unprofessional—"

"So unprofessional."

"And sneak off to fool around. Where would this private place be?"

He opens his eyes, his face full of excitement as his mind scans the blueprints of his house with supersonic speed. "There's a storeroom just past the pantry that's not being used."

I pull back my sleeve and check my watch. "They still have twenty-three minutes for their lunch break."

"Really?" he asks, his voice almost breathless. "Are you sure?"

"About the time left, yes. But the rest, no, I'm not," I say with fire coursing through me. "I've clearly lost my mind. Last night I made the very sane determination to protect myself and slow our relationship."

Will nods, the ends of his mouth turn down. "You did, even though I wanted to veto the idea."

"But today I'm fairly certain I'll internally combust and leave behind a pile of sparkly ashes if I don't kiss you soon."

"Kiss?" he asks.

I nod. Although on second thought I'm pretty sure a kiss won't be enough for either of us. I give him a sexy smile and decide to elaborate.

"With tongue. And touching of the fondling variety."

"Probably more like groping."

"Perhaps some biting. I'm in a biting mood," I add.

"Hot damn!" He stands quickly and grabs my hand. "What are we waiting for?"

Chapter Twelve

When Will pulls open the storage room door, I hesitate.
"What?" he asks.

I take a peek. A row of almost full size reindeer are suspended from the ceiling.

"This is weird."

"It's the only room downstairs with a door lock," he explains.

"Gotcha." I step inside and take in my surroundings. This must be one of his storage spaces for his Christmas stuff. It's like a prop warehouse in January after the holiday decorations come down. To my right are the huge pieces of a child-size gingerbread house and a pile of oversized lighted candy canes. I spy a large group of full-sized elves. God only knows where he keeps Santa's sleigh.

When he closes the door and turns the antique lock, the light fades to a dusty dimness. The one small window opposite the door renders all the stored figures and decorations like focal points in a Vermeer painting—if Vermeer had lived in the twenty-first century and had a highly exaggerated love of holiday decorating. I watch the motes dance in the beam of light around the piles of Christmas stuff.

"This is overwhelming," I say softly.

"You're overwhelming. And it's my turn to touch you." His voice is low and sexy.

A moment later his lips are working their way up the soft skin of my neck while he pulls me tightly against him. His hands move over my curves as he kisses me slow and deep.

"Ohhh." I moan, hoping everyone is still outside on break.

I slide my hands under his shirt and up his chest as I kiss him back. Everything about him feels perfect—the planes of his chest leading up to his powerful shoulders, the hard and soft of his kisses, the way he pulls me so close. I feel his want all the way through me.

I pull back and grin. "Can I?"

He smiles. "Please."

My wandering hands go down over his fly. I sigh happily that he's completely aroused. He groans when I elevate my touch from stroking to groping and his eyes roll back with pleasure. A minute later his hands are all over me and my moans get louder between each mind-bending kiss. He starts sliding his hands from over to under my clothes, when someone suddenly starts pounding on the door.

"Sophia, I know you've got him in there, and we're behind schedule! We have four more setups to shoot today."

We freeze in horror. I recognize Stu's voice and my mind goes numb as I realize the full extent of how incredibly awkward this is. There's no way to get out of this gracefully.

Will's body tenses up and he gets a wild look in his eyes. As he pulls away from me, he starts mumbling insults to himself in a hushed voice about making bad choices.

When he finally finishes his rambling thoughts, I feel as if he's going to float away and it terrifies me. I have no idea why this man has brought out my wild side, but I'm getting turned inside out too, and I can't stop myself. I don't want to lose him.

I grip his shoulders hard as my fingers dig into his flesh.

When I was young I thought that love was finding the perfect Ken for my Barbie, a mix-and-match guy you could walk hand in hand with over the rainbow. It took a lot of years and disappointments to learn that's a load of crap.

Love is an explosive crash on a collision course of desire and expectation. Even in its quietest moments, when your lives easily braid together like the plaits in a girls hair, there's still darkness lingering. My experience with my ex, Marcos, taught me to always search for the darkness so you're not broadsided like I was when it comes.

He also taught me that love is a madness. You let go of logic and move to crazy town. Today it's the desperation of an unsteady mind that's willing to abandon all reason to hide in a dusty storage room to be with *the one*. With Will there's no going back now.

We frantically try to figure out what to do, exchanging whispered words.

"Why did I agree to this?"

Will's question takes my breath away, and with it, I sense his spirit float even further away, lingering in the storage room rafters and likely to head out the window within moments. In my mind I reach for him, grab his ankle, and hold on.

We may have met because of a reality show, but the real reality is sometimes it's worth going down the rough road to get to love. And as I pull him back toward me, our eyes meet. He knows it too.

There's no going back for him either.

After a quiet moment, we pull ourselves together and exit the storage room. We bolster ourselves for a monumental amount of teasing and snide comments, but the crew is surprisingly low key. Other than an eye roll from Stu and some bossiness from Lindsey, everyone stays classy.

It's a good thing because ten minutes later Helena shows up to join the shoot. After introductions they gather for a discussion in the kitchen. "So my role in this episode is to explore why our culture places such importance on the holiday ritual of decorating in a broad sense, and then what it means specifically to you, Will," she says with a confident smile.

"Really? Why would anyone care about what it means to me?" Will asks, confused.

"Well, the point of shows like this is to make people examine their own intentions. When they view people on reality shows, they are constantly comparing their own ideals as they watch. The effect is fascinating."

"I like to watch our hoarding show because I always clean my house afterward," Lindsey adds.

"Exactly. You'll either be inspired by the people you see, or do whatever you can to never be like them," Helena says.

"Can't you just be entertained?" Will asks.

"Of course, if the personality is entertaining enough, a lot of the other expectations may be lowered."

"I don't want to know where I fit into all of that," Will says, shaking his head.

"You don't need to. That's my job," Helena replies.

Helena and Paul decide the family room would be the best place for an on-camera chat with Will. He follows me in when the guys finish their prep.

"So, Will, I've been told this is your favorite room, can you tell me why?" Helena asks once the camera is rolling.

He smiles. "I think because of the trains. I've always loved trains. The set in the back belonged to my grandfather and whenever I spent Christmas with my grandparents, he'd let me help him with the setup."

"So you're keeping their memory alive in this room," Helena states.

"If you say so, but I also think the trains are amazingly engineered. Did you see this one in action?" he asks, pointing to the tracks. He flips the switch on the remote control and the train starts chugging along.

"I can understand why you'd enjoy that," she replies, smiling. "Now let me ask. Many people decorate for Christmas, but only a small handful decorate to the extreme you do. To what do you attribute your desire do this… to set yourself apart?"

"I don't know, maybe I'm nuts." He jokes.

"Nuts? Are you worried about your behavior? Perhaps that it's too extreme?"

"What makes you say it's extreme?" he says, teasing.

"I know you're joking, Will, but I'll answer anyway. You have to spend an extraordinary amount of time and money on your efforts here. By keeping this up, you're possibly avoiding something in your real life, do you know what it is?"

"Nope. Do you know?" he asks, baiting her.

"Well hearing that you're single, I would explore the idea that you are avoiding an emotionally intimate relationship."

"Because I decorate a lot for Christmas? I don't buy that. Besides, my grandparents started all of this, and they were married for fifty-seven years. You can't say they were avoiding an emotionally intimate relationship."

"Actually, I could suggest that as a possibility. They could've used their time-consuming hobby to avoid each other. That happens often in long relationships that appear on the surface to be stable."

"Hardly," he scoffs before standing and pulling off his mike. "Okay, this has been fun but I'm done."

"Will?" Lindsey says, "There's just a few more questions. Can't you hang in there just a little longer?"

"No. She doesn't know anything about my grandparents, and I'm not going to sit here and hear her say shit about them."

"I'm sorry if I upset you, Will," Helena says.

"Nobody told me this involved me getting my head examined." He looks at me with an angry stare. "If I'd known I would've never agreed to talk to you."

"Let's take a break, and then we can explore an approach you're comfortable with," Helena suggests.

Will watches me walk out of the room. I pull out my phone and make a call while I head to the backyard. Romeo runs up to me and sticks by my side. A minute later Will comes outside looking for me just as I shut my phone down in frustration.

He scowls as he sees us. "Traitor girl, traitor dog," he calls out.

My call had gotten heated. Will might not have been able to hear what was said but it's pretty obvious I'm not happy.

I pace back and forth several times trying to calm down.

When I finally look toward the house, I see he's still on the deck and I walk over to join him.

"Thanks for standing up for me in there," he says sarcastically as I get close.

"Will—" I say. I'm just as frustrated as he is.

"So who was that on the phone?"

"George."

"Your boss?"

"Yeah. I called him to find out what the hell is going on."

"And what did he say?"

"He reminded me that they often have academics on the show to explore people's behaviors and I was being dramatic. That if I didn't think the line of questioning was appropriate, I needed to redirect it."

"Really?" Will asks, sounding unconvinced.

"That's what he said." I huff.

"So, you're pissed. Why?"

"I feel like I never really got control of this show, and I'm not sure why. Lindsey is treating me like she's my boss, Paul is being especially obnoxious, and then this woman comes in and asks you things out of left field that I wasn't expecting. I know I'm new to this genre but they treat me like I've never done a show before."

"This isn't making me feel any better." Will warns me.

"Sorry. And I'm sorry that I didn't speak up during that segment."

"Why didn't you?"

"I kept thinking her strategy would make sense, suddenly pull things together. I didn't think she was going to analyze you the way she did or be disrespectful about your grandparents."

Will squints at me and tips his head.

"I'm sure our groping session in the storage room thirty minutes before didn't help matters either. I need to get my focus back."

"Maybe we both do."

"Will, I promise I'm going to do everything I can to make this right by you."

He doesn't respond and he folds his arms across his chest.

"I'm hoping you'll still like me when this show is over," I add.

His expression softens, and I breathe a sigh of relief.

"I *think* I'll still like you… maybe."

I smile sweetly. "Fair enough. And I'm glad because I *know* I'll still like you."

Now that we have an approved set of questions for Helena, things go much smoother. I finally manage to keep a respectable distance away from Will, consequently the team seems more relaxed. Perhaps they're assuming that, despite whatever went down in the store room, our flirting is over. I use that to my advantage and regain control.

I approach Will during the afternoon break. "So, the guys were talking about the way you help some of the local homeless people. They were wondering if they could interview one of them. I was thinking about Hank."

"Interview Hank? What would they ask him? He has a lot of pride. I wouldn't want them to humiliate him."

"They said the focus would be on your relationship with him and his friends, and discussing some of the ways you've helped him."

Will purses his lips together, but then suddenly his eyes get wide and he smiles. "Would they pay him for the interview?"

"That could be arranged."

"It would have to be cash," Will says.

"We could pull it from our petty cash fund, and I could authorize it."

"Okay. If you pay Hank, I'll help them find him and let Hank know it's okay *if* he wants to do it, and that's *if*."

"All right. I think it will be a nice addition to the segment," I say, smiling.

That night at dinner, Will's spirits are high. "We're almost done. All we have left are the outside shots and this three-ring circus will be over."

"Has it been completely awful for you? I ask, hoping his answer is no.

He takes a sip of his beer. "Pretty awful, but not completely awful."

"Well, I'm glad to hear that," I say, laughing. "Can I steal another fry?" I reach into his basket, not waiting for his answer.

"Sure. You're enjoying my dinner more than your own."

"Stupid salad. Why didn't I get a burger like you?"

"I don't understand girls and their eating sometimes." He holds up his burger and offers me another bite. "You're going to have to eat to keep up."

"Yeah?" I ask, grinning.

"Definitely." He lifts his beer bottle to his lips.

"When you drive me home will you come up for a while?"

"Do you really have to ask?" He teases.

"We can finish that kiss we started in the store room." My face heats.

He bites down on the fry and chews it thoughtfully before looking up with a wicked half smile. "Does this mean we're moving ahead? I'm still not going to drag you into my bed. You'll have to tell me when you're ready."

I nod, stealing another one of his fries. "Moving ahead, still slow but moving forward."

"You sure? No more back and forth?"

"I'm in, both feet." Tilting my head, I study him. "How about you? For a minute in the storeroom, you were slipping away."

He nods, his darkening gaze moving over me, and I run my fingers along the very trail he kissed down my neck in that dark, dusty storage room. I rest my hand on my cheek and nervously wait for his reply.

His eyes blaze with a light he shines like a lighthouse on a foggy night. When we connect he looks younger and hopeful, an even better version of his already amazing self.

He looks like a man in love.

"I'm in," he says.

Chapter Thirteen

The next morning my face is a little raw from our make-out session the night before. I'm still surprised we didn't go all the way but we were both exhausted and agreed it wasn't the right time. I want the first time we make love to be full-on fireworks, not sprinkler wands that quickly fizzle out after you wave them around.

Will picks me up and takes me to breakfast so we can have some time together. I have to work all afternoon and into the evening so it's our only chance for quality time. Before he takes me home, we swing by his house to search for a notebook Lindsey worries she left behind.

As we step out of his truck, I notice a man standing in the yard next door.

"Who's that?" I ask.

"Fred, my asshole neighbor." Will frowns when the man crosses the lawn toward us. "He never talks to me, so whatever he wants can't be good."

"If it has anything to do with the shoot you should let me handle it."

"No way," he says.

"The filming agreements are our problem. We arranged them. Honestly, it would be smart for you to stay out of it."

He falls silent.

"You know I'm right."

Will steps out of his car and turns to face Fred.

"What's up?" he asks with a stony expression, his hands passively jammed in the pockets of his worn jeans.

"That filming crap was supposed to be done this week. You moved it and we're not happy about it," Fred says.

Although he looks pretty average as middle-age men go, the way he's glaring at Will and gesturing dramatically puts me on edge. He keeps running his thick hand over his bald head as he talks.

"First of all, I didn't move it. Mother Nature did. They couldn't shoot the outside stuff in the rain."

I move over to Will's side of the truck. "Hi, Mr. Hoffmeyer. I'm Sophia Worthy, and I'm from the production company. I'll help you with your concerns."

I turn to Will. "Will, why don't you take care of Romeo while I handle this?"

"Sophia," he says, shaking his head.

"Please."

He looks very tense and he keeps glancing over at Fred, but I stand my ground until he finally gives in. "Be careful," he says quietly. "I'll be right inside."

Once Will is out of sight, Fred Hoffmeyer gives me a once-over.

"You his girlfriend or what?"

I ignore his question and decide to take the polite, professional approach. "Listen Mr. Hoffmeyer, I'm sorry if the rescheduling of the exterior shoot has inconvenienced you. But it's a big storm that's supposed to hit tonight, possibly even late this afternoon."

"Well, that's too bad, isn't it?" He sneers.

"Yes, it's unfortunate. Believe me, we would all like to finish this up."

"The thing is, miss, the weather's not my problem, and if this thing is going to take two weeks, I want to be paid twice."

"Although I wasn't the one dealing with you, I do know that you're being paid for three days, plus two for the setup and takedown of the yard decorations."

"We have an ordinance that says he's not allowed to put that garbage up until the week of Thanksgiving."

I mentally note the irony that his house is the neighborhood eyesore. His lawn is near dead, and the paint's peeling off the wood siding. I try to keep calm by reminding myself that I wouldn't want to live next door to someone who drew those kinds of crowds next to my house during the holidays. I just wish he didn't have to be such an ass about it.

"Well, I'm very sorry you think of the décor as garbage, but we are well aware of the ordinance and have obtained a special permit from the city. As long as it's taken down the day after the shoot, all is good."

"It's garbage!"

"Again, I'm sorry you feel that way, but as we just discussed, you're being paid for the days of the setup and takedown as well, so I'm not sure I understand your conflict. The number of days in our agreement hasn't changed."

He points toward Will's front door. "That ass thinks that just 'cause he's good-looking he can treat the rest of us like he's better than we are."

Oh geez! Will wasn't kidding about this nut job.

I get a very unsettled feeling and realize that this guy isn't going to be easy. He's not rational, and it's going to be a challenge to talk any sense into him. I glance at the house where Will's watching from the window. A moment later he steps through the front door and onto the porch. He folds his arms over his chest, spreads his legs in an authoritative stance, and glares at Fred. As much as I feel safer having Will close, I get the feeling he's just going to escalate things.

"You're going to pay for this, asshole, and she will too!" Fred yells. The rage in his eyes waves all kinds of red flags. I'm going to have to come up with another strategy for us to deal with this guy.

"Sophia, I need to talk to you. Come here please." Will's voice is measured and strong. It makes my stomach flutter with nerves.

I nod and briefly turn back to Fred. "I'll let our production company know about your concerns, Mr. Hoffmeyer. I'll have Lindsey contact you tomorrow."

"You better, or we're gonna shut this thing down," he grumbles, spitting on the ground before returning to his property.

Will's entire body is tense when he opens the front door and leads me inside. He slams the front door shut.

His anger surprises me when he swings around to face me. "Do not do that, Sophia!" he says with gritted teeth.

I look up, surprised. "What are you talking about?"

"I warned you about him, but you insisted on trying to reason with that madman, and you put yourself in danger." He's shaking.

Danger? Why's he being so dramatic?

"Will—"

"I can't let anything happen to you. I don't care what he does to me, but now he knows who you are. He's a crazy fucker. I thought you'd have more street smarts than that."

"Hey, I have street smarts!" I argue.

"Not that I can tell. I should have never left you alone with him, but I made up my mind that I wouldn't be so controlling and overprotective as I've been in the past. But maybe I should stick to my instincts after all."

"I see," I say quietly.

He slams his fist against the wall and heads to the back of the house, leaving me in the foyer. I hear the back door slam shut.

I sit down on the third step of the main staircase facing the big kid's Christmas tree and take a deep breath.

Controlling? Overprotective? Those are definitely qualities I'm not comfortable with in a man. This insight into Will is troubling.

I slowly stand and steady myself before heading to the backyard. He's on the lawn, throwing a tennis ball to Romeo. The dog jumps up into the air to catch the ball and then charges back to Will and drops the ball at his feet.

Will sees me and then picks up the ball and throws it again. I wait as the two boys go several more rounds before I interrupt.

"Can we talk?"

He nods, drops the ball, and joins me on the step. He rubs his hands over his knees before sitting down and taking a deep breath.

"I'm sorry I yelled," he says finally, slipping his hands in his back pockets and tipping his head down.

"And I'm sorry I worried you. I thought I could handle the situation, and although it didn't go well, nothing bad happened?"

He sighs. "Not yet."

"Please don't worry. Lindsey knows how to handle him."

"So you'll stay out of it?" he asks.

I can hear the earnestness in his voice and see the worried look in his eyes.

"Yes, I will."

"You promise?"

I take his hand in mine. "I promise. Thank you for wanting to protect me. That's a noble thing, even though I can take care of myself."

"I care about you more than you realize. I can't let anything happen to you."

I smile and rub my fingers over the top of his hand. "So this is a side of you I haven't seen before," I say softly.

He looks at our joined hands. "I wish you'd never seen that side. In my wise old age I've tried to outgrow it."

I laugh. "Yeah, you're *so* old."

He sighs. "But our past always catches up with us, doesn't it?" He has a troubled, dazed look in his eyes.

"What do you mean?"

"As I mentioned before, I was pretty wild when I was young—especially in high school."

"Yeah?" I say, not sharing that Steph has already told me a little about his rough years. I want him to feel comfortable enough to tell me himself and know I won't run for the hills.

"I made some bad choices and even ended up in juvie for six months. If Grandpa Joe hadn't gotten involved, I'd probably be in prison now."

"What did you do to end up locked up for six months?"

"I beat up a guy so badly I could've killed him. He was threatening my girl," he says.

"Are you exaggerating? Seriously... *could have killed?*"

His face blanches. "Believe me, I'm serious."

"Well do me a big favor and please don't kill your neighbor. Visiting my boyfriend in prison isn't exactly on my bucket list."

"No, I guess not." He fights back a smile.

"What?" I ask, sensing his shift in mood.

"You called me your boyfriend."

I blush. "I did, didn't I?"

"You sure did. And don't give me that *you're a man and you're a friend stuff.*"

"Does that mean you don't find the idea of being my boyfriend disagreeable?"

"Disagreeable? On the contrary, I'm all for that idea... *girlfriend.*" He gives me a crooked smile.

He leans forward and kisses me chastely as he casts his gaze down.

"What was that halfhearted kiss all about? That's not like you at all." I take his chin in my hand, encouraging him to look at me.

"My past doesn't scare you? I'd be lying if I said I wasn't worried that you'd second guess dating me after hearing all of that."

"Will, I wasn't a perfect teen either, even though you can't really compare shoplifting to attempted murder; still neither one of us was perfect."

"Shoplifting, really?"

"What can I say? It wasn't one of my better choices. I've never been good at not getting the things I really want."

He nods.

"I believe in living in the moment, and not basing how we move forward always on what happened in the past," I say.

He pulls me into his arms. "I'm relieved. Telling you about that has weighed heavily on me."

"So can we seal the deal? Can I get a real Will kiss now?"

I watch him as he slowly brushes his fingertips across my lips.

"Ready?" he whispers.

"Sure am," I say with a sweet smile.

The kiss is soft and slow and perfect. I feel the tingle all the way to my toes, the same toes that a moment later feel something slobbery wet roll over them.

Romeo has just offered his ball as part of our love fest, his tail wagging furiously.

"She's mine, dude," Will says, patting his head. "But if you're good I'll share her once and a while."

Over the next few days, Will and I get together whenever we can. It's not as frequent as I'd like since I'm busy at True Blue with endless scheduling and production meetings. Meanwhile he deals with a leaky roof from the big storm and a pile of other chores. By the weekend, we're ready for a break. On Saturday I bring over lunch, and when we're done we decide to take Romeo to the dog park.

Will gathers the leash, ball, and dog treats. The minute Romeo sees the leash he barks at the back door and then the truck door until he's loaded inside. Will secures him in his car seat that tethers him to the seatbelt so he can stick his head out the window. I get to snuggle in between Romeo and Will.

I fasten my seatbelt and turn to Romeo "Excited are we?"

He barks happily and whines at the window until Will rolls down the glass.

"That dog seems part human at times. I wonder what he'd say if he could talk."

Will laughs. "Oh, he'd say plenty. When I was deciding which dog to take home from the shelter, he just kept barking at me until I chose him. Well, it wasn't barking, exactly. That would've annoyed me. It was these weird sounds he makes when he's trying to get my attention."

"You were meant to be together. I'm sure of it."

After we drive a few blocks, Will spots Hank rummaging through a recycling bin. His shopping cart is overflowing with bags of cans and bottles.

"Trash day is a working day for Hank," Will comments. "I thought we might see him today."

He drives alongside him.

At first Hank jumps a little and his eyes get wide when we pull up. Not everyone is okay with the homeless in the area picking through their recycling bins, but when he recognizes us, he relaxes.

He walks right up to Romeo's window, reaches in, and rubs him under his chin.

"How's my little friend," he says as Romeo leans into his hands appreciatively.

"Hey, Will. I was hoping I'd see you." He turns to me and smiles. "And good to see you again, Miss Sophia."

I wave. "Hi, Hank. It's good to see you again too."

"Are you guys still okay for setup Wednesday? I'm sorry again about the rain delay."

Hank shakes his head. "Stupid rain. I shouldn't complain. It doesn't rain much here but when it does, it messes everything up."

I imagine that for all my complaining when it rains or we have a heat wave, I don't have to endure anything like people who live on the street do.

Will reaches for his wallet. "Let me give you some of your pay in advance."

Hank holds out his hand. "No need, but thanks anyway. Do you know those crazy people you said wanted to interview me just to talk about you?"

Will and I smirk at the crazy reference.

"They gave me a hundred bucks! That's the easiest money I've ever learned. We didn't even talk ten minutes."

"Was it okay? Were they polite and everything?" Will asks.

"Sure, it was easy because they just wanted to talk about you. And don't worry, I told 'em you weren't an ass." He chuckles.

"Well, that's a relief. Thanks."

"I'm joking. Actually I told 'em the truth—that you're the best man I know."

"Sounds like I should give you a bonus for lying on my behalf."

"Oh, you stop now. I mean it." Hank turns to me. "He is."

I take Will's hand in mine. "I agree."

"Enough of the Will fan club," Will says, putting the car into gear.

"Are you taking the little man to the dog park?" Hank asks.

"Yup, so we're going to head out."

"Have fun. And nice to see you again, Miss Sophia."

"Likewise, Hank."

I hold Will's right hand as he steers with his left and think about the contrast of Will the angry protector versus Will the kind friend to the homeless. I sense life will never be dull as long as I'm with him.

At the dog park, Romeo gets busy checking out all the female dogs.

"He has a favorite, but I don't think she's here today."

"Yeah? Please, please tell me her name is Juliet!"

"Nope. Desdemona, but they call her Desi."

"Geez! Well they must make quite a pair."

"She's a purebred Irish setter, easily twice the little guy's size, but he pays no mind to that. You should see them try to go at it. We have to constantly pull them apart as they frown on that stuff at the dog park."

I laugh, imagining it. "Poor Romeo, never satisfied."

"Well, not for a lack of trying."

"Speaking of Irish things, I've been thinking of going to Ireland next summer," I say, testing the waters.

"Wow, Ireland? You're quite a traveler. Have you always been that way?"

"Oh no, my parents couldn't afford big trips with a larger family and four kids to put through college, but I think I was born with wanderlust. As soon as I scraped the money together, I started traveling the world. It's one of the reasons I work so hard... to fund my trips."

"Who are you going with? And it better not be that Marcos dude," he says warily.

"No. So far I'm going by myself, but I know this really handsome man that I may invite. I bet he'd be really fun to hang out in pubs with."

Romeo runs over to check in. Will throws his tennis ball half the length of the park, and the little guy takes off after it.

"That'd be cool. I'd love to go to Ireland with you."

"Great." I feel excited just thinking about it.

"My tattoo has Irish origins."

"It does?"

"Yeah, it's a Celtic symbol called a Dara Knot from the Irish word for oak tree." He lifts up his sleeve a little higher.

"I've wanted to ask what it meant," I say, running my fingers over it gently.

"Why didn't you?"

"I was afraid it was for an old girlfriend or something, and then I'd go from admiring it to resenting it."

He lifts his eyebrows. "I still don't believe you're the jealous type."

"Oh, I am. And... I'm a bit possessive, too."

"I'll keep that in mind."

"So what does the symbol mean?"

"It's a reminder that like a tree's roots, we have vast inner resources under the surface that can lend wisdom and stability no matter what shit is going down around us. That idea has gotten me through some rough times."

I smile. "I bet it has. You're amazing. And as for your tattoo, I like it even more."

Chapter Fourteen

Tuesday in the production meeting at work, I learn that the one time I'd like my schedule to ease up, it's jam-packed. "What do you mean I have to do a shoot over Thanksgiving in Massachusetts? What about my Thanksgiving?" I ask. My parents are going to have a fit, and I'd been thinking about asking Will come home with me.

"You have to go during Thanksgiving as this subject, Dorothy, doesn't want to recreate her major production another time."

"We'll be filming her actual Thanksgiving?" I ask, not hiding the skepticism in my voice. "There's no way that's going to work."

"Sophia," Rachel says in her calm, controlling voice. "She does an authentic Plymouth Rock recreation and meal for fifty-three people. There'll be lots to work with."

"Fifty-three! She must be psychotic. When will this nightmare air anyway? Thanksgiving a year from now?"

"George has this all figured out. He's creating multiple uses for our footage," says Rachel.

"Always the economist," Paul adds.

"For example, Will's Christmas segment will air the weekend of Thanksgiving, and a much shorter piece of it will be part of the mixed holiday celebration that comes out the week before Christmas."

"I really wanted to be home for Thanksgiving weekend." I huff.

Lindsey folds her arms and slumps in her seat. "Join the club. I have to be in fucking Toronto that weekend. My mom's going to kill me for missing her favorite family holiday."

"That sucks," I say to Lindsey.

"We both have to be in Malcolm, Georgia, in early November for the Easter lady," continues Lindsey.

"Yes, she sounds especially colorful. Did you read her file? She's bedazzled every Easter thing she could get her hands on." I'm less than enthused.

"Bedazzled like a rhinestone queen. And let us not forget the overweight husband who wears a fur bunny suit. But who am I kidding? Who could forget that? It's burned in my memory like a bad dream," says Lindsey.

"Chubby hubby probably terrorizes the little kids," Paul says.

"I bet he's one of those furry freaks who get off wearing fur costumes head to toe. Being the Easter Bunny lets him think his kinky obsession is legit," says Lindsey.

"Should I feel bad that we're making fun of all of these people?" I ask.

"Don't feel too bad about it. The real TV production people sit around and make fun of us for having to produce this dreck, so it all comes full circle," Paul says.

"I feel worlds better now. Thanks, Paul," I say.

Rachel turns to me. "Listen. As long as we're respectful at the shoot, and treat these people well, I think it's fine for us to let off a little steam in the privacy of our home office."

"Yeah. For example I treated Mr. Christmas *really* well." Lindsey chimes in.

"Not as well as you wanted to." Paul points out.

"It's just as well I didn't go by the shoot like I'd planned," Rachel says. "I don't need any more guys with weird tendencies for boyfriends. All the reports I got back indicated he was surprisingly smart and very easy on the eyes."

"He isn't weird at all." I try not to sound defensive, while pretending Rachel doesn't consider Will a potential conquest.

"Well, you would know," Paul says, raising his eyebrows.

"No, Rachel's right... he was fine. So different than most of the yahoos we deal with. I still can't figure out why he does all that crazy shit, but I'd plug in his Christmas lights any old time." Lindsey fans herself dramatically.

Rachel turns to me. "Speaking of Will. Have you talked to him about the shopping trip?"

My mind fills with dread. "No, I haven't. I'm sure he won't want to do it, and I'm nervous to ask."

"Quit dragging your feet. I want him on board before the exterior shoot this Wednesday."

"Okay." I agree glumly.

On the drive to Will's home, I call Lindsey using my Bluetooth.

"I'm on my way over to Will's to check up on their progress for tomorrow. You got things straightened out with Hoffmeyer, right?"

"That guy's such a psycho," Lindsey says.

"And that's why it's so important he's taken care of *before* the shoot."

"We were able to make some cuts in other areas, so I could get more money. I feel like we're being extorted."

"We are, but I truly feel like Will's safety is at stake. This is important. Thanks for arranging it," I say.

"No problem. The only thing is that it's taking extra time to get the check cut since it wasn't in the original budget. If he says anything can you remind him that I promised I'd have it to him Friday at the latest?"

"Friday?" That's worrisome.

"It's the best we could do. I told him that."

"Yeah, but did he listen?" I say to myself after we disconnect. *I sure as hell hope so.* I'd want this shoot to end on a high note without creating any more problems for Will.

Will is precariously balanced on the top of his slanted roof with a string of lights looped around his neck. He gives off an air like he's the Paul Bunyan of Christmas. His confidence is appealingly macho as he yells directions to the guys in the yard while preparing to hang the lights. At one point he widens his stance, folds his arms over his chest, and surveys the progress, the confident command of which makes me all hot and bothered.

"Sophia!" he bellows. All the guys stop their work and turn to see who he's so excited about. He abandons his lights and works his way down the ladder.

When he finally reaches me, he hugs me so enthusiastically he lifts me off the ground.

"Wow! Now that's a greeting!" I exclaim.

"I'm just glad to see you." He sighs before kissing me. A few of the crew let out a whoop and holler, and Will pulls back and laughs.

"How's it going?"

"We've had a few issues, but overall okay. I'm doing the high-risk stuff and the trim along the rooftop. I don't care what those inbreds next door think. I'm leaving it up after the shoot through Christmas. I just won't turn it on until Thanksgiving."

I feel nervous and remember my conversation with Lindsey.

"Are you sure that's wise?" I ask.

"Let him sue me," he says, sounding very cavalier.

I take a step back and turn toward the front yard. "Hank came right up and said hello when I pulled up. Do you want to introduce me to everyone else?

"Sure," he says, holding out his hand. "Let's do it."

After we make the rounds, Will takes me into his garage workshop where he's making some repairs and adjustments to some of the animated figures. "I'm having trouble with this Santa's workshop elf. He's holding a hammer in his hand and his arm is supposed to move up and down, but it keeps getting stuck." He gently lifts up the elf's shirt to check the wiring.

"So you fix this stuff yourself?" I ask as he works.

"Yeah, being a scenic guy comes in very handy with this house. Between what Gramps taught me and what the guys show me at the studio with animated props and characters, I can pretty much fix anything."

"You said a while back that your Grandpa was always teaching you how to fix stuff. That's so cool."

"Yeah, he was great—all self-taught. This was his workshop. Sometimes when I'm in here late at night I almost feel like he's with me." He stands and picks up a worn chisel.

"Maybe he is."

"I'd like to think that's true," Will says. "He was my hero. I'd like to think he's keeping an eye out for me. I don't think that stuff is creepy at all."

While Will gets back to work, I wander through the room. I study the old-fashioned peg board mounted to the wall with brackets holding well-worn tools, burnished with age and use. I run my hand over on the gnarled yet polished work surfaces. Every scratch and groove in the wood is a sign of hands at work. I close my eyes for a moment and imagine Will as a boy, standing next to his grandfather as he teaches him his craft.

"My dad's not handy at all," I say absentmindedly.

"No?"

"I mean he's great and everything, but he has no clue how to fix something. When our stuff broke it ended up in the trash bin."

"Yeah, that's pretty common nowadays. It takes a certain mindset to hold onto things that, with some attention and pure elbow grease, can still have value."

Later when I get ready to run a few errands, Will invites me back at dusk to view the finished product in its full glory.

"Shall I get some takeout?"

"That's a good idea. I'm probably not going to be up for cooking tonight."

"Hey, there's something I forgot to ask you earlier," I say nervously.

"What's that?"

"Since they've expanded the holiday thing into a series, they've decided to add something."

"Add something?" Will asks, making a face. "Like what? Are they going to lock me in a dungeon and torture me, because that's what any more of this would feel like."

I scowl. "I can't tell you how awesome you make me feel about my job."

He shrugs. "Sorry, but I've got to call this like I see it."

I crumble a bit with defeat. "Okay, I guess I'll have to tell them no. But don't you even want to hear what it was?"

He studies my face. "Okay, okay… what is it?"

"Going shopping in a holiday superstore." I smile as if it's a great idea.

He starts laughing uproariously. "Shopping! Are you serious? Why would anyone want to watch that?"

I feel the sting of his comment. "You haven't watched a lot of reality TV, have you? Viewers really like to see how experts like you put ideas together."

"This was Paul's idea, wasn't it?" Will asks.

"How'd you know?"

"Just a feeling," Will grumbles. "So where does this stop? Are they just going to keep coming up with things? We'll never be done, it will go on and on, forever and ever."

"Yeah, and that would be awful. Imagine... we'd have to keep working with each other."

"Like I said, torture, pure torture." He pulls me into his arms and hugs me.

"Okay, I'm telling them you said no. Absolutely not, under no conditions, will you go shopping, no matter how much I beg you to."

He kisses the top of my head and rubs my "back. "Well, if it's *that* important to you, of course I'll do it.

I grin. "You will? Why would you do it, if you hate the idea so much?"

"Haven't you figured it out yet, woman? I'd do anything for you."

When I pull up just before six, Will and Hank are leaning over some type of electrical panel. It looks as if the rest of the crew is gone.

"You think that's okay? I followed what you told me, but I wasn't sure if I put that last plug where you meant," Hank says, biting his thumbnail.

"This looks good. I couldn't have done this without you and the guys' help." Will pats him on the shoulder.

"Anytime, you know that. I appreciate the work."

"Looks like you guys are done," I say as I approach them.

Will smiles and loops his arm around my waist. "Yeah, you ready to be amazed?"

Hank's eyes get big. "You haven't seen it before, miss?"

"No, this will be my first time. I saw a little picture of it, but I suspect that's nothing compared to being here."

"Oh yeah, you've got to see it! It's the best Christmas house around... in the whole world, I bet," Hank says enthusiastically.

"Well, let's see it then!"

"Okay, go stand over on the side walk, front and center," Will instructs.

"Yes, sir," I grin as I walk away.

"Ready?" he yells when I'm in position.

I give him a thumbs up.

Will turns to Hank. "Give us the countdown, man."

Hank rubs his hands together. "Five, four, three, two, one... Merry Christmas!"

Will quickly flips circuits two at a time as each area of the yard and house snap on. With each pop, the glow from the yard gets brighter and brighter.

I blink several times and realize I've been holding my breath until the scene is completely lit and animated.

"Wow!" I cry and clap my hands happily. "This is unbelievable."

The gingerbread house, which was in dusty pieces in the storeroom last week, is assembled and proudly glowing with lights while animated gingerbread men wave from the windows.

Across the path is a Ferris wheel at least ten feet high, and each seat holds elves and Christmas characters as the large wheel slowly rotates. There's a family of snowmen near the front door, shimmering with tiny white lights.

An animated Santa is on the roof, waving from his sleigh. Attached to the sleigh is an entire team of reindeer who are aglow and ready for flight. Even the trees surrounding the yard are full of little lights.

The more my gaze wanders, the more I discover. I finally glance at Will. He's staring at me intently. When our eyes meet he turns and looks over at the displays, then back at me and grins.

I grin back, clap my hands and yell, "Bravo!"

Will turns to Hank and shakes his hand.

"Bye, Sophia!" Hank calls out.

I wave back. "Bye, Hank... thanks for helping!"

Will walks toward me slowly, smiling the entire way. A feeling comes over me, and I almost fall backward from the impact. As my mind tries to wrap around this sudden emotion, a series of puzzle pieces take shape in my mind: the way Will shook Hank's hand with honest gratitude, the commanding image of him on the roof when I arrived, the delight he expressed without reserve when he saw me, the joy I saw in his face when observed my reaction to what he's created.

I have no idea why this particular group of simple events link together to create a shift in my deepest feelings for Will. Maybe my stubborn head finally just needed to catch up with my body that adored him from the start.

Regardless, this very moment is a silent explosion under my skin, a life force pulsing through me. My whole heart is opening so that his heart fits perfectly inside mine. Despite my resistance—back and forth, up and down and overthinking—my heart has stepped up to run this show. *I hope you're ready for me, Will Saunders.*

I am in love.

As he approaches me, he's unaware that every molecule in my body has shifted. I try to tone down my doe-eyed stare.

He's a little worse for wear from the dirt and grime of setting up all day, and his T-shirt is torn on one side.

I raise my eyebrows and study where the fabric is torn.

"Caught it on a sharp edge of the rain gutter on the climb down from the roof," he explains. When he runs his hand through his hair, I note his hand is covered with scratches.

"Are you hurt?" I ask and inspect the damage, running my fingers up the skin of his side to make sure he's okay.

"Fine," he says, brushing it off like it's nothing to be climbing across tall roofs and setting up holiday fantasylands in your front yard.

I kiss him. "This is amazing. It's a million times better in person than the picture in your file."

He smiles and I wonder if he can tell yet that I'm suddenly loopy with love.

"Let me show you around," he says. The entire yard is laid out thoughtfully with paths lined with candy cane lights leading from one display to another. It's a far cry from the yards in my parents' neighborhood haphazardly filled with inflatable, puffy Santas, and wire reindeer that have seen better days. In contrast, each of Will's displays tells a story and has the quality you'd expect from a theme park, it's put together so well.

He takes my hand and leads me down the path, past the choir of singing polar bears to the oversized train set with boxcars full of wrapped gifts.

I survey all the packages. "I'm surprised this stuff doesn't get stolen when you're not around."

"People have tried, but these boxes are empty and everything is wired down." He pulls on one of the fixed packages to demonstrate, then points to other figures in the yard. "Everything is secured. If people are really determined, they can get something, but we've had surprisingly few problems over the years. Grandma Della used to always say it was protected by the Christmas spirit."

"I love that." *Who am I kidding?* I love everything right now because I'm in love with Will.

"So, what's your favorite thing so far?"

"It's all great but I'd have to say the gingerbread house, the detail of it is amazing and vintage. Where'd you find it?"

Will grins. "It's my favorite too. It was one of the last big projects Grandpa and I did together before I started getting into trouble and stopped coming over. Grandma helped us decorate it."

"You guys cut out all this trim detail?"

He nods. "Gramps could do all that stuff. He was a craftsman although he didn't consider himself one."

I squeeze his hand. "I'm glad I got to see this before shoot day. Just the two of us."

"Me too," he says as he adjusts the top on a lantern. His eyes are constantly moving. I imagine it must be a monumental job maintaining all of this throughout the season.

From the corner of my eye, I catch a glimpse of something over by the Hoffmeyers'. Someone is watching the spectacle from a window. I'm not sure if it's Fred or one of his grown sons, but it unsettles me.

"Hey, I've got our dinner still in my car. Why don't you turn off everything, and we'll go inside."

"Good idea."

I set the table and get dinner unpacked while Will jumps in the shower. When he returns to the kitchen with wet uncombed hair and bare feet, I sigh. Combine that with his white T-Shirt, jeans, the fresh scent of soap and that grin, and I'm swooning—hard.

He steps behind me as I attempt to fill our plates. He pushes my hair over my shoulder and tenderly kisses my neck before wrapping his arms around my waist and pulling me closer.

"Thanks for doing this," he says softly.

"Picking up takeout?" I ask, laughing to cover my nerves. "I should've cooked for you."

He rubs his chin across my soft curls. "I don't care about that. It's the way you're with me, all of it. It's how you look out for me and care about all the stuff I do, even my extreme hobby."

I lean my head back against his shoulder. "I do."

"You know where I came from and the shit that goes along with my screwed up past, but you like me anyway."

"It's not so hard to like you," I say with affection in my voice.

He kisses my shoulder and his hands start moving over me. "No?"

I take a sharp breath when his strong hand cups my breast. "Not hard at all."

I slowly turn to face him. The intensity in his eyes goes straight through me until my knees feel weak. A moment later he's kissing me, his hands sliding down to my backside, as he leans into me.

"Oh God, I'm so hungry," I say, gasping between kisses, my entire body so finely tuned to his touch.

"You want me to stop? The food's getting cold." He slowly grinds his hips against me as his fingers press deeper. "We really should eat."

"Eat?" I ask, blinking, as if I've forgotten what that means. "No, no," I correct him as my cheeks color. "Actually I was hoping…" I bite my lip and close my eyes knowing that the words I'm about to say will change our course. Even if I'm not brave enough to tell him that I'm in love with him yet, I can show him.

"You were hoping?" he asks, waiting patiently for me to finish my thought.

I need him to understand. "I was hoping you'd show me your room."

"My bedroom?" he asks, his eyes hooded with desire. He looks down and clears his throat before looking back up with a dark expression. "What are you hungry for, Sophia?"

I move close enough to slowly skim my cheek along his jaw. "For you," I whisper.

He edges even closer, and his lips brush across my ear. "Are you sure?" He pauses. "If I take you up there…" He closes his eyes and takes a sharp breath.

I shiver and wonder for a moment if we'll even make it upstairs. I feel like I'm going to combust. "Please, take me."

He holds out his hand and I grab it and hold on tight.

When we get upstairs, he throws the door open and flips the light switch. I gasp as the room glows with a soft splendor. It distracts me from all the passion surging through me, but it's distracting in a wonderful way.

"Do you like it?" he asks breathlessly.

"Like it? Wow... this is unbelievable."

I scan the perimeter of the room where small trees, bare of leaves line the room. They're all white and accented with tiny twinkly lights. The effect as the light shimmers from the pearl iridescent walls is ethereal. To complete the theme, the coved ceiling sparkles with mini lights imbedded in the ceiling. They subtly blink in random intervals.

"It's magical." I notice the silver sleigh bed with cobalt blue bedding in the middle of the room. Compared to the rest of the house, the bedroom is stark but with elaborate details and effect. It has a sexy elegance.

"I got the winter forest idea from a picture book I remembered. It's a little over the top. I got help from my friends at the studio."

"I like that about you. You do everything with flair," I say stepping into his arms.

He gently pushes my hair back over my shoulder. "I try. I wasted a lot of time when I was younger; I want everything I do now to mean something." He runs his fingers down my cheek as he gazes at me.

"I think you're amazing." I kiss his fingers as they graze my lips. "Everything you do, everything you say, just makes me want you more."

The expression in his eyes grows in intensity. He closes his eyes for a moment while he takes a deep breath. When he opens them again, his fingers curl under the edge of my sweater.

"May I?" he asks.

I nod silently, biting my lower lip in anticipation. He pulls the sweater up over my head, my hair falling back feeling windswept and wild. He can't contain his smile when he looks at the sheer bra covering my breasts.

"Beautiful," he says softly. His hands roam over me, and I feel every touch intensely.

While I slip off my bra, he pulls off his T-shirt. When we face each other and embrace, I hum at the glory of skin against skin, the perfect contrast of my softness pressed against the hard contours of his sculpted chest. His next kiss is defining, unrestrained passion as if every moment we'd shared until now led to this one.

His searching hand moves up my torso, gliding across my skin, his powerful fingers gentle as they explore. Caressing my breasts, with each of his feathering strokes, my nipples harden. I ache with desire, imagining his tongue circling my nipple, his warm lips pressed against the softness of my breasts. I'm already undone and we've just begun.

Meanwhile my hand explores lower regions, making a trail along the denim at his waist. When my fingers finally rub along his fly, I discover the most defining evidence of what I do to him. I moan when I find him so hard, and he welcomes my grasp, groaning with pleasure when my fingers tighten around him.

Following, he leans forward, his forehead pressed against mine, panting as he takes in the sensation of my hand moving over him.

"I've wanted this so much. I need you."

I tug his waistband with my other hand. "I need you too."

He watches while I undo his fly. I help him push everything down until he's fully exposed.

"Oh, Will," I say as I hold him in my hands, slowly moving over him as he watches. My fingers explore, circling and stroking him slowly from base to tip. I've never seen such a beautiful man and I tell him that as he leans forward to gently take my nipple between his lips. I moan as I rub him against me. I can feel our restraint unravel.

"I need you in my bed, Sophia. Now!"

I love the urgency in his voice and stare intently at him as I undo my jeans and kick off my shoes. He does the same and pulls back the linens on the bed before turning to me. He opens his arms.

"Come here," he whispers. When I'm back in his arms he says in a strained voice, "Do you know how many times I've imagined this since the first time I saw you?"

"Tell me," I say as I ease back onto the bed. He joins me and sinks down by my feet, lifting my foot and brushing his lips along my ankle. "I imagined kissing you at our first meeting as I watched you eat that macaroon."

I smile. "I thought so. I was flirting with you."

He continues to kiss his way up my calf and the sensation makes me shiver. "That had occurred to me. And why were you flirting?"

I take a deep breath as I feel wet kisses trailing up my inner thigh. Every touch and kiss confirms that he is the sexiest man I've ever known. I fall back onto the mattress happy to surrender to his attention. "You were fascinating and just so damn good-looking."

He laughs softly right as his lips graze the top of my thigh. "And..." he prompts me. His tongue circles over my most sensitive spots, teasing, arousing. I'm overwhelmed with the most exquisite pleasure, each spark and sensation more delicious than the last. I run my fingers through his hair.

"And sexy," I gasp swaying my hips invitingly. I want him inside of me so fiercely that I can barely breathe.

His tongue continues to circle upward as he moves higher near my belly button. I lift my head and our eyes meet for a moment, his full of excitement.

"And you were charming," I say rising up to my elbows. He smiles and a moment later my nipple is between his lips. I moan, not sure how much longer I can remain lucid enough to speak. I lift my foot and run it down the length of his leg as my head falls back with the sensation of his mouth on me. "So, so charming."

The more intensely his kisses, the more undone I become until I have my legs tightly wrapped around him, intent on pulling him closer.

"Will," I beg.

"Yes, yes," he replies, lightly biting my neck as his body rises over me, every muscle in his body tense with anticipation. He kneels and rolls on the condom before leaning back down.

He lifts my arms over my head and holds my wrists down, pinning me to the mattress.

"Will," I gasp, every fantasy I've had of him has led to this.

He watches me squirm as I wait for his touch. His gaze falls over me with his silent smile, making me feel beautiful.

"No one ever... ever...has made me feel like this." My head falls back as if in a dream. I open my eyes as he brushes his lips up my neck, and tastes me with warm kisses.

Our hunger overtakes us as he devours me, sinking into me so completely it transcends everything. When we are finally hip to hip, I am electrified by the perfection—the delicious stretch and fullness of him inside of me. I want to cry knowing that my love for him is exquisitely captured in this perfect moment.

"I'm so done for," I whisper with a love-soaked smile, endlessly opening beneath him.

"Breathe, love, this is just the beginning," he chants, this man who gives me everything and more. His strong hands hold me until I'm weightless, falling toward him.

The room rocks back and forth with each thrust, the exhilarating anticipation of climax building. We keep going up, up, up, and when we climb high enough, reaching the edge of the cliff, I swear I see the stars in his eyes.

We are wound tightly together, letting the reality of what we've done soak through us. I rewind moments over and over in my head. I grin internally and slowly skim my hand from one side of his chest to the other. I don't have to look up to know he's smiling. I can feel his happiness; it's that big.

I realize all the lights in the room have faded to the faintest glow. What time is it anyway? It felt as if we made love endlessly, and I laugh to myself, wondering if I'll even be able to walk tomorrow. I kiss his shoulder.

"Hey, beautiful," he whispers, stroking my hip with his fingers.

"What time is it?" I ask.

He turns toward the small table next to the bed and lifts up the clock. "Eleven-thirty."

"Wow. I guess I'm spending the night." I giggle.

"You aren't going anywhere," he says, pulling me closer.

"Good thing we aren't shooting in the morning. I'm not sure I'd have the energy. You wore me out."

He chuckles, his voice sounding rough from exhaustion. "Yeah, we got pretty wild. You wore me out too."

I lift my leg and curl it over his muscular thigh. "I was out of practice. It'd been a while."

"Really? I couldn't tell. But it's been a while for me too, so we're even."

I'm happy to reconfirm that there isn't a rotating door on his grand bedroom.

"I'm glad to hear that. I wasn't sure what to think when you first brought me in here. This room screams sex."

"It does? That wasn't what I was going for… but I guess it's an added bonus if you like it. We were inspired for sure," he says, sounding genuinely surprised.

He lets out a big yawn.

"I guess we should sleep," I say.

"Please."

"But one more thing, okay?"

"Just one?" He teases.

"Uh-huh, only one."

"What is it," he whispers, and his voice wavers on the edge of sleep.

"I really like you. Really," I say quietly.

He presses his lips into my hair and gently kisses my head. "I really like you too, Sophia."

"Good, glad we got that settled," I say. I close my eyes with a smile on my face, as the soft blanket of sleep slowly eases back over us.

Sometime before daybreak, I stir awake just enough and realize Will isn't spooning me. I turn onto my back and reach for him, but he isn't there.

"Will?" I sit up in bed and don't see him in the bedroom or hear him in the adjoining bathroom. The bedroom door is open and I notice a faint light coming from the hall. I get up, find one of his T-shirts, and slip it on over my head before quietly padding into the hall.

I slowly explore, confirming he isn't upstairs and decide go downstairs. *Maybe he's checking on Romeo?* I get alarmed when I can't find him in the kitchen or family room. The last place I think he'll be is in the dining room, but sure enough, that's where I find him.

I gaze at him from the doorway. He's leaning forward with his elbows resting on his knees while sitting in a chair against the wall. His gaze is fixed on the treasure chest. In the dim light I can't read his expression and it worries me. Why has he left our bed to linger in a room he created from a place of loss?

"Will," I say softly.

He looks up, his eyes wide with surprise. "Hey, what are you doing up?"

"I was wondering the same. Do you mind if I join you?" I point to the empty chair next to him.

He smiles. "I don't mind."

I slowly settle in the chair, leaning back and taking in the silence. My heart is pounding so hard I wonder if he can hear it.

"I come down here sometimes if I can't sleep. This is a place I like to think things out."

"So you've got a lot on your mind?"

He nods. "Yeah, there's a lot going on."

Everything in this room looks different in the dim light. The iridescent walls have lost their shimmer, and many of the ornament shapes are hard to identify. It reminds me of a film I saw about divers and how dark the ocean is when they dive deep.

"So you come to the room you created for Andrew when you need to work things out?" I feel sad as I say it.

"Does that weird you out?"

I look at the treasure chest. "Yes and no. I think I'm a little unnerved because earlier we were making love, and now you're here. I'm not sure how to feel about that."

"Right after this room was done I used to sit and talk to Andrew pretty much every night. I haven't done that in a while. Now it just makes me feel peaceful being in here."

He skims right over my concern, and I wonder if he even heard me. "Is it strange having me in here?"

He traces the scratches on the back of his hand with his finger, and then looks up. "No. The significance of this room is part of me, part of my past. It's right that I would share it with you."

"I'm glad you feel that way."

"Losing Andrew changed my entire life. And even though all these years have passed, it's still with me."

"I understand. Can I ask you how he died?" I ask gently.

Even in the dim light, I see the agony flair in his eyes.

"Andrew was the ideal big brother. He was fun and imaginative, protective and bossy. We even had a secret language with each other. I've heard twins have the same thing…. He only tortured me occasionally." He grins.

I laugh. I learned quickly how to give it right back to my siblings, but it could be exhausting.

"So like me, Andrew inherited the holiday gene and always came up with all kinds of adventures for us around the holidays. Around that time my dad's company was doing transport for a piano manufacturer. If he had access to empty piano crates, he'd haul them home for us to use as clubhouses. He'd just cut out openings for windows and doors out of the sides and we were good to go."

"Cool," I say, imagining it in my mind.

"That year we had one we played in all the time and dad strung strands of lights around the crate during Christmas. Andrew convinced me that we were explorers living in the North Pole, hunting reindeer for food, and keeping watch for Santa."

"How cute." I picture Will with a plastic bow and arrow stalking suburban backyards with his brother.

"So one Saturday I was crawling through the door to go inside the clubhouse and I scraped up my side because the opening was too small. I made such a scene about it that Andrew decided he'd fix the problem. Dad was at work that day, so Andrew went and got dad's saw out of the garage and starting sawing away while I cheered him on. It didn't occur to either of us to turn off the Christmas lights and move them out of the way."

I close my eyes, suspecting what's to come.

Will stops and when I glance up, his eyes are haunted as if he's reliving it. "It happened so fast, Sophia. One minute we're laughing and he's proudly making progress as he cuts away, and the next there's a horrible noise—I'll never forget that sound—and he falls over flat."

I gasp at the visual and cover my mouth with my open hands.

"I knew it was really bad. I screamed and ran into the house to get my mom, but by the time we got back, he was gone. He had the live wires clutched in his hands. He'd cut not just through the lights but the big extension cord and there was some issue with the outside lighting so it didn't trip the circuit breaker."

"Oh, God. How horrible. I can't even imagine."

"My mom went completely nuts. They had to sedate her, and she was never the same after that day. She blamed me, she blamed my dad, and she even blamed Christmas. I felt like my life was over even though Andrew was the one that was gone."

"So that's why your family no longer celebrated Christmas."

He nods. "Not only did we never have it again, it was the worst time of the year in our house. Everything was gray and empty. Dad would drink more than usual and mom would sink into a catatonic depression. I hated being there and as soon as I got old enough, I stayed away as much as I could."

We sit silently for a minute, and I think about what this means to the Will I know now.

"So all of this" —I gesture to the house— "is to make up for what you lost?"

"Yeah, although it wasn't premeditated or anything. It just sort of happened over time. I told you about that studio job where I worked on a Christmas movie. It was this big overdone production—every inch of the house was Christmasized. At first I approached it unaware of how it would affect me personally. As the project went on I realized how happy I was working on it. I would get there earlier than I needed to, and hang around longer at the end of the day."

"How interesting. Your reaction was instinctive. It gave you back some of the joy you missed out on as a child."

"Exactly. So when they offered the props in lieu of pay, I jumped at the chance even though part of me was worried I'd lost my mind. Where was I going to put all that stuff when it wasn't Christmas?" He laughs and shrugs.

"Fast forward a few years and here we are," I say, grinning.

"Yes, indeed. Here we are."

"What do you imagine Andrew would think of all this?"

"I've often wondered that. I think he'd love it."

"I bet he would." I scrunch up my nose. "Maybe not all the glitter and mermaids in here… but everything else."

"Yeah," he says with a wistful smile.

I scan the room, seeing it in a new light. It occurs to me that this room is different from the rest, but I decide not to bring it up.

"What were you just thinking?"

I sigh and my expression falls. "Just that this is the only room with no Christmas lights."

"No. Pity the girl I was dating who surprised me by hanging some in here a few years back."

"Oh, no."

"Believe me, it was a short lived relationship," he says.

I smooth his T-shirt down over my legs and get up. "I'm going to go back to bed. Come up whenever you're ready, okay?"

He takes my hand and stands. "I'm ready."

After walk back to the room, we crawl under the covers and into each other's arms. He smiles and runs his fingers over my cheek.

"What?" I ask.

"All that talking and you never asked me what I was thinking about downstairs. I talked to Andrew about something important."

"Really? What did you talk about?"

He links his hand in mine and squeezes gently. "I told him I'm in love with you."

"Oh, Will!" I press my hand over my heart to keep it in my chest. I'm overcome with emotion. That's when an idea hits me. I peel the covers off me and swing my legs over the side of the bed.

"I'll be right back," I say.

"Hey, where are you going?" he says, grabbing the back of my make-shift nightie.

I turn back and grin, my eyes dancing. "I'm going to talk to Andrew and tell him I'm in love with you, too."

His smile is so big I'd swear the sun's burst in his room.

"Come here you!" He tackles me and pins me to the bed with his body. A moment later he begins expressing to me all of his love, without using a single word.

Chapter Fifteen

The sunrise is brilliant the next morning, illuminating a crystal blue sky and leaving every shadow sharply defined. Fine dew lingers over the manicured lawns with the quiet hush fading as the sounds of a new day fill the air. Fall in Los Angeles never feels like autumn, just a cooler version of a sunny day.

Will surveys the front yard before I head out to work. I'm relieved to see all the decorations exactly where they'd been left the night before. The neighbors have been prepped for what's happening this evening, but one never knows how people will react to a yard of Christmas stuff in mid-October. Hell, it's not even Halloween yet.

"So I'll be back before the truck shows up," I say, feeling glum as Will hugs me good-bye.

"Why are you pouting?" He places his fingers under my chin and lifts my face to greet him.

"I'd rather hang out with you and Romeo today."

"I'd rather you did that too. Take the day off!" he says enthusiastically. I sigh. "I can't."

"Well then don't pout, baby. You'll be back here before you know it, and we'll be here waiting for you."

I lean over and give Romeo a pat. "See you later, handsome." His tail wags furiously.

I kiss Will next. "And see you later too, handsome."

I get into my car and when I roll down my window, I overhear Will talking to Romeo.

"Hey, Romeo, we sure know how to pick 'em, don't we?"

Romeo barks.

"You said it dude, she's quality."

That afternoon, the trucks aren't even fully unloaded before the yelling starts. It's like herding cats. The crew is more irritable than usual.

"We have to figure out what shots are most the important so we can prioritize the shoot and make the most of our time before we lose the light." Aaron points to his makeshift schedule.

"I don't think it's going to be a problem. This place is like a damn theme park—there are almost no black holes." Stu argues.

"I thought we'd already mapped this out. Paul and I agreed that we were going to start with a pan of the overall house and yard, and then zoom to the roof with Santa and the sleigh," I say, my arms folded over my chest.

"That's so expected." Terry rolls his eyes.

"Do not get fucking artsy on us, Terry. We have four hours to get everything and this isn't a Merchant Ivory film. As our Sophia said, Santa and the damn sleigh—this shot isn't optional." Lindsey puts her hands on her hips and glares.

"And then the tight shots of the most animated stuff like the Ferris wheel. We need enough light for that," Aaron says.

"Sure, fine." Lindsey sighs.

I watch Will as he stands on the front porch with his arms folded and observes the argument. He had hoped to be an observer tonight, but Lindsey and I informed him earlier that he's expected to say a few things on camera. Now we're waiting to find out what that is exactly.

"Tell me when you want everything fired up," Will yells when there's a lull in the arguing. I smile at how comfortable he is with everyone now.

"Thanks," Aaron calls back. "Will do."

Lindsey looks at her watch. "Probably in about thirty minutes."

Will waves. "Okay, fine."

I get busy with details but I smile at him from a distance just before I touch base with Lindsey. He winks at me and I beam in response.

"How's it going?" I ask Lindsey.

"Fine. This should be pretty straightforward as long as they can get everything to read on camera."

I nod. "Isn't it amazing?"

Lindsey laughs loudly as I scan the yard. "It's so typical of me. I haven't really looked at anything from the perspective of a viewer... just the potential problems with the shoot. Now that you mention it, it is amazing. Those singing polar bears are a hoot."

"Can you imagine what the kids think when they see it?" I ask with reverence.

"Yeah, but where the hell does he store all this crap?"

"He's got it figured out, but who cares. I think it's really special what he's created here."

Lindsey shakes her head and laughs. "Damn, girl, you've got it bad."

She looks at Will who's looking at me. She nods toward him. "I guess that works since he's obviously got it bad too."

I smile but don't encourage her. "Oh, Lindsey," I say with a loud sigh before wandering off to find Paul.

I watch Will with amusement as they mike him up for the next take.

"Will, say something so we can make sure your mike is working," Terry says.

"What should I say?"

"Whatever you want as long as you're talking. Pretend you're Santa Claus."

"Testing, testing. Ho, ho, ho, Merry Christmas," Will says, rolling his eyes.

Terry nods. "Good, thanks."

Aaron motions for Paul to start.

"So, Will, you showed us the amazing, over-the-top, Christmas décor in your house, but you hadn't warned us that the best stuff is outside. This is crazy," Paul says.

"Well, that's one way of putting it," Will says dryly.

"Now I've heard that your house is really well known in the area, and you get a lot of visitors over the holidays. Is that true?"

"Yeah, from the day the set up goes live, there's usually a crowd along the fence looking at everything. It pretty much stays that way until after New Year's."

"A crowd? Wow! Your neighbors must love that," says Paul.

"No, not really," Will answers honestly.

"Aw, where's their Christmas spirit? Don't be Scrooges, neighbors," Paul says.

"That probably isn't going to help," Will says, shifting his weight uncomfortably.

As if on cue an old Pontiac slowly passes by the house and a young man leans out the car window and yells, "Hey pretty boy, your house sucks and you do too!"

Will grits his teeth and clenches his hands into fists as the car tears into the driveway next door.

As I watch Will's reaction I'm horrified that anyone would do that, let alone your next door neighbor.

Paul waves to the car enthusiastically. "Love you too, asshole!"

"Can you say that on TV?" Will asks, his eyebrows raised.

"No, Aaron stopped shooting. Do we need to do a retake, Aaron?" Paul asks.

"We're okay. I'm sure we can salvage the front end of that," he replies.

Paul turns to Lindsey. "I thought you took care of those losers."

"Yeah, Lindsey," I grumble as I put my clenched fists on my hips and glare at her.

"Okay, okay. Let me go over there *yet* again. They've become my all-time favorite people… *not*!" she snaps as she heads next door.

After Lindsey returns, I take her aside. "Are we good?"

Lindsey frowns. "Not exactly. They just told me that since the check is late and won't be here until tomorrow, they want to triple, not double their fee. I told them it was impossible."

"Are you joking?" I ask with disbelief.

"I wish I was," Lindsey says, shaking her head.

"What are we going to do?"

Lindsey chews on her lip. "We should talk to George first thing in the morning. Maybe he'll get the lawyer involved."

By the time the guys are done shooting, quite a crowd has gathered behind the picket fence. "It's much too early in the season for this kind of spectacle," an old man walking his dog, observes.

"We're filming a special. The set is coming down tomorrow so enjoy it while you can," Lindsey announces loudly.

"Can't you leave it up?" a young boy asks, looking disappointed.

"Sorry, the owner's not allowed to, but he'll have it back up around Thanksgiving," I say.

"That's great! It's super cool. The best Christmas house ever!" he says.

Will steps up next to me. "Super cool? That's high praise. Thanks, dude," he says to the boy as his parents pull him along.

He turns to me and smiles. "You're getting a taste for what it's like."

"Do you come out and talk to the crowd often?" I ask.

He shrugs. "It depends on my mood, but I usually do at least once a night. People tell me great stories. It's usually pretty interesting."

I eye the production van. "I bet. Hey, it looks like they're almost packed up. How much longer do you want to keep everything lit?"

"Let's give the crowd a ten minute warning and then shut it down."

I nod and give Lindsey the direction. While she makes announcements to the crowd, I whisper, "Would it be okay if I stay with you again tonight?"

He grins. "Of course, you don't need to ask. I always want you here."

His smile is warm and it carries to his eyes. It melts me when he looks at me like that.

The crew says their good-byes to Will, and I pretend that I'm going to use the restroom before leaving. I say good-bye to everyone and head into the house. When the coast is clear, I come back out and we say good night to the group of neighbors still left at the fence. Will turns off the lights one circuit at a time until the yard is dark except for the landscape lighting and front lanterns. He takes me by the hand and we go inside.

"The three-ring circus is officially done. I think we need to celebrate," he says. His grin is boyish as if a heavy weight has been lifted off his weary shoulders.

I smile, glad to see the giddy relief on his face, even if I was the one who introduced this distress in his life.

"Champagne?"

"Yes."

I pull two glasses out of the cabinet while he digs around in his refrigerator. "They gave us champagne when the last series ended," he explains as he finds the bottle and pulls it out. "I've been waiting for something to celebrate."

"Perfect."

"Sorry I don't have those fancy champagne glasses, but we can use wine glasses," he says when I set out tumblers.

"I keep telling you I'm not fancy." I insist.

"Hmm." He pops the cork and pours two healthy glassfuls.

I lift mine up. "Here's to getting through!"

"Hell yes! It's over!" He laughs, his energy invigorating.

I expected we'd be exhausted but as it turns out, Will is amped up and he gets me going. As we work our way through the champagne bottle, my flirting accelerates and he teases back.

"Did I tell you earlier how hot you looked during the yard set up yesterday, all manly doing your manly stuff?"

He laughs. "No you never mentioned that. Manly stuff, huh?"

"Yes, you looked good enough to eat. Now that I mention it, you look that good now too."

"You're all talk and no game," he says with a salacious grin.

"Oh yeah? Are you challenging me?" I ask.

He nods. "Are you up for the challenge?"

Game on, I think as I wink.

I hook my fingers in his belt loops and pull him out of the kitchen. He smiles and lets me lead while he watches the sexy commanding smile on my face. I'm about to show him that I'm not just flirting anymore.

"Where are you taking me?" he says, his voice laced with longing.

"You'll see." I bite my lip as I tug on his belt loops more firmly.

Once in the hallway I steer him toward the living room door. "In there," I say, still pulling him along. I'm already so aroused that every part of my body is humming and I haven't even begun to do all the things with Will that I've been picturing in my head.

He pauses to turn on the twinkle lights, before I pull him to one of the couches. I slide my fingers out of his belt loops and run my hands over his shoulders. He watches me with dark eyes. I can feel his heart pounding as I run my hands down his chest. I trace a light trail back and forth with my hand, moving lower and lower on his abdomen. I stop at the top of his jeans.

This man. He just does something to me—wild things—deliciously dirty things. My mouth waters and my fingers twitch in anticipation.

I make him wait a moment while my gaze moves over him. Clothes can't hide his sexy body but I know the fun will really begin once I get them off. I look down and see he's hard and straining against his jeans. Another wave of desire curls through me and I as stare he pushes his hips forward invitingly. His ragged breath is all I can hear.

"Okay?" I ask, dipping my fingers just inside the waistband, teasing him.

He swallows thickly and whispers, "Yeah."

"I've dreamed of doing this to you. In here... like this," I say with a sigh.

I slowly unzip his fly and drag his jeans and boxers down his thighs. He pulls his T-shirt over his head just before I wrap my hand around him and slowly move up and down his length.

"Sophia," he moans.

"You're perfect," I say with longing.

I gently push him back until he settles down onto the couch. Something about the way he surrenders, his gloriously naked body draped against the cushion makes me feel sexually powerful. His erection is at full attention as he pulls his legs apart, an invitation I can't wait to accept.

"And look at you. I love that you've figured out what you want," he says, with a wicked smile.

"I have," I say, hungry for him as I sink down to my knees. My heart is pounding knowing I'm finally going to take him in my mouth.

His eyes grow wide as I kiss the head of his cock before sliding my tongue down to the base and back up. I wrap my lips around him, loving how he feels, watching him, and listening to his reactions—the unbridled yearning in his ragged breath and the passion in his eyes. He slowly slides his fingers through my hair, his expression drunk with pleasure.

Every place he touches me while I make love to him, becomes an erogenous zone, sizzling and sparking causing me to moan and press my thighs together. There's an ache between my legs, as I imagine him touching me where I'm wet for him.

I take my time, playing and teasing. I savor the taste and feel of him, anticipating the moment when he can't hold on another second and I guide him to cum in my mouth. I moan with satisfaction as I feel his climax building, but when a flush moves across his chest and his hips begin to rock, he tucks his finger under my chin and guides me up.

"Straddle me, love," he whispers

The ache between my legs can't be denied. I stand and make a show of sliding off my jeans and taking off my sweater and bra.

He groans as he watches me. I'm so wound up with need that I have to fight to stay focused as I climb onto his lap. He leans over and fishes a condom out of his jeans pocket.

I grin. "You're prepared."

"And with you, always hopeful."

I feel in command as I lift up and slide him against me. My eyes roll back with pleasure.

"Does that feel good?" he asks, as he watches with hooded eyes. "You're in control here."

I press over him and let my head fall forward as I catch my breath. "You feel so good... so perfect. I like controlling you."

One of his hands circles my nipple while the other runs over my hip and caresses my behind. "You know what *I* like?"

"What?" I whisper.

"Watching you like this. Teasing me, making me crazy for you."

I smile, swiveling my hips to just barely skim over him when all I want is to have him inside of me. I bite my lip as I hold on to my last threads of restraint.

He studies me in awe. "Do you have any idea how beautiful you are?"

"You make me feel beautiful," I say, my need for him flaring. He makes me feel like poetry in motion—my desire brushing across my lips, tumbling over my shoulders, across my breasts, and sinking between my legs. I want to be his everything—like none other.

His expression hardens. "I want you, baby," he says with a groan.

I quickly realize he's undone, and sheer desire has pushed him to the edge. As his words roll over me hard, I take a sharp breath and slowly sink down on him until I can't take any more of his length. Every nerve in my body is buzzing with brilliant sensation. My hips slowly begin to move as his hands hold me, guiding me.

He watches me with a dark expression, something akin to pain, even though I know it's the pleasure coursing through him.

"Is this what you want?" he asks breathlessly as he fills me.

"It's everything I want," I chant. I grab his shoulders and use the leverage to take him harder. My eyes glaze over with drunken pleasure as his moans accelerate.

He knows the moment I take flight. The pop of each light explodes inside of me until I'm shimmering with sensation. He tightly holds onto me while I cry out, taking him with me to our place of light.

Still buzzed and blissed out, he wraps us up in the throw blanket, and we curl up on the couch. A few more sips of champagne added to our exhaustion, and we doze off. Sometime later I feel him kiss the top of my head.

"Baby," he whispers.

"Hmm?" I reply.

"Let's go to bed."

"Good idea," I mumble, still not opening my eyes until he gets up and pull his jeans back on.

"Why don't you go on up," he tells me. "I'm going to let Romeo out, and then I'll join you."

"Sure," I say. "Give him a pat on the head."

I'm already in bed when he returns to join me.

"Everything okay?" I ask.

"Yeah... it's all good," Will says, pulling off his jeans. "He hates being locked up, and loves it when I let him loose. When I left, he was running circles around the yard."

"How cute," I say, yawning and already half asleep.

When Will crawls into bed and spoons me, I embrace the warmth of skin against skin, his heart beating so close to mine.

"Good night, beautiful," he whispers before I close my eyes and let sleep take me under its hypnotic spell.

Chapter Sixteen

I sense that it's still late at night as I break through the surface of a heavy dreamlike state. When I open my eyes, I'm disoriented.

Am I in the waking world or in a dream? Then I hear the anxious barking that I thought was part of my dream. I clear my head. I'm curled up next to Will in his bed. There's silence for a brief moment, and then another round of frantic barking. This time it startles me. It sounds like Romeo, but why is he in the front yard?

I sit straight up in bed and listen again. Not only does it sound like Romeo, but the light shining through the window is too bright for this time of night.

What's going on?

I gently shake Will's shoulder. "Will, wake up. Something's wrong."

His eyes pop open and he blinks several times. "What?" he asks, but as soon as he hears the barking, he sits up and tips his head toward the window. He gets out of bed and trudges to the front window while rubbing the sleep from his eyes.

When he examines the yard, he gasps and leans into the glass. I jump out of bed and join him at the window. Something large in the front yard is on fire and the flames shoot high into the dark night. My foggy mind spins, wondering what would burn with such ferocity?

"What the fuck?" Will growls. I follow his gaze to the man with a hood pulled down low over his forehead. He's waving a burning stick at Romeo as Will's determined little guy lunges and barks like a crazed beast.

I see the fierce rage tear through Will. It frightens me, snapping me completely awake.

"Sophia, call the fire department!" he yells even though I'm standing next to him.

"Oh my God!" I cry out, everything hitting me all at once. I rush to the bedside table, grab my cell phone, and dial 911. My hands are shaking so badly I can barely hold the phone.

"Tell 'em to send the police too and that the arsonist is still outside!" Will yells.

While I'm dealing with the emergency operator, Will finds his jeans and snatches them off the floor. He yanks them on and turns to the door as if he's going to run out of the room.

"Shoes!" I yell.

While I frantically give information to the dispatcher, I move back to the window to describe the fire's progress. Will quickly pulls on his sneakers and joins me to peer out the window one last time. The flames are higher now but haven't spread to other displays, and the arsonist is still fighting off Romeo.

"Get 'em, Romeo," Will says under his breath.

Right before Will turns to run downstairs, the guy lifts up his torch and when Romeo lunges the man arches his leg back and then swings it forward full force. The powerful kick hits Romeo right in the chest and sends him flying backwards. There's a pitiful cry at impact, but then complete silence when Romeo hits the ground. From our view he looks lifeless on the damp grass.

"ROMEO!" Will screams, pain and terror filling his eyes.

"No!" I cry as he flies out of the room and pounds down the stairs. I yank on my clothes and charge down the stairs, while praying that Romeo's all right.

When I get outside, Will is kneeling over his beloved dog, his hands frantically touching him.

"Romeo, come on, little guy," he chants. He looks up, and his unshed tears glisten in the firelight. I've never seen a man so broken.

"I can't tell if he's breathing! Help me!" Will cries.

I run to him and fall to my knees on the damp grass. I gently push Will back, place my fingers to Romeo's neck, and put my face just inches from Romeo's nose. I pick up a weak pulse and the faintest of raspy breaths.

"He's alive, Will! But we've got to get him to the vet."

"I'll get the car keys." Will drags his fist across his eyes, brushing the tears away.

I regard the arsonist. He has a look of grisly fascination on his face and then he sneers, almost satisfied. The fire is growing higher and it finally dawns on me that it's the gingerbread house, Will's childhood project full of memories of his grandparents. We can't leave for the animal hospital. The arsonist will make sure the fire reaches the house. I feel nauseous.

"What about all that?" I ask, nodding toward the fire as Will jumps up to run inside.

"I only care about saving my dog. The fire department and police are on their way. They can deal with the rest," he shouts over his shoulder, and he starts for the door.

"Ohhhh poor, poor, pretty boy. His rat dog is dead!" The arsonist's voice pierces the silence of the night and overwhelms the sound of the cracking fire.

Dread flares in the pit of my stomach. A man like Will can only be pushed so far.

"Will!" I yell, but it's too late. I barely recognize my lover with that murderous expression on his face.

"I'm going to kill you, mother fucker!" he screams and changes course, charging the arsonist.

I let out a piercing scream as Will tackles the guy to the ground. He rips the torch out of the arsonist's hand, and for a split second I think he's going to beat the man senseless with it and set his head on fire. But Will hurls the torch to the street, and then lays into the man with flying fists and grunts. One particularly hard punch snaps the guy's head back, making his hood slide off.

Is it Darrell Hoffmeyer from next door? Will told me that he's the one that yelled at him from the car during the shoot.

Will delivers blow after blow, not seeming care that his hands and clothes are covered with blood.

Darrell frantically tries to stop Will, but eventually curls in a ball trying block the blows. Will's natural strength topped off with his explosion of adrenaline appears to be much more than Darrell can handle.

"Help! Help me!" Darrell yells at the top of his lungs between blows. "Darrell, Darrell, where the hell are you?"

I recognize the voice of Fred Hoffmeyer and spy him running down the sidewalk toward Will and Darrell. I'm stunned realizing that they're responsible for this vicious attack. Fred is trailed by a younger man, probably his other son.

"Darrell!" Fred yells, his anger escalating.

"Dad! Help!"

I have a powerful instinct to get Romeo to safety and help Will. I gingerly lift Romeo until he's cradled in my arms. I hear a garbled yell and I snap back up.

A moment later, Fred and his other son tear a crazed Will off Darrell. I blink in horror. Will looks like a savage all covered in blood. His expression is terrifying as he curses and fights them. He spies me holding Romeo.

"Get to safety. Get Romeo out of here!" he yells.

My heart feels like it's going to explode out of my chest and my mind is a collision of thoughts and sounds: the fire snapping as it roars, Darrell groaning in agony, clanging metal, Fred cursing, a siren far in the distance. I'm overwhelmed with conflicting instincts to protect both Will and Romeo at any cost.

Darrell sees me and he pushes himself up while his father and brother are having a go at Will.

I realize as I glare back that the sirens are getting louder, and I sigh with relief.

Darrell stands on shaky legs and turns to the Will mêlée. He stumbles behind Will and surprises him with a neck lock. Fred takes a swing and guts Will in the stomach.

Darrell snaps something at his brother and nods toward me.

"She's got his fucking dog; go break the little bastard's neck. That'll show this fucker."

The brother instantly takes off toward me.

"No!" I scream and run toward the driveway, clutching Romeo to my chest. If I run toward the house, I'll be cornered, so I make the only choice left. I run down the middle of the street in the direction of the approaching sirens.

The brother runs after me and is gaining ground. I glance behind me. I see a flash of silver out of the corner of my eye and reach deep inside to sprint faster. He's close—so close I can hear the swish of his pants as he runs and can almost feel him reaching me. I imagine his fingers grazing the ends of my hair, and dread surges through my body. A second later there's an explosive crash behind me and the sharp smack of something hitting the pavement.

I look behind me, and I skid to a stop. The brother is sprawled like a rag doll across the pavement. He's out cold. I turn around, still clinging to Romeo. *What happened?* He probably has a head injury if that smacking sound was his head hitting the unforgiving surface. But what's more startling is the sight of Hank shaking and clinging to his shopping cart. His eyes are wide and his mouth agape as if he's just realizing what he's done.

He points a shaking finger at the flattened man. "He was trying to hurt you," he says as if he needs to explain his actions.

Just then a fire truck rounds the corner. It barrels right up to the house with no hesitation. The flames in front are a beacon, directing the truck to Will's home.

Thank God, there's help now for Will too.

Gasping for breath, I start to crumble as the trauma of the night hits me. I look down at Romeo, so still in my arms, and cry out as the tears fall.

Hank's expression turns to panic. "I'm sorry. I'm sorry, Miss Sophia. I had to stop him. You're Will's girl."

My heartbreak sets in. "It's okay, Hank. Truly. I can't believe you were even around. How did you know?"

"The middle of the night is the best time to collect cans & bottles in this area since the trucks come early in the morning." He looks down, refusing to make eye contact. "I was on the next block over and saw the flames. As I got closer I heard your scream."

"Oh my God. I'm so grateful you were so close."

"Me too." He relaxes and smiles timidly.

"Thank you for saving us." I give him a warm, grateful smile.

He straightens his stance and looks me in the eyes. "I'm just glad I could."

I study the unconscious man on the side of the road. "You should go. I'm the only one who saw you, and let's just say…I didn't see what happened since I kept running." I wait, hoping Hank gets my drift.

He eyes the injured man and his shoulders curl in and his eyes dart toward the fire trucks. Yes, I must go. If they arrest me, Miss Sophia…"

"Go," I say, nodding in a direction that takes him away from the house. I wait until he's disappeared into the shadows.

Romeo's breathing is labored. "Come on, Romeo. Help is here," I whisper. I hurry back, scared to see what shape Will is in.

"Please, please," I chant to myself. "Please let him be okay."

The police pull up just before I get to the front gate. I'm relieved that three of the firemen have pulled the fighting men apart while the others deal with the fire. Will's cursing still, his eyes narrow and full of fury. He's pretty battered up, but at least still in one piece.

When he sees me still holding Romeo, he furrows his brow, scans the two of us, and then turns to look in the direction I came from. I realize I'm breathing in gasps as I wipe my tears from my face.

As soon as the police intervene, the men start yelling.

"He tried to kill me!" Darrell yells, pointing at Will.

"And you fucked us over, did that TV crap and didn't pay us!" Fred yells, his face redder than normal.

"You set my house on fire and tried to kill my dog, you bastard!" Will roars back.

Fred looks around frantically once he sees me. "Where's George?" he yells.

I step up to the policeman and point to George. The policeman immediately radios for an ambulance and backup.

The firemen have put out the blaze, leaving the smell of smoke and charred wood wafting around us.

"Are you okay? What about Romeo?" Will calls through the chaos, an urgency in his voice.

"I'm fine, but we need to get him to the vet hospital."

A minute later the ambulance and the police backup show up. The scene becomes even more intense and chaotic as Will, Fred, and Darrell are all apprehended and George is loaded in the ambulance. Meanwhile one of the policemen questions me about the events and asks what happened with Romeo. He gets the information for Romeo's vet from Will and calls ahead to alert them.

The police decide to take everyone to the station for questioning and to file charges with one of the cars escorting me to the animal hospital.

They're about to load Will into the backseat of one of the squad cars when I rush over. I realize we haven't had a moment since this crisis started. One minute we're peacefully sleeping in each other's arms and the next, being questioned by the police. I rest my hand on his shoulder.

"I'm so sorry for all of this, Will," I say softly.

"Me too. I think I'm in shock." His face is twisted in pain as he gently cradles Romeo's head in his hands. He looks up with the saddest eyes. "Please, baby, get word to me that he's going to be okay. Please."

My heart skips. "What do you mean, *get word to you*? I'm meeting you guys at the station for the questioning."

He shakes his head and lets it drop. "This isn't good, Sophia. I'm just saying, I'm not sure how all of this is going to go down."

The change is almost instant. It's as if a thin suit of armor, like the ones in futuristic sci-fi films, slides over his skin. I can see him toughening up right before my eyes, morphing him into the street kid of his youth.

He grits his teeth and his voice is rough. "I don't want you to see me like this." He grimaces and looks away. "I'm screwed."

"But none of this is your fault. They did this!"

He shakes his head, defeated. "Doesn't matter. No one ever said life was fair."

I feel the final piece of his armor lock in place as the policeman pulls him away.

As the hours pass during the night that never ends, a deep feeling of remorse takes shape in me, twisting and turning until I'm completely saturated with it. This is all my fault. If I'd never coerced Will to do the show, none of this would've happened.

Romeo is in intensive care with something called pneumothorax because one of his broken ribs tore a small hole in his right lung. The vet informs me it's very serious but assures me that Romeo's one of the toughest dogs he's seen. He has a fighting chance. I cling onto hope, as I can't imagine what it'll do to Will if his little guy doesn't pull through.

At the station, the questioning and confusion drones on and on. As Will warned me, he's in a really bad position since Fred and Darrell are pressing charges against him and the savage nature of his attack on Darrell only makes things worse. As a result, he's arrested and held overnight.

Darrell earns a similar fate for the arson crime and attack on Romeo. By four in the morning, Fred is allowed to leave to go be with George at the hospital. They've received word that he's conscious now, but they're keeping him for observation.

The desk sergeant insists I go home and get a couple of hours of rest. I linger for a while, feeling horrible about leaving Will, but finally agree. I can get help for him first thing in the morning.

I get into my car and the illuminated clock on my dashboard screams five twenty-two. I count the hours back in my head. Seven hours ago my world was right. Will's enchanted house made me believe my life was a fairy tale with my dashing prince and his faithful dog. If someone were writing my life story that section would be written in pink with little hearts doodled in the margins.

Will has changed my world in so many ways. Until tonight our future was destined to be an endless strand of Christmas lights burning brightly in the darkness.

I turn on the ignition and shiver from the cold night air. Could things be bleaker? As I pull out of the parking lot I pause, not knowing where to go. Will's or my place? Or perhaps I should go to church and pray for our world to right itself now that everything's been turned upside down.

Chapter Seventeen

When my alarm goes off at eight in the morning, I want to hurl it against the wall. I feel disoriented and shaky as I sit up and try to get my bearings. I barely remember changing into my pj's and crawling into bed after the night from hell.

I stumble into the kitchen and start a pot of coffee. After finding my cell phone, I sit down to make a few calls. I'm on my fifth call before I finally get True Blue's attorney, Martin Rasner, on the phone.

"You spent the night at the police station with the client?" he asks, sounding very concerned. "Can you explain why you were with him that late in the first place?"

Flustered, I get defensive. "We were making plans for the... next shoot," I stutter. "Do you have a problem with that?"

"Oh, that's very convincing, Sophia. Late night planning meetings with young male subjects are always such a good idea," Martin says dryly.

"Martin, we need to get him out of jail this morning at nine, on the dot," I snap.

"Sophia, if he beat the crap out of his neighbor and ended up being locked up, why is that our problem? He sounds like a big boy—all grown up. He can figure it out on his own. I don't want us any more involved than we already are."

"Let me be clear. His neighbors attacked him because they had been promised money from us for the inconvenience from the shoot, and we hadn't paid them yet, so they were enraged," I say finally feeling sharp and awake.

"They hadn't been paid yet? The paperwork wasn't signed?" he asks, his voice now on edge.

"No, they hadn't… And no, it wasn't. It's a long story, but regardless; this is what set them off. So, as you can see, we need to step up and do the right thing."

"Damn it! This has lawsuit written all over it. You've spent time with him. Do you sense that he's litigious?"

I pause for a moment. In my heart I'm certain Will isn't that way, but right now I need everyone doing whatever they can to help him.

"Oh, yeah. I'd worry about it. The last thing he said before they cuffed him and dragged him off was that we'd be hearing from his lawyers." I lie, telling tell him what he needs to hear to take action.

"Fuck!" Martin swears. "Okay, I'll meet you at the station at nine sharp."

I tap my foot while Martin signs Will's paperwork at the release desk. I want to check the time but I forgot to put my watch back on in my rush to get to the station. My stomach's churning as I try to imagine what mood Will might be in when they get him out.

I study the desk clerk and realize that there must have been a shift change. No one looks familiar, and the entire night now has a dream-like quality—well, more nightmare than dream. I close my eyes, take a deep breath, and listen to the low drone of the fluorescent lights. When I open my eyes again, everything has a sickly yellow-green cast. It's that very light Will walks under when he's finally escorted to the waiting area.

When he spies me sitting with Martin, he eyes us warily, and stops a few feet away. Martin stands and approaches him.

"Will, I'm Martin Rasner, the attorney from True Blue Entertainment. We've secured your release after your hellish night." He pulls out a business card and hands it to Will. "Here's my contact information if you need it."

Will takes the card without looking at it and jams it in his back pocket. He won't make eye contact, and I have no idea if he's trying to formulate what he's going to say, or if he's just not going to say anything at all.

I note that Martin doesn't extend an apology for what happened or True Blue's part in it. *Of course not.* He's a lawyer and the last thing he would do is say anything that puts his client in a bad position. It leaves a rancid taste in my mouth.

There's an awkward pause. Finally Martin turns to me.

"Are you sure you're okay driving Will home? I can do it."

"No, no, I insist," I say.

Martin studies me silently. "Okay, check in with me before lunch." He turns to Will. "Take it easy. This will be behind you soon."

Will finally looks up and glares at Martin, who steps back.

Martin spins and walks out the door.

I turn back to Will. "I'm sorry, so sorry, Will," I say softly, trying to hold back the tears.

He closes his eyes and tips his head back.

"I need to get out of here," he says with a chilling emptiness in his voice.

I'm almost glad he walks behind me to my car so he can't see the tears I brush away. The drive back is excruciating. I tell him about Romeo's condition, informing him that I got an update from the vet while Martin was signing the paperwork. He listens to me while gazing out the passenger window.

Will only speaks once during the entire drive. "I swore I'd never be back in one of those places ever again. I swore." He shakes his head and falls silent again.

It's so tense in the car, I fear anything I say will upset him, so I remain silent too. When we get close to his neighborhood he digs his fingers into his knees.

"I need to see Romeo now. Just drop me off there."

It stings that he doesn't want me there. When I approach the building, I pull into the lot and park, ignoring his drop-off instructions.

As we step out of the car, he turns to me.

"What are you doing?"

"I'm coming with you," I say, trying not to sound hurt.

"This is my problem," he says, his eyes cold and gray.

"Will…" My voice sounds sad.

He turns and walks to the entrance.

I follow him several paces behind and take a seat in the back of the waiting area while he checks in. If I were him I'd need my space and time to process everything that happened.

He can be angry and short with me in the short term and I'll try to handle it. I just hope that when he looks back he'll realize that I was, and am, there for him.

Once he's checked in, he's taken back to the vet's office, and I follow several steps behind him. He glances over his shoulder, looking annoyed like I shouldn't be there.

"Will, please. I care about him too." I say quietly.

He turns back without saying a word. He asks Daniel, Romeo's vet, several questions before asking to see Romeo. The veterinary assistant walks us back to where Romeo's being observed.

"Oh, buddy," he says, his breath catching in the back of his throat. "Romeo."

He turns away and blinks. His shoulders sag as he looks back at him.

"Can I touch him?" he asks the assistant.

"He's sedated so he probably won't react. Just be careful of the tube."

Will gently skims Romeo's fur with his fingers.

As I observe, I think how peaceful Romeo is. *Too peaceful.* It's haunting.

Will leans in close. "Hey, my brave little man. Thank you for protecting us. If you hadn't barked so loud and woken us up to the fire…well, who knows what could have happened." His voice is shaking as he talks, and he looks off to the side for a moment and grimaces.

Just watching Will with Romeo reminds me of the whole chaotic scene and how seriously in peril we were last night.

"Wow, he saved you?" the assistant asks, awestruck.

Will flinches like he's forgotten he's not alone. He brushes a hand under his eyes and nods without raising his head.

"He sure did," he replies.

"Such a brave dog, a great dog," she says with a sweet voice.

"The best dog ever." He swirls his fingers on top of Romeo's head.

My eyes flood with tears and I hold in a sob.

"I think we better let him rest," The assistant says after giving Will a few more minutes with Romeo.

"Okay, just one more thing." Will leans even closer to Romeo. "Fight hard, little guy. You're a champ and you will pull through this. I'm going to be here a lot until I can take you home. And when I do, I'm going to take the best care of you." He sighs and I can feel the conviction in his words.

"It's you and me always, Romeo."

I try to steady myself and not linger on the meaning of those words.

As Will walks back to the waiting area, he acts like I'm not there. I can feel the anger roll off him.

"Ready?" I ask, stepping closer to get his attention.

He silently nods and follows me outside to my car.

I've driven several blocks with my hands tightly clutching the steering wheel before I break the silence.

"Do you feel better now that you've seen him?"

Will stares out his window. "We still don't know if he will pull through. You heard Daniel. He's stable now, which is the most we can hope for at this point. It will take a few days to know for sure."

I nod solemnly. "But there's reason to be hopeful. Romeo's under great care and I bet he was glad that you checked on him."

"Yeah," he says quietly. "But he was sedated and didn't react to me being there. At least I got to touch him and talk to him. Maybe he knows on some level that I'm there for him."

My breath catches. "Oh, Will."

It's silent for several minutes before I speak again. "I wish we could have gotten him in right away." I regret running down the street and holding him. That must have only made things worse.

"Yeah, well if only it hadn't happened at all," he replies with a shadow of anger behind every word.

The resulting silence is so big it fills every nook and cranny in the car, the kind of deafening silence that makes your head hurt. I'm almost relieved when I pull up to Will's house so we can get out of the damn car.

He's staring at the yard when I park in the driveway.

"The gingerbread house," he says, as if he's just realized that it's gone.

I almost don't recognize his voice. It's so different, an intense intonation of misery mixed with resignation.

"It's gone. I'm so sorry, Will," I whisper.

"You're sorry? You have no idea," he says, mostly to himself.

I turn to him after I pull my keys out of the ignition. "Can I come in?"

He rests his hands on his knees and takes a deep breath, staring out the front windshield.

My heart pounds wildly as I realize things are even worse than I feared.

He finally shakes his head. "I don't think it's a good idea."

"No? I thought you could use the support. I can be there for you," I say weakly.

He grips his knees with his hands and loosens before doing it again. "I've got to get my head on straight, Sophia. I'm really angry right now, and it would probably be better for you not to be around me."

His words gut me while I stare at the steering wheel. He hasn't verbally blamed me yet, but I'm sure it's just a matter of time. Nothing he could say would be harsher than what I've already said to myself.

"When I can see you?" I ask. I hate the neediness in my voice.

He opens the car door and steps out. He doesn't even lean in to face me.

"I'll call you." He closes the door and walks away.

I feel so hollow I'm not sure I can breathe. I back out of his driveway carefully and drive home extra slow, my vision blurry with the first of the day's many, many tears.

Chapter Eighteen

The meeting at True Blue is unusually somber until Paul pipes up.

"As Stan Laurel would say to Oliver Hardy, Lindsey, 'Well, that's a fine mess you've gotten us into!'" Paul turns to our irritated line producer and wags his finger at her.

"Screw you, Paul," she says, giving him the finger. "It's not my fault that dude and his inbred offspring are all off their rockers!"

"Besides, Paul, you got the quote wrong. It's 'you've gotten *me* into.'" Aaron points out.

"Oh, shut up," Paul says, emphasizing each word while rolling his eyes.

"How bad was the fire?" Rachel asks, her expression tight.

"It could have been horrible, but thankfully it was damp out and there was no wind. The worst of it was he lost the gingerbread house he had built with his grandparents," I say.

"That sucks. That thing was amazingly crafted," Aaron adds sadly.

"Yeah but at least his fucking house didn't burn down. With all that turn-of-the-century woodwork, it would have been an architectural disaster," Paul says.

"Did Will really spend the night in jail?" Aaron asks.

"Yes, he did."

"We have a very thorough investigator. Apparently Mr. Christmas has a history of violence, so attacking his neighbor was not a well-thought-out plan. Clearly our client screening was not thorough enough." Rachel adds, not so helpfully.

My stomach sinks. So much for sealed records.

"Will? Violent?" asks Lindsey, surprised.

"Well, he did threaten to beat the crap out of me during the interior shoots," Paul reminds them.

"People," Rachel says in her take charge voice. "Why do I not hear about these things when they happen? I shouldn't be hearing about this after the fact or not at all. That doesn't cut it. I'm the one dealing with management, and they are not pleased with what's happened here."

"I can imagine. So as I was saying, Will was going to beat my face in or something, and Aaron had to take him for a drive to cool him off," Paul says.

"Was it really that bad, Paul. Or are you being dramatic," I ask.

"Honestly, it was really macho and sexy hot." He folds his arms over his chest and grins. "But that's how I like my men."

Lindsey rolls her eyes. "You like your men angry? That's messed up."

"And you like 'em soft, since you're such a badass. Am I right?"

"Can we stay focused, please?" Rachel says, frustrated. "Legal is looking into everything. There's a chance we may not even be able to use the footage."

"What? So the whole shoot is a wash?" Aaron looks ready to lose it.

I feel like I'm going to throw up.

"I don't know for sure. We'll just have to wait and hear what legal decides on the risks and liability," Rachel says.

"I'm so pissed off. I mean those fucking white trash neighbors of Will's were trying to blackmail us. It was extortion. They're the ones that set his place on fire and tried to kill his dog. They should pay for all this," Lindsey says.

"The vet bills are staggering and our budget is blown sky high." Rachel's lamenting sounds shallow and self-absorbed.

My rage builds. "Will's world almost collapsed that night. Are we really just concerned about money? What about Will?"

The room goes silent and everyone stares at me. Finally Lindsey clears her throat.

"So, Sophia, some of us were wondering how you happened to be there when this happened in the middle of the night?" she asks carefully.

Rachel has a smug look as she tips her head and studies me. She taps her pencil on her pad waiting for my answer. "Yes, why was that?"

Paul rubs his hands together with delight. "There's so much we can do with this!"

"Such as?" Aaron asks, confused.

"Well, how about she was licking his candy cane? Or hanging his Christmas balls." He grins like the Grinch, a devious look on his face. "Did he *cum* down your chimney?"

"Shut up," I snap, disgusted.

"What? I'm sure you have a lovely chimney," Paul says, widening his eyes to play innocent.

"Enough!" Rachel yells. "Sophia, since you have a *special* relationship, is Will still on board, or should we expect a call from his lawyers too?"

"Sounds like that lawsuit line is getting long," Lindsey adds.

I'm silent for a moment, twisting my hands on my lap.

"I really don't know. He's pretty angry, and he's not talking to me right now," I finally say.

Their fake sympathetic nods only make things worse. I stand on unsteady legs and excuse myself, thinking I can escape to the bathroom. I want to splash water on my face and wash away my part in all of this. Paul starts talking about me before I'm even out the door.

"Poor thing," he says, shaking his head. "Heartbreak is the worst."

"And that's why there's a rule not to get involved with subjects. Too many things can go wrong," Rachel says.

"And that's not even the half of it," says Paul cryptically.

Rachel eyes him warily and nods, but I'm too upset to even care what he means.

By Saturday I'm beside myself. Will still hasn't called, and I'm climbing the walls. I finally decide to confront him. I'd rather have him be clear and break up with me instead of leaving me hanging.

When I pull up to the house, there are several men in the yard, taking the displays apart. I get out of the car, aching for the gingerbread house that is no longer.

I'm so deep in thought, Hank startles me when approaches.

"Miss Sophia, how are you doing?" His tone is so gentle that it wrecks me. He must be aware of how Will feels about me now.

I turn and try to give Hank a genuine smile but it falters.

"Not so good, Hank," I answer honestly.

"Nah. Will neither. That was a dark night," he says, shaking his head.

"The darkest. How are you doing? That was a rough night for you too."

"Thanks to you, I was lucky to get away. I was just worried about Romeo and Will, and I didn't know when or if I'd hear anything."

"I'm so sorry about that."

"So, Will told me about visiting Romeo at the vet place."

"Poor Romeo," I say.

"I bet he makes it. He's a great dog." Hank smiles encouragingly.

I nod. "He will."

I survey the yard. "You guys are taking it all down?"

"Yes, Will says he can't stand to look at it anymore. He said he may take it all down inside too." He lets out a sad sigh.

"Really?" I can't hide my surprise. For some reason I didn't expect he'd want to take down everything.

"It's all ruined now. Everything's broken," Hank says obliquely.

"And Will?" I want to know if he's said anything about me, but I can't bring myself to ask.

"Hard to say. I've never seen him like this." Hank glances at the house.

I pull my shoulders back. "Well, I better go face the music…find out if he wants to see me."

"Don't give up on him, Sophia. He'll come around, but right now, he's in a bad way. He's sick with worry over Romeo and all. Just try to understand."

"Thanks, Hank. I'm really glad I saw you." I squeeze his arm gently with affection.

He gives me a compassionate smile. "Me too. I'm behind you, Sophia. If he lets me, I'll tell him that you're the best thing to come along in a long, long time."

I trudge up to the door and ring the bell. By the time I ring the doorbell a second time, my hands are trembling. I'm about to return to my car when the door opens.

He looks more wary than surprised to see me. Yet, as we regard at each other, for the first time since I woke him up that night, I feel like he's really seeing me.

"Hey, Will." I press my hands together. "I was hoping we could talk for a minute."

He takes a deep breath, nods, and opens the door wider for me to come inside.

"Let's go out back," he says as he leads me down the main hall. "Do you want anything to drink?"

I'm relieved he's being civil at least. "No, thanks," I say softly.

He grabs his coffee mug and then holds the back door open. We both sit down on the deck stairs at the same time.

"How are you doing?" he asks.

"Not so good," I admit. "How about you?"

"Lousy, although better than I was last time I saw you."

"Well, that's good. Progress at least." I try to be encouraging.

"I was gearing myself up to call you."

"You were?" I sigh. "I was losing hope. But at least we're talking now."

With a far away look in his eyes, he presses his hands down over his knees.

Could this be any more awkward, I wonder.

"Will—"

"Sophia, before you say anything there's something I need to say."

"Okay," I reply quietly, trying to prepare myself for the worst.

"The other night, when everything went to hell and I went nuts, I never had a chance to thank you."

I look up, my mouth falling open as I blink. I wasn't expecting this.

"I may be furious about what happened with the production company and my bastard neighbors, but that doesn't change the fact that you saved Romeo. I saw how you risked your own safety to protect him from George, who would've killed him."

"I'd do it again. All I could think about was helping you and Romeo."

He takes my hand in his. We sit silently for a moment. I relish reconnecting with him no matter how faint and unstable the feeling is.

"Will, you have no idea how terrible I feel about everything that happened. If I could go back in time, I'd change everything. But I can't, can I?"

He shakes his head. "No."

I wipe a tear off my cheek. "I mean just thinking of Romeo in the hospital…"

Will squeezes my hand.

"And when I saw your gingerbread house on fire. It killed me. I know what that house meant to you."

"I know you do," he whispers.

"I'm so sorry." I put my free hand over my eyes as the tears streak down my face.

He doesn't let go of my hand and we sit quietly for a minute, both deep in our thoughts. He finally lets go, gets up and paces for a minute in front of the deck with his hands in his back pockets.

"The thing is, Sophia, those hours I spent in the holding cell, I went to some really dark places. It felt like the lowest days of my teen years… the rage, the self-loathing…all of it."

"How horrible."

"It was. Since then I've had a lot of time to think about how I'm not as together as I thought I was. I lost control of myself so quickly. It scared the fuck out of me. And then I thought about all of the shit that annoying Helena woman said about why I do the Christmas thing. I wonder if maybe she's right. I'm just doing it to cover up stuff I should be dealing with."

"I think you're being too hard on yourself."

"Or maybe I'm just really fucked up," he says, his shoulders slumping.

"Come on. That was a terrifying night."

"I think it's a lot more than that, more than just a really bad night. I need to slow things down between us until I figure some stuff out."

I lean forward, resting my face in my hands. "You're breaking up with me? I wish I could say I'm surprised, but after what happened, I came here expecting it."

He lets out a frustrated sigh. "No, we're not breaking up, just slowing things down. As it is, Romeo's coming home tomorrow, and I'm taking the week off so I can care for him until he's stable. If he does well, I'm thinking about taking him with me for a few days to visit an old friend who lives in Solano Beach."

"Is this friend a guy or a girl?" I ask, not able to hide my distress.

His eyes widen. "Oh, it's a guy. His name is Richard. He's a great friend and got me my first job at the studio. When they lived here, he and his wife Lorraine were kind of like my surrogate parents. Romeo loves them, and he really loves hanging out at the beach. It'll be good for me too."

"When do you think you'll be back?" Maybe he's just using the time to clear his head.

"I have to be back for work the following Monday. I also promised Steph I'd come to her birthday party that Saturday. So we'll head back Saturday."

"Steph invited me too. Do you mind if I'm there?"

He sits back down on the step and takes my hand again. "Of course I don't mind. I told you we're not breaking up."

"Right," I say, not sure I believe him, but his hand feels warmer and his hold more confident now that he's shared his thoughts. I wish I felt the same instead of this sinking feeling, but I'm only steps away from stumbling into emotional quicksand.

"Well, I leave for Georgia the Monday just after, so you'll have plenty of time away from me." His ambivalence leaves my heart aching and feeling even less grounded than before.

I gaze one more time at his hand with his fingers curled over mine before pulling away and standing.

"So, I guess I'll get going."

He stands as well. "Yeah, I've got to get back outside and check on the tear down. Hank's taken it over, and I'm glad for it."

"I think he's worried about you."

His expression falls. "Yeah, that makes two of us."

He opens the back door to the house and we step into the kitchen.

"Hank is my hero. I still can't believe he showed up that night."

Will furrows his brow. "I can't get him to talk about it."

"Really? He was mortified after he did it."

"He was probably scared he'd get in trouble with the authorities."

"I'd give anything to have seen it clearly. It was just a blur," I say.

"So, you didn't see him coming?" Will asks.

"No, not at all. I just remember running with Romeo in my arms down the middle of the dark street toward the sirens. I had turned to see where that George guy was. He was just a couple paces behind me and gaining fast. I saw a flash of silver out of in the corner of my eye. The sirens were so loud the sound of the cart got lost.

"George was so focused on me that he must not have seen Hank coming at him from the side. I heard the sound of an explosive crash. It happened so fast. I skidded to a stop and looked behind me. George was sprawled on the pavement like a rag doll."

"Holy shit."

"It took a second for it to compute. That's when I saw Hank holding onto his shopping cart for dear life. He was completely shaken."

"Oh, Hank," Will says sadly.

"You know, now that I think of it, right before I started running I heard a noise that sounded like clanking metal. I bet it was his cart as he pushed it down the street. It had that kind of noise. He told me he'd seen the flames and was coming to check on the house."

"What if he hadn't been out collecting cans that night?" Will asks with dismay.

Suddenly the doorbell rings, so Will steps forward to answer it. When he pulls it open, it's Hank who seems glad to see that we're calm and apparently getting along.

"Speak of the devil," Will says.

Hank looks back and forth between us. "I just came to ask what we should go into the garage storage first," Hanks says, biting on his thumbnail. "Were you really talking about me?"

"All good stuff, my man," Will says.

Hank's eyes narrow like he's not convinced. "Are you sure?"

"It's about how you saved me the other night, Hank," I say to reassure him.

Hank stands tall and nods. "I'm just glad I was there."

"We're so grateful," I say.

Will looks warmly at me with a twinkle in his eye and I feel a surge of happiness sensing that maybe things are going better than I'd hoped.

Hank nods and gives us a gentle smile. "I'm just glad to see you two together and happy."

"Me too," Will says, taking my hand.

I swoon internally.

"So give me a second, Hank, to say good-bye to Sophia, and then I'll be out to help."

"Sure thing."

When the door closes, Will pulls me into his arms and gives me a long hug. I settle into his arms, soaking up every sensation, knowing it will have to carry me for a while.

"Thank you," he whispers as he holds me.

"For what?" I ask.

"That's the first time I've smiled in what feels like days. And you were brave to come over here considering what I was like last time you saw me."

"I didn't feel brave. I just missed you so damn much." I admit.

"I missed you, too."

"Good."

He laughs as we pull apart. "Good?"

"Yes, and I want you to miss me this week, too. A lot."

"Really? What things would you expect me to miss most?"

"Maybe how I feed you cupcakes, or how I'm always touching you, or how we love to laugh, and how sweet I am." I pull on a lock of my hair and twist in in my fingers.

"Well, I'm sure I'll miss everything about you," he says.

"That works for me," I kiss him on the cheek. "Let me know how Romeo's progress goes?" I open up the door and step out on his porch. I feel a powerful swell of sadness hit me as I head down the porch stairs.

"I will." He leans against the doorjamb, looking at me with a forlorn look in his eyes.

I'd like to think that he doesn't want me to go.

"Bye then," I say and turn.

"Bye for now, Sophia."

As I walk to my car, I can feel him watching me. Despite my melancholy, my entire being feels so much lighter. Will's attitude is more promising than I could've hoped for when I arrived.

Chapter Nineteen

I throw myself into research for my upcoming shoots at work to keep myself busy and my mind distracted. The out-of-town location shoots are always twice as tricky as we have to plan flights and hotels, transport the equipment, and learn each city's policies for permits and restrictions.

Lindsey handles these details. She asks me three different times if I have plans to see Will, and after the third negative answer, she finally stops asking.

As much as I try to get excited about the bedazzled Easter lady, my inspiration falls flat. Everything regarding holidays now is measured against Will and consequently comes up short. There's just no way a large man in an oversized furry bunny suit can compare to snow falling indoors while making love in a winter forest. I sigh and lean my chin into my hand while I remember Will's enchanted house and all the experiences I shared with him there.

In my low mood, even Paul acts nicer to me. He corners me at the coffeemaker Tuesday morning.

"Have things gotten any better with Mr. Christmas?" he asks as he stirs milk into his coffee.

"You heard he's not doing the shopping segment, right?"

"Yeah, I heard. I expected that. For what it's worth, Will's the only guy I've ever interviewed on these reality shows who I thought was cool... someone I'd actually hang out with."

"That's sweet. He *is* cool. He's one of those people I will never forget."

"Well, maybe you won't have a reason to. He's sweet on you," he says.

"At one point, maybe. But not like he was before. Not after that night."

"Still a delicate little buttercup, are we? I adore you for it, of course but men are more pragmatic, girlfriend. The next time you see him, wear something sexy, and he'll forget everything but the quickest way to get your panties off."

"You're such a romantic, Paul."

"No, I'm not. I just call 'em as I see 'em," he insists with a shrug.

That afternoon I scan the blog of our newest client, Bonnie Miller. The blog's title, *The Easter Bonnie* makes me cringe a bit. Between her Easter collection and festivities, blog, Facebook page, Pinterest and Instagram, this woman's self-promotion of her Easter obsession is staggering and reminds me how different this experience will be compared to my experience with Will. I'm on the About Me page when my phone lights up and I see it's Will calling.

"Hey, how's Romeo?" I ask, trying to tone down the excitement in my voice.

"He's good. Not a lot of energy, but he's worlds better than last week."

"Oh, I'm glad to hear that. Thanks for calling to let me know."

"Yeah, I had another reason to call. I wanted to ask you a really big favor."

"Sure. What is it?" I ask.

"I was wondering if you could babysit Romeo for a couple of hours after work tonight. I'm sorry it's such short notice."

"You mean dog sit?" I ask, laughing.

"Honestly it's like taking care of a baby," Will says, sounding sad. "I asked Jeremy, but he has plans, and you two are the people little man is most comfortable with."

"Aw, he likes me."

"He really does. Even though I took the week off work, they called earlier because they are having some big problems getting scenic finished for one of their other shows. They asked if I could be another hand tonight. And Romeo's not ready to be left alone yet."

"Of course I'll babysit. What time do you need me there?"

"Six-fifteen. You sure you don't mind? You don't have plans?" he asks, sounding relieved.

"No plans and I'm excited to see him." *And you.*

When I pull up to the house, I grab the little stuffed bunny I bought for Romeo, my purse, and takeout dinner.

"Is that a chew toy for Romeo?" Will asks with a grin after he opens the door.

"No, it's a stuffed animal," I say, smiling as I hold it up. "Isn't it cute? My dog Buster had one when I was growing up."

Will laughs. "What's he supposed to do with a stuffed animal?"

"I don't know. Whatever anyone does with a stuffed animal. Maybe he'll want to sleep with it. Buster did."

"Well, if your scent's all over it, he probably will. That was sweet of you. Thanks."

I step inside and he gives me a hug. When he releases me, I step back timidly, aware that things are still awkward between us.

"Where's Romeo?"

"The family room. He's asleep, but he'll probably wake up when he hears us talking." Will leads me down the hall and opens the door.

From the look of things, they've been living in this room. Romeo's bed and water dish are next to the couch, medicine bottles are lined up on the coffee table, and bedding is folded and piled next to the couch.

"What's that for?" I ask.

"I'm sleeping down here so I'm near him. Now that he can walk around, I'm worried he'll take on the stairs."

I squeeze his arm gently. "Such a good daddy."

Will smiles and leads me to Romeo's dog bed. I peer inside and am happy that Romeo's doing pretty good. They shaved his fur where they did the surgery, but the stitches are healing well.

"He looks better than I'd hoped," I say softly to Will.

Romeo's eyes pop open, and he stares wide-eyed. His tail starts thumping along the side of the dog bed.

"Look who's here, little man. Your very favorite girl," Will says.

I lean down and rub the top of his head. "I'm your date tonight."

"And she brought you a present!"

I hold the bunny up to Romeo, and he sniffs it but doesn't act interested.

Will takes the bunny from me and holds it to my chest. "Here, give it a hug and rub it all over your chest and neck to give it your scent."

After Paul's little speech earlier, I changed into a low-cut, fitted blouse. As Will watches me with the bunny I catch him staring at my cleavage.

When I set the bunny back in Romeo's bed, he sniffs it, then scoots over and rests his muzzle against the soft part of the bunny's midsection.

"Aw," I coo.

"That's my guy," Will says, grinning.

Will quickly explains what I need to do while he's gone. He reminds me not to share any of my dinner with Romeo and then gives me the TV remote in case we want to watch Netflix.

"He likes romance movies," Will says rolling his eyes.

"Just another reason to adore you," I say to Romeo, patting his head.

After Will leaves, Romeo eyes me intently while I eat my dinner, eventually stepping out of his dog bed and sitting at my feet. His big brown eyes are distracting.

"Daddy said no burrito, my friend."

Romeo keeps staring at me so I decide to turn on a movie. I scan through Netflix's current romance selection. "Hey, what do you say we try to find a romance with dogs in it?"

Halfway through the selection I find what I want. "Look Romeo! It's a movie called, *Must Love Dogs*! It's perfect." I click on the selection and lean back on the couch. He steps closer as if he wants to sit up here with me.

"Hold on, little guy." Mindful of his incision site I carefully lift him up to the couch. He scratches a spot on the cushion right next to me and settles in.

I stir at the sound of a door opening and closing.

"I'm home," Will calls out.

I blink. I must've fallen asleep. I'm stretched out with my legs on the ottoman next to the coffee table and Romeo on my lap. I think about sitting up, but I'm so tired I can't be bothered. My eyes fall to half-mast.

As Will steps into the room, he grins. He looks at Romeo, looks at me, then nods to his dog and shakes his head laughing. Meanwhile Romeo is wide-awake and completely enthralled with something on the television. I rub Romeo's back lovingly, and he wags his tail as Will gets closer.

"Lucky dog," Will says, smiling.

Will gently settles onto the couch next to us. "So whatcha watching, dude?" He turns to study the screen and laughs softly. A minute later the credits run, and Will leans back on the couch and studies me.

"You're home," I say with a sleepy yawn.

"Just got here. It took less time than I thought it would."

I yawn again, covering my mouth with my free hand. "Oh, that's good."

"Aww, you're tired," he says, nudging me.

"Yeah, I haven't been sleeping well at all. I'm so sorry I fell asleep, but he really seemed fine, and we got cozy together."

"He's never looked happier, and you found the perfect cheesy movie for him."

"Awesome, don't you think? There were times we were watching that I actually thought he was smiling. Crazy, right?"

Will shrugs. "He probably was."

"So, it went okay at work?"

"Yeah, it was fine. Thanks a lot for doing this. I felt so much better knowing he was with you."

A huge smile spreads across my face. "I was happy to do it."

I sit up a little taller and put my feet on the floor. Glancing down, I notice that my neckline has plunged dangerously low, and I blush as I adjust my top.

Will doesn't say anything as he scratches Romeo behind the ears. "Dude, how did you score getting to cuddle on her lap? You're one lucky little man."

I laugh. "He was just nice to me, that's all. If you're nice, I'll let you sit on my lap too."

"Yeah? I'm pretty sure I'd crush you," he says, his eyebrow arched.

"I'm willing to give it a try," I say playfully.

"I'd rather have *you* sit on my lap."

My heart thumps in my chest. "Can I?" Just the idea of being that close to him again is irresistible.

He looks unsure about it too, but he gently lifts up Romeo and settles him into his bed right next to his bunny.

He then sits back on the couch and holds his arms out, welcoming me. "Come on," he says quietly.

I get up, gently ease myself onto Will's lap and circle my arms around his neck. He takes a deep breath and sighs.

"Is this too much?"

"Too much?" he asks weakly.

"Am I too heavy for you?"

"The real question is can I handle being this close to you?" he asks himself out loud as he gazes into my eyes. "I'm not sure I can."

I lean in close, taking in every detail—his strong jaw line, his beautiful soulful eyes, and the thundering of his heart under my hand as it's pressed over his chest.

"I'm not sure I can either. I miss you so much," I whisper.

He closes his eyes shut and lets his head fall back on the sofa. "Why am I such a mess?"

"Maybe you miss me too," I say, my voice raw and vulnerable.

"Yes, I miss you. I can't stop thinking about you, Sophia." He groans, pulling me closer.

I soak in his warmth but I'm torn. I can feel how much he wants me, but he also said he's not ready. He may never be ready for me again. Am I strong enough to pull away and give him the time he needs? Can I follow through with what I should to do?

"I'm going to go. I don't want you to do anything you're not ready for."

He digs his fingers into the arm of the couch. "That may be a good idea. I'm still angry and mixed up about the shit that happened last week. I'm not blaming you, I'm just questioning some of the decisions I've made. I haven't been this angry in a long time."

"I'm sorry," I say softly, my heart aching. "Why don't I go. You're leaving tomorrow to see your friends and clear your head. Why don't we talk when you get back?"

He nods and hugs me one last time before letting me up.

We're silent as I pet Romeo good-bye and walk to the front door.

"Thanks, again, for everything," he says as he pulls the door open.

I smile. "I care about you guys. Both of you." I look down at my feet and then out the open door, unsure what it will be like the next time we are together. It occurs to me that he's calmer, and it's my chance to say the words that have been tied up inside of me since that morning at the police station.

"Will, for whatever part you hold me responsible for that night and for all the ways you may never forgive me, just know one thing and believe it's true. You're a wonderful man. Don't let who you were in the past stop you from who you are meant to be. Because even if you decide not to be with me…you, Will—the Will I fell in love with, the guy who makes magic for kids and takes interest in homeless people…that's the Will I'm going to hold in my heart the rest of my life."

He leans back, his mouth hanging open at my heartfelt plea. I can see the anguish in his eyes.

I clear my throat and hold up my hand to indicate that I'm not quite done.

"So, please be *that guy*, be *that Will*. He's amazing."

When I finish I'm not sure how to wrap things up. I twist my hands nervously.

"Okay then," I say, quickly moving away before he seems to realize I'm really leaving. By the time I get to my car, I'm swallowed up by the darkness.

As I drive off, he stands under the light in his driveway and takes several steps toward me as if he wants to run after my car. As tempted as I am to turn around and go back to him, I keep moving forward.

Chapter Twenty
True Blue Entertainment Studio

Paul stands in Lindsey's cube, wasting time and debating whether to go back to work or not.

"I've decided the Internet is the porthole to hell for anyone with an obsession." Disgusted, Lindsey closes another window on her computer.

"And you just figured this out?" Paul asks in a mock surprised voice. "We all work in reality TV, thanks to the Internet. It's six degrees of separation for anything deviant or obsessive."

"We could probably do a show where we try to figure what people are into based on their Google search history," Lindsey says.

"Yeah, it could be a game show. Instead of *What's My Line?* it could be *What's My Obsession?* as we go through their hard drives."

"They'd nail me first round." Lindsey rolls her eyes.

"Really? Do tell!" Paul says enthusiastically.

"It's too embarrassing! I'm not going to tell you."

"I know, you have a large My Little Pony collection," Paul teases.

"Yeah right. I know for a fact that you do though."

"That's old news. So what is yours then?"

Lindsey folds her arms over her chest, and shakes her head defiantly.

Ah, come on. I'll tell you my other obsession, if you tell me yours." He grins.

"We already all know your other obsession is porn. You tell us all the time."

"True, I'm too transparent. But keep in mind… it's not lowbrow shit with no production value."

"No, of course not. I'm sure the stuff you like is shot in black and white with lots of artsy set up shots." Lindsey scoffs.

"Damn straight, sister," he says with a huff.

Someone clears a throat, and Lindsey and Paul turn. Rachel leans against the wall behind them. Apparently, she's been listening to their conversation. Her arms are folded over her chest and her eyebrows are knitted together, making her look very stern.

"What?" Paul raises his arms dramatically.

"It's awe inspiring to witness the sheer depth of the people that work here," Rachel says.

"Depth? Our noble leader speaks of depth. This from the woman who buys Louis Vuitton fake handbags at one of those knockoff shops downtown," Paul says.

Rachel gives him an irritated look.

"I never said there was depth here. There's no doubt that we're swimming in the shallow end, here at the truest bluest of entertainment studios," Paul says.

"Paul!" Lindsey exclaims, surprised he's being extra feisty with his boss.

"On that happy note, Paul, why don't you join me in my office for a minute," Rachel says.

He glumly follows her to her office and closes the door.

"Yes?" he asks.

"I wanted to make sure you have everything set for the in-studio stuff next week while Sophia is in Georgia working with Luis and the team on the Easter segment."

"You're worried?" he asks.

"Well, Sophia's still hung-up on that Christmas fellow. I'm thinking if she knew what tone the show is going to have, she would choose to protect him, rather than make her job the priority."

He nods. "She's more than hung-up on him. They're doing the wild thing. I would venture to say she's in *lurve*," he says, rolling his tongue. He bats his eyelashes dramatically.

"Shit, it's worse than I thought," Rachel says, shaking her head. "Not that I can blame her. He's tempting."

"Yes, he is, although they did have a falling out over the location screw-up with the neighbors. I'm not sure he's hung-up on her anymore—that poor delicate buttercup. She was quite broken up about it."

"Well, what happened was pretty horrible. All right, that tells me my instincts are right. I want her kept as far away from postproduction as possible. I'll keep her overloaded with other stuff until the show airs."

Paul nods. "Got it. I do feel rather decadent about it, knowing him and how he will take it... not that it matters. We're too far down the road to turn around now."

"Exactly. Full steam ahead."

"If only he was wearing that reindeer T-shirt. He's just too good-looking—like an actor playing the part of a holiday nut." Paul leans closer to the screen in the postproduction bay to watch the footage again a week later.

"I was going to ask. You have to have an impressive ability to suspend your disbelief to accept that this guy is behind it all," Alex says, waving to the longer shot of the lavishly decorated living room as she edits.

"Have you gotten the footage from our studio shots with Helena? Her behavior analysis is jarring." Paul widens his eyes as he says *jarring*.

"I just got it, and yes, it is. I'm doing the same layout we do on the baby beauty pageants—shots of them doing their stuff before cutting to the analysis or contrast comments."

"Exactly."

"He's going to look really bad. Does he understand what's coming?" she asks.

"Of course not."

"I never minded doing manipulative editing to those mentally unstable pageant moms using their daughters to achieve their own unfulfilled dreams. They're asking for it. But I have to admit, I feel bad making this guy come across as an unbalanced loser. He's really a good guy."

Paul sighs. "Ah, what we must sacrifice in the noble responsibility of providing entertainment to the masses."

"You're so dramatic." Alex rolls her eyes. "Sometimes I wonder if you're the unstable one."

"Why else would I work here?"

Chapter Twenty-One
Sophia

As I get ready for Steph's birthday party, I feel a combination of a sinking fear mixed with a bubbly thrill. I'm like a girl going to my first dance. Will is going, and I wonder if he will return from his time away inspired to see me, or resolved that he's done with our relationship. I put on my cutest dress and kitten heels to sway him in case he's on the fence.

When I arrive at Steph's place, people are scattered through the house and in the backyard. Between Steph and her three roommates, there are a lot of people jammed into not a lot of space. After pouring myself a plastic cup of wine in the kitchen, I wander through the crowd until I find Lindsey and Luis, the director for the Georgia shoot.

"Hey, girl," Lindsey says as I join them in the backyard.

"Hi." I smile and turn to the director. "Hi, Luis. I'm looking forward to working with you on the shoot in Georgia."

"Likewise." He studies me as he takes a sip from his beer bottle.

"Luis was telling me about some great places we can eat at while we're in Georgia. I love soul food! Everything's fried," Lindsey adds.

I scrunch up my nose in disgust. "Everything?"

"Ah, that may have been a slight exaggeration," he admits. "Do you like to dance, Sophia? I know of a really cool place not far from the shoot. I think it was a barn, but you wouldn't believe the music. I heard the guy who DJ's is originally from New York but wanted to bring the vibe back to his home town."

"Sounds great. I *love* to dance," Lindsey says, her voice more animated that usual as she tries to turn his attention back to her.

"Me too," I add for good measure.

"Good. It sounds like we're all going to have a fun time."

I take a drink of my wine and nervously scan the crowd for the twentieth time, checking if Will's arrived yet.

"Sophia, did you hear me?" Luis says, leaning in close.

I startle and step back, not realizing he had spoken to me. *How long was I daydreaming?*

"I'm sorry, what did you say?"

"I asked if I could get you more wine? I'm getting another beer for Lindsey and me."

"Oh sure, that would be great. Thanks, Luis."

I lean against the stucco wall of the garage and try to focus on what Lindsey is saying—something about the hot new intern with all the tattoos when I suddenly feel like my heart is being tightened in a vice.

About twenty feet away, some adorable young blonde pulls Will into the backyard as he laughs in mock protest. My breath catches, trapped somewhere in my throat since I've forgotten how to breathe.

He's so perfectly handsome. I sigh heavily. *Is he already with someone else?*

It feels like someone's hit me. Judging from the way I collapse inwardly, I'm pretty sure I just got slammed in the stomach with a sledgehammer. My hand is quivering so I set my plastic cup on a patio table. I look down at my party outfit. It reminds me of the sharp contrasts of this fateful evening: how very fine I felt when I put it on earlier and how completely foolish I feel now.

The girl drags Will over to a circle of people that includes Steph. He's wearing a fitted black T-shirt that shows off his physique. I almost turn away as I remember running my hands over every inch of the bronze skin and sinewy muscle under that shirt. When my gaze drifts to his worn jeans, I realize he's wearing the pair I pushed off him in the living room the night I claimed him for my own.

He's moved on.

He's moved on.

The chant thunders in my head to the pounding rhythm of a tribal beat.

The blonde vixen, who's dressed like Liesl from *The Sound of Music* and probably dressed that way to throw competition like me off her trail, has her hand on Will's chest, the chest my hand should be on, and he laughs at something she's said.

NO! An inner scream howls in my head. I die a thousand deaths and imagine a future of saying prayers in the abbey among my sisters of the Broken Heart Order, trying to remember what life was like when I had the Internet, sexy lingerie, and Will.

I shake my head. *Dramatic much? Holy hell, woman, get a grip.* I bite on my thumbnail and take one final look at the man who now will forever personify "the one who got away" before getting the hell out of this party.

I slowly peek out from under my lashes, and blink several times when Steph points my way. Will stares at me, wide-eyed. He seems thrown by my outfit, kitten heels and all, but at least his gaze is on me and not hot Liesl Von *trap-my-man*.

He takes a step in my direction when I feel a finger trace along the skin of my arm.

"Here you go," Luis says with a smile as he hands me the glass of wine and leans against the wall next to me before passing Lindsey her beer.

"You okay, Sophia? You look like you've seen a ghost," he says.

I smile and lie. "No, I'm fine. Thanks for the wine."

"No problem."

I glance at Will. He's turned back to his group, and judging from the frown on his face, he doesn't look happy.

I manage to gulp three large sips of wine before Lindsey tries to take my cup away.

"Slow down, cowgirl. How are you going to meet a cute guy if you're all drunk and sloppy?" she asks.

"Ah, you're no fun," Luis says with a laugh.

Over the next half hour, Luis does his best to engage me in their conversation as I sullenly drink my wine. Will glances over periodically with an undefined expression on his face. I'm grateful Luis filled my glass generously. I can get a good buzz without having to peel myself off the stucco wall for a refill. But eventually Luis and Lindsey move off to talk to other people and I wave them on, insisting I've spotted someone I want to say hi to.

For a moment I try to gather the courage to go at least say hi to Will, but as I step forward a mysterious cowardly force pushes me toward the house instead. I convince myself it would probably be better to talk to him when I'm not about to have an emotional breakdown.

I wander through one of the darkened bedrooms, groping for a light switch or lamp so I can find my purse and jacket. The feeling that I'm not alone alerts me to someone's presence in the room. I spin around and gasp when I see Will leaning against the door.

"What are you looking for?" he asks in a low, studied voice.

"My stuff," I say, pushing my hair off my face.

"Stuff?" he asks, his eyes narrow with a suspicious look.

"My purse and jacket," I explain, exasperated at the complete failure of the night.

"Are you leaving?"

"Yup." I move some of the stuff around on the bed but still can't find my stuff.

"With that guy?" His voice is tight, his gaze penetrating even in the low light of the room.

I stop moving the jackets around and stand straight up, surprised.

"Guy? You mean, Luis? Hardly." I huff at the ridiculous idea.

He relaxes his arms and slips his hands into his back pockets.

"What about you and Liesl? I'm sure she's willing to climb the Alps with you."

He tilts his head to the side with a look that reminds me of Romeo, and I almost implode with how unaware he is of his off-the-chart adorableness.

"Liesl?" he asks.

"Von Trapp… the 'Sixteen Going on Seventeen' hussy that kept touching you." *And there he is with the tilted head again. If he does it once more, I'll fall to my knees.* "You know, the blonde you came to the party with."

"You thought I was trying to make *you* jealous? Steph told me you weren't at the party yet. Then when she spotted you, I was going to go right over until I saw you with a man already."

"Luis," I say remembering the frown on Will's face when he saw us.

"The name of the girl I was with is Dawn. She was Steph's sorority sister. Her car is in the shop and she lives near me, so Steph asked me to give her a ride."

"So you're not *with her*?" I swallow and try my best not come off like a whack job.

"No. Actually, I was hoping I was *with you*."

"Yeah?" I ask, hope firing up with a roar.

"Yes. I was just waiting for my moment." He slowly walks toward me.

"You were?" I feel weak as he steps up close. "Oh God. I almost lost it out there." I gesture toward the backyard. "I was having crazy, insane thoughts because I thought I'd lost you already. I can't bear the idea of it."

"You don't have to." He gazes at my lips like he's planning an epic kiss.

"So you don't want the pretty, bright-eyed Austrian that wears dresses made of curtains."

His eyes are bright as he shakes his head. "You crazy girl. I spent my time away getting my head straight and planning how to get things back on track with us. Can't you see I'm still crazy about you?"

"Thank goodness!" I grab his shoulders and propel myself into our embrace.

He groans, half pleasure, half pain, and tightens his arms around me. The kiss and ones that follow are so intensely passionate that I forget where we are.

"Sorry, sorry, we just need to get our jackets," a high voice behind us says.

Embarrassed, we break apart and wait as the girl grabs two jackets and hands one to a guy before turning to leave.

"Get a room!" The guy teases as they laugh and rush into the hallway.

Will insists I leave my car and ride with him. Besides the fact that I've had too much to drink, he explains that the idea of being separated again, even for the fifteen-minute drive, is unbearable.

The entire drive to his house I'm touching him and he moans with appreciation. I run my hand up his arm and over his shoulder as he silently maneuvers the truck through the near deserted streets. A few moments later, I move my hand down his chest, to his thighs and, finally, between his legs. With his free hand he reaches over, slowly working his fingers up my thigh, but when he swerves the truck, he gasps and peels my hand off his erection.

"Close call," he says under his heavy breath, his eyes wide. I'm not sure I've ever seen him so pent up. It's no secret I feel the same.

The fourth time my hand recklessly wanders, I grip him so firmly he gasps even louder. He swerves again but this time over to the side of the road and stops.

What's with me tonight? I'm a wild woman.

He watches my hand moving slowly over him and then takes in the hungry expression on my face as I lick my lips and lean into him.

"Oh, baby," he says, moaning. "I'm going to have to make you sit on your hands or we'll never get home. I'm three strokes away from taking you right here."

I peer out the window nervously then back at him. "I could be game." My desire outweighs my logic.

He peels my hand off him again, and curls it up in his hand. He looks at me as if I'm the only thing he's ever wanted.

"We haven't been naked together since the night of the fire. I want to make love to you in my bed tonight, not in my truck. Do you have any idea how much I thought about making love to you since I've been gone."

"No," I whisper, suddenly feeling like the most desirable woman on Earth. *Who needs push up bras and strappy high heels to feel sexy when this man does it all with a single look?*

I scoot to the far end of the seat, and gaze out the window with a grin. "I'll be good, I promise. At least until we get to your place."

"We'll be home in five," he says, and I wonder if he says it more for him than me. He clears his throat, adjusts himself, and hits the gas.

Once we're home, he stops to quickly check on Romeo. After that, everything's a blur until we're both naked and stretched across his sheets. Our need for each other is acutely visceral, we can't stop touching and stroking each other while we kiss and kiss and kiss. We roll over and under each other from one end of the bed to the other in a sensual dance.

There are so many things I want to say, but I show him instead by arching under his touch and calling out his name as if he's answered all the questions in my heart. With my crazy comments at the party, he can

tell that I thought I'd lost him. It seems to make him even more determined to show me what I am to him.

"I've always wanted you to be mine," he says in a low voice as he
spreads my legs open wide.

I nod, biting my lip, my whole body humming in anticipation.

When he finally takes me, his passion consumes me, making it feel
like we'll fall through the sheets to the center of the Earth. He thrusts
into me slowly, watching me with laser focus as he cradles my face in
his hands. My climax splits me open, spilling my joy all around us as he
gathers up all he can.

Afterward we lie in each other's arms, stunned.

"I've never…" I can't find the words.

"My neither." He runs his hand through my hair and presses soft
kisses across my forehead.

I sigh with a smile, content.

"Stay with me," he says softly. I'm hoping he means not just tonight
but all the days that follow this one.

"I'd like that." I cup his chin and gaze intently into his eyes. "There's
something I need to ask you."

"Okay." He turns so he's completely facing me.

It's good but still I'm worried. "I hope it doesn't freak you out."

"Maybe you should just tell me."

"Oh God," I say nervously.

"Why don't I go first? There's something I want to tell you," he says.

"Go ahead."

"I had a lot of time to think about everything while I was in Solano
Beach. I thought about how I was still letting my past drag me down,
and how I would feel if you weren't in my life. It made me realize how
much you mean to me."

"And?" I ask, hopeful.

He kisses me gently and then looks into my eyes. "I didn't think it was
possible, but I'm even more in love with you."

I smile, a thousand-watt grin. "You are? Really? After everything…
are you sure?"

"Yeah, I'm sure. I was assuming you could tell a few minutes ago,
when…"

"I was hoping," I say with a sweet smile, my intense gaze softening. "I know I'm far from perfect."

He presses his fingers over my lips. "Shh," he says. "I think you're perfect for me. So, what were you going to ask me?"

"It doesn't matter now," I say, grinning.

"Really? Why's that?"

"Let's just say I was going to ask if this was more than sex for you? I wanted to know if I could still be your girl. But now it's resolved."

"Indeed it is."

I push him onto his back, crawl on top of him, and raise my arms to the ceiling.

"This ought to be good," he says, grinning.

"I love you... so much!" I exclaim.

He laughs and pulls me down into his arms before kissing me.

"Glad we got that settled."

"All this good stuff and I have to leave Monday for my shoot. And I'll be gone for weeks." I lament our upcoming separation with a pout.

He looks up at me with depth in his eyes as he slowly traces circles on my back. "I'll wait for you."

Chapter Twenty-Two

So far, Georgia ends up being a better trip than I feared, and it probably would be great fun if Will were with me. Our hotel is on the edge of Atlanta, so there's lots to do. Of course with our shoot schedule, even if we have the time, we're usually too tired at night after our long work days.

Bonnie the Easter lady couldn't be more welcoming and excited about the show, which is a sharp contrast to Will. Frankly it's a relief because I don't have it in me to convince another unwilling subject.

Despite all the amazing food, I can barely eat since I'm in that love state with a silver umbrella floating above me and making everything sparkle. Every hour a Will thought slips into my mind. What would Will think of Bonnie's Easter Bunny collection? Is Will taking Romeo for a walk right now? Is Will naked in the shower soaping up his sexy body? Those steamier thoughts make my pulse race and my cheeks flush, which leads to Luis asking me if I'm all right.

"I'm great," I answer every time with a huge grin.

I even buy a snow globe to give Will from a shop next to our hotel. The intricately sculpted memento has a winter theme with a couple that resembles Will and me kissing while the snowflakes fall around us.

"Will," I say into the phone with a long, sad sigh.

"What baby? What's wrong?" he asks.

"They've just extended our trip."

He groans. "How much longer will you be gone?" he asks with a tight voice.

"You're mad," I say with regret.

"Yeah, I'm mad and I'm disappointed, but not at you. I know this isn't your fault."

"Believe me, I'm disappointed too."

"So what in the hell is so important that you have to stay?"

"Shooting an Easter segment in November wasn't a great idea. We're supposed to be shooting an elaborate egg hunt reenactment, and it hasn't stopped raining for a week. I was so excited when last night's forecast predicted four days of sunny weather starting tomorrow, but then I got the call."

"Who called you?"

"Rachel. Among other things, they've found a guy about an hour from here who thinks he's a leprechaun. His entire house is Saint Patrick's Day themed… green for days. Can you imagine?"

"Is everyone on this series a complete kook besides me?" he asks warily.

"It's looking that way," I admit. "It's starting to have the disturbing edge of that documentary, *Grey Gardens*."

"So how is that going to make me look?" he asks, reiterating what I've been worrying about. "It reminds me of that saying about being judged by the company you keep."

"I think it's going to make you look even more cool and amazing than you already are," I say, worried that I sound completely full of shit.

"Sophia? Be straight with me," he says with a low voice.

"I don't disagree, Will, that every reality show has nuts on it, but there are sane people too. That's what keeps it interesting, you never know what you're going to get."

"At least it will all be over soon. My show's airing in a few weeks."

"True. I can't wait until your fan mail starts pouring in."

"I'm sure I'm being paranoid, and no one I care about will watch it, or if they do, not even make it past the first commercial."

"Right!" I say, stifling the thought that he totally discounted what I do for a living.

"I mean who has time to watch that kind of crap anyway?"

I grit my teeth before commenting, "You mean the crap that my career is based on?"

"Oh, don't take it that way. You know what I mean, baby." He backpedals.

"Not exactly. You want to explain it to me?"

"What is the value in reality TV anyway? I thought everyone considers it garbage."

"The value?" I say, trying to manage my temper. "What about other popular programming? What's the value of watching grown men in stretchy pants throw a ball, try to land on top of each other, and then slap each other's asses?"

"Are you really going to compare the value of our nation's favorite pastime with reality TV?" he asks, his voice edged with mock horror.

"Football is so stupid." I'm riled up.

"Stupid?" he asks in a dramatic voice as if he can't believe I said it.

"Do we have a bad connection? Yes, I said football is stupid. Idiotic, really. I mean what's the point?"

"Right, right football, a strategic game of elite athletes competing, thus allowing men to vent all their pent-up testosterone is of equal value to a human leprechaun in his very own shamrock fantasy land."

"Well I think so. You know what it is, Will?"

"No, but I'm pretty sure you're going to tell me," he says sarcastically.

"Entertainment. Escapism… a way for people to forget about their problems for a while and focus on someone else's problem."

"So that makes me a problem?" Will asks.

"Why are you being like this?" I ask, exasperated.

"It's what you just said… someone else's problem!"

"Mr. Literal strikes again. Can you lighten up just a bit? What the hell?" I want to growl.

"I'll lighten up as soon as you stop saying stupid things about football."

There's a long silent pause. I try to calm down and not throw the phone across the room.

"Stupid?" I say calmly. "You just called my comment stupid, which in my mind is equivalent to calling me stupid. So, on that happy note, I'm going to say good night. I get enough abuse from my job to have to get it from you. When you are ready to apologize for the insults, give me a call."

I shut off my phone and toss it on the armchair before falling back onto my hotel bed in frustration.

What was that? I flip through the television channels trying to stay distracted. We've never had this type of stupid argument before.

About an hour later my phone rings, and I feel a wave of relief.

"Hello?" I answer, sounding very timid.

"I'm sorry, Sophia," he says before taking a big breath. "I'm sorry I was a bad boyfriend and said that your work is garbage. I didn't mean it. I think I was just mad you weren't coming home, so I took it out on the easiest target."

I sigh. "Oh, Will. I think that's why I got so snippy. I'm sorry too. I know you don't mess with a man's football. I'm just missing you so much."

"You are?" he asks.

"Desperately. I can't stop thinking about you, night and day. It's making me crazy," I say, sounding breathy.

"Me too. I'm off my game at work and the house has never felt emptier."

Listening to his voice makes me feel desperate for him. I stretch out on my bed and run my hand through my hair. "I love you so much. I'm just aching for you."

Something in my words and desperate tone must spark something in him because his voice changes from sad to a tone of sexy intrigue. "It sounds like you need me. Like you wish I was there."

"God, do I. You have no idea." I squeeze my thighs together, getting excited about where this call might go.

"What would you do with me if I were there?"

I imagine him leaning back on the couch and stretching his legs out in front of him. I pause and then sigh.

"Well, I'd give you a kiss you'd never forget. Then I'd slowly take your clothes off." I picture my hands on him and it makes my skin feel hot.

"All of my clothes?" he says, sounding eager.

"I'd do it slowly, kissing and touching you everywhere, until you were completely naked." I remember the time I was on my knees, pleasuring him.

"I'd like that," he says with a moan.

"Have I ever told you how much I love your body? You have such an incredibly hot body."

"I'm glad you think so," he says with his sexy voice. "Just hearing you say that turns me on, baby. You have such a hot body too. My jeans are getting tight just picturing you on my bed."

"You're turning me on too… so much." I slide my fingers between my legs.

"So after I'm naked, what would you do then? I'm unzipping my fly, baby, so keep talking."

I lean back, feeling his fire burn over me. "I'd put you on my bed, and do everything you desire."

"Would you straddle me, Sophia? I want to watch you make love to me." He sounds so turned on, worked up in the best way.

"You sexy man. I like it when you watch me. I can almost feel your strong hands on my hips pulling me down over you." I say, my breath speeding up.

"Do you know what you do to me? I'm stroking myself, love, picturing your beautiful body as you move over me and it's making me crazy." His voice is heavy with want.

"Are you *really* hard?" I ask with a groan.

"So hard for you. I wish you could see how hard. I wish you could wrap your hand around me and feel for yourself."

"Oh God," I gasp.

"Touch yourself."

"I already am."

He gasps, sending an excited thrill straight to my core.

"I'm picturing you spread out on my bed. Are you wet for me?"

"Do men like football?" I tease in my sexiest voice.

"I like you much more than football."

"That's the hottest thing you've ever said to me, handsome." I'm baffled why it turns me on even more. My fingers move faster as my legs fall farther apart. I swear I can hear him stroking himself between his ragged breaths.

"Sophia," he says with desperate edge to his voice. "The instant replay, I'm on top of you, inside of you so deep, kissing your breasts… you feel so damn good…" He groans.

"Harder, Will," I beg.

"As hard as you want, baby," he says forcefully.

My gasping breath picks up until I'm panting.

"Come on, love," he whispers, letting out a long groan as he lets go. I remember how he looks with his eyes shut tight, the most raw pleasure coursing through him.

I can almost feel him inside me when I cry out then moan with my release.

"Did you?" he asks with a hopeful voice.

I fight to catch my breath, barely able to hold onto the phone. "Touchdown," I say with a satisfied sigh.

Chapter Twenty-Three

The next week passes agonizingly slowly, and I keep hoping some kind of miracle happens and I'll be home for Thanksgiving. I tell Will that I'm tempted to get on a plane just to see him, even if just for one night, but with my shooting schedule, it's impossible.

Every night when we talk, I realize I'm sounding more and more forlorn. The work's really getting to me. I'm trying to put on a brave face, but I'm very unhappy with these segments. They're becoming more and more cartoonish. Part of me wishes I'd stayed with the cooking shows.

That afternoon we break early on the leprechaun shoot and I head back to my hotel to regroup and check my messages. I'm alarmed when I notice that Will has called my phone repeatedly. *Naturally* he would need to speak to me on a day I'm shooting in the boonies where there's no signal.

I access my voice-mail messages and listen to Will's voice. He sounds angry. *What's happened?* I take a deep breath and listen.

> *Sophia you need to call me as soon as you get this message. I just saw the ad for my show and I'm ready to kill someone. It has a photoshopped picture of me wearing the idiotic shirt that says "Mr. Christmas." Did I mention there are reindeer antlers on my head? I look like a complete moron!*
>
> *I don't know how to stop this, but you have to do something. They've turned me into a fucking clown. People are already putting copies of this shit around work. Do you understand? This will ruin me!*

I'm heading home now to figure out what to do. I'm wait-
ing to hear from you… Call me NOW!

Reindeer antlers? Mr. Christmas T-shirt? *What the hell?* I break into a cold sweat and grip my phone while my mind races. *Who I should call first?* I look at my phone again and see a long list of calls from Will. Do I dare to listen? I look back at his first call. It was made over two hours ago. My stomach sinks. If he was this mad two hours ago, what's he like now?

He's texted me too so I read that next. There's an image of the print-out of the ad. It's hard to read with all the wrinkles in the paper, but I can make out enough of it, and I'm horrified. He's attached an ominous message—*Explain this.*

I curl over as if I've been punched. Something about seeing the picture makes it even more agonizing than hearing about it.

What's going on? Is there any way to fix it?

Chapter Twenty-Four
At the True Blue Entertainment Studio

"Paul, you've got to take this call," the receptionist says.

"Why? Who is it?" he asks warily.

"That Christmas guy you guys shot a while back. He's pissed off and demanding to talk to you."

"Why me? I don't want to talk to him."

"He wanted management but Rachel isn't around. He's pretty worked up and keeps calling. Can you please, please just talk to him?"

"Oh, hell… All right, put him through."

Paul lets the phone ring five times before he picks it up. "Yeah?"

"Hey, Paul. It's Will."

There's a long silent pause.

"…from the Christmas special shoot."

"Yeah, sure." Paul rolls his eyes. "What can I do for you, Will? You know Sophia's on location. I can get you her number."

"Oh, I have her number, but unfortunately, I haven't been able to reach her today."

"Well, you know how crazy shoots can get, I'm sure she'll call you back later."

"Right, right. So I saw an interesting ad this morning, Paul."

There's a shorter pause.

Paul clears his throat. "Oh really. What was it?"

"It was me, dressed up like a Christmas clown."

"Really? Imagine that." Paul smiles wryly.

"So enough with playing nice, Are you going to tell me what the fuck is going on?"

"Not much to say, Will. You know how those advertising people get. I wouldn't worry about it if I were you."

"Right, public humiliation has always been high on my list of what I hoped to achieve in my life." Will's words are thick with sarcasm.

"I see you've lost your sense of humor. Oh, wait a minute… I don't remember you ever having one."

There's another long pause filled with tension.

"I certainly don't have a sense of humor right now. I want to see the tape for the show," Will says in a low voice.

"Of the show? Sorry buddy, that's not going to happen." Paul shakes his head at the audacity of Will's demand.

Will decides to up the ante to try to scare Paul into submission. "Paul, did you hear about what I did to that guy that set my yard on fire and hurt my dog?"

Paul coughs but doesn't respond.

"I have a temper, Paul, and I'm really, really unhappy right now. If I were you, I'd show me the tape."

"Are you threatening me? That's not a good idea. Do you really want to spend the holidays in prison? I'm sure they would put you with a very friendly cellmate who would appreciate your good looks."

"Show me the fucking tape," he says with a tight voice.

"There's this thing. It's called an agreement, which is essentially a contract, that you signed authorizing us to pretty much do whatever we fucking want with you and your footage," Paul says calmly with just enough sarcasm to boil Will's blood.

"So as you can see, big boy, it's not my problem if you didn't read the contract. It won't do you any good to beat the crap out of me."

"But it would make me feel better," Will says with a sneer.

"And I may even enjoy it, but that's a whole other story."

"So you don't know where Sophia is and why she's not answering her phone?" Will asks, fed up with Paul's games.

"Wasn't she doing that leprechaun today? Well, not *doing* him, but you know what I mean. Yeah, why don't you harass her instead of me? She actually likes you and might be more fun to threaten."

"I'd never threaten a woman."

"Well then why are you threatening me? I'm gay so that's considered bad form as well in most civilized circles."

"Who said I was civilized?"

"Touché! Well, this has been grand… a lot of fun, Will, but I have work to do. Why don't you lighten up and embrace the experience. Any publicity is better than no publicity, and surely you don't do your house up with all the crap unless you really crave the attention deep down."

"You don't know anything about me, Paul."

"Good, and let's keep it that way."

Chapter Twenty-Five
Sophia

I look down at my phone again and know that even though I don't have answers, I can't keep Will waiting another minute, wondering why I haven't responded. I'm wound tight like a coil about to spring; every part of my body tenses as I call him.

"Damn it, Sophia!" Will yells as soon as he picks up. "I was starting to wonder if you were ever going to call me back."

"I'm sorry! This crazy-ass leprechaun lives in a dead zone. I had no cell reception or Internet all day. I just got your messages."

"*Really,* how fucking convenient," he says, his tone dripping with angry sarcasm.

"What are you talking about? I'm stunned, I feel sick, and I don't know what to say."

"Well, you better think of something. This shit's going to ruin me."

"I swear, I didn't know anything about it." My response only pisses him off further.

"Aren't you the goddamned producer? What's wrong with you? You should know all about it!"

"Please don't yell at me. I feel bad enough. When they booked me for these other shoots, I talked to everyone in postproduction and told them what I expected. I have no idea what happened," I say.

"What you *expected? What you expected?*" he yells.

"I confirmed several times during the shoot that this was going to be an upbeat and positive portrayal. Please, let me make some calls and find out what happened. Maybe it's just the ad that's misleading."

"I highly doubt that. You make your calls and demand that they fix it."

"Okay, I'll do it now. Are you going to be available when I call back?"

"What do you think? I can barely function I'm so pissed off. I've been watching the phone all day, and I'll continue glaring at it after we hang up."

"I'm so sorry," I say with a sad sigh.

There's a long angry silence. "You promised me."

"Will...," I say softly.

"You promised."

Fueled by Will's rage, I pace the floor of my hotel room until my defeat turns to fury. I beat the hell out of the pillow on my bed and sit down to refocus on making calls.

When I get Rachel on the phone and tell her about Will's call, it's as if I don't know who I'm talking to. She's short-tempered and impatient with me as if she can't believe I'm questioning her. It doesn't bother her in the slightest that I knew nothing about what happened.

Of course, it doesn't, I think. *She must be behind it.*

"Why are you worried about this? You need to focus on your current project, not what's already finished," Rachel snaps.

"I'm worried because the ad that came out today makes the show look like a parody on people who love the holidays. That isn't the show I am producing, and that isn't what I promised these people."

"And therein lies the issue. Why do you think we finished that episode without you? It sounds like you care more about keeping him happy than doing what's best for the production. You got *way* too interested in Mr. Christmas, didn't you?"

"Yes, we're friends, but I fail to see what that has to do with this matter."

"It has everything to do with it. We decided to change our point of view somewhat after viewing the footage. Part of that decision was what we got on camera. The other part was the kind of clients we'd secured for future episodes."

"You did change direction and didn't tell me!"

"We did, and it's not the first time or the last we'll do it. Our top priority is always to make the most compelling show we can. This is entertainment television, not educational dreck. Did you forget that?"

"No, of course not," I say.

"And furthermore, from what I hear from the team, you are a lot more than *friends* with Mr. Christmas."

Thanks team, for throwing me under the bus, I think as I silently steam.

"You know that according to your contract, that's a no-no. And now you can see why," Rachel adds.

"So are you going to fire me?"

"Don't be dramatic. I'm just making a point."

I think about it for a moment. "How would you prove the nature of our relationship anyway—put a camera on us and turn it into an exploitive reality show?"

"Check yourself, girl. I thought you liked your job." Rachel warns me, and I know I'm close to stepping over the line.

"I thought so too," I say glumly.

"Well, I'm sure you like your pay and *having* a job. So get your head on straight and take care of business."

I want to scream at Rachel, but I fight to keep my cool or I won't have a chance in hell to fix this. I try a different tactic.

"Rachel, we're just going to screw Will and make him a laughing stock? He's such a good guy. Can't we be better than that? I'm begging you to help me fix this wrong before it ruins him."

"Sorry, no can do. He may be mad now, but he'll get over it. If he's really into you, both of you will laugh about it one day."

I seriously doubt that, I think silently. It's hard to laugh with someone when they've shut you out of their life.

I end the call and I hang my head while tears fill my eyes. Even if Rachel agreed with me, there would be no way to fix the show at this late date. Not only does the possibility of losing Will make me heart sick, but the harsh reality of the lack of ethics in my line of work is glaring in my mind like a neon sign.

When I went to film school, I had the most noble of intentions to make documentaries and right the wrongs of the world. I think back on my conversation with Will about documentaries and my path. He was right all along about reality TV. Instead of making a positive difference,

I'm doing work that creates problems, rather than solving them. The resulting gloom makes me feel lower than pond scum.

I'm moments away from crawling under a rock when I have a wave of inspiration. *What if they just cancel the show completely?* As much as I know that would never happen, I'm desperate enough to try. I pick up my phone and call George, the big boss.

"George Starrett's office," his assistant Janice answers.

"Hi Janice, it's Sophia, one of the producers on Rachel's team. I was hoping I could speak with George."

"Oh, hi hon. You're part of the team doing the new holiday show, right?" says Janice, her voice softening.

"Yes, that's actually what I wanted to talk to George about."

"Let me tell you. I saw the ad for the show a few days ago when it came in for approvals. It looks like a riot! Congratulations! I'm hearing great stuff about it."

"Uh, thanks. So, is George available?" I ask hesitantly.

"He's on his way to New York for a big meeting with our sponsors. I doubt he'll be back in the office before Thanksgiving. Can I leave him a message?"

"No, that will be too late," I say, feeling ill. "Does he read e-mails?"

"I read them and only forward what's important. Is something wrong, dear?"

"Well, I have a serious concern about the Christmas show I was hoping to discuss with him."

"That's really something you should work out with Rachel," she says in a maternal tone.

Why is it executive assistants sometimes think they're running the company?

I scrunch up my face and grip the phone harder. "I didn't really get anywhere with Rachel."

"I see… And you hope you might with George."

"Yes," I say, breathing a sigh of relief.

"George will most likely defer to Rachel. He has a lot of respect for her. I'll let him know you want to talk to him, but you should be prepared that it may be futile. He doesn't like to get involved with these types of issues."

My heart sinks. "Yes, I understand… I just hope he gives me a chance to make my case. It's really important to me and, I believe, to the company."

"Okay, I'll tell him. Is this the number he should reach you at?"

"Yes, thank you so much, Janice."

As I set my phone down, the truth hits me hard; I can't change anything. I bend over and the tears fall fast. I know I'm going to lose Will over this. How could I have been so cavalier about the studio's intentions? I acted like a novice, never taking control of the show like an experienced producer should have. Will gave me his trust and I've destroyed it.

I curl into a tight ball on my hotel bed and let the tears fall until I feel raw all over. I cry as I remember what we were, and torture myself imagining what we could've been. My extreme self-flagellation provides a proper beginning to what I imagine to be the season of darkness looming ahead of me.

Just the idea of spending Thanksgiving in some anonymous Massachusetts hotel room while Will is at home tossing his memories of me into a roaring bonfire is enough to make me crack like an abandoned Easter egg.

When Will answers his phone, he sounds angry and any courage I had mustered up before the call, disappears.

"Sophia?" he asks when I don't say anything.

"We're over, aren't we?" I ask, surprising even myself that I went there. This time he's silent for the longest moment of my life.

"You can't fix it, can you," he says, his tone starting to ice over.

"I don't think I can," I say softly.

"Wow. There you go. You're easy on the promises and short on the fixing."

"I tried, Will."

"Evidently not hard enough."

"I don't blame you for hating me. I'd probably hate me too if I were in your shoes," I say, defeated.

"I would've never given you the chance to."

"Noted," I say right before a sob escapes, and I can't hold back the tears.

"Look, I've got to go. I can't talk to you right now. I've got to figure out what I'm going to do."

I almost don't recognize his voice. It sounds empty, as if he's talking to a stranger.

"All right. I'm so sorry, Will. You have no idea how sorry I am."

"I'm sorry too... about a lot."

"I hope one day you can find it in your heart to forgive me."

"Me too," he says before hanging up.

I don't get a call from George, and I stumble through the next few days in a thick haze. I feel like Jane Eyre on the English moor after leaving Rochester. At least Jane Eyre didn't screw Rochester the way I've screwed Will. I flail along internally from sunup to sundown, finally passing out at night, half delirious when exhaustion finally takes me. I almost miss my flight to Boston I'm in such a fog of depression.

Luckily the huge Thanksgiving reenactment shoot is a complete nightmare. Everything goes wrong from the weather to a good chunk of the group coming down with stomach flu. The resulting complications create a powerful distraction from my pain. I work myself hard until I fall asleep late each night while going over notes on my laptop in my room.

Every time I think of Will, my heart shatters again, so I do my best to push him out of my mind. The moments when I slip, like when I see them setting up the Christmas tree in the lobby of my hotel, take my breath away. I even mourn the loss of Romeo, crying when someone walks past me with a dog that looks like him.

I count the hours to when I can leave the hell of this shoot and get home to the hell of my very empty apartment.

As each hour passes during the shoot on Thanksgiving day, my urge to call Will gets stronger and stronger until I finally pick up my phone during a break. When the call goes to voice mail, I end the call without leaving a message.

I kick myself for even trying because now I feel even worse than before, and I didn't think that was possible. I head back to the set.

"You okay?" Aaron asks after he sets up his camera for the next shot.

I shake my head. "Not really."

"It's Will and the show, isn't it?"

I nod, not hiding my disappointment.

"He'll come around. Guys are bull-headed, but once we cool off we realize the truth and come around," Aaron says.

"Yeah, and what's the truth?"

"That we can't stand to live without the girl we love." Aaron nods. He looks like he's lived through the war zone of love.

"Not to be rude, Aaron, but you're divorced. Should you really be giving me advice on relationships and how the guy will come around?"

"I'm exactly the right person, because I know what it's like to have the right woman and then lose her."

"I'm sorry. I didn't mean to sound bitchy with my comment."

He shrugs. "It's okay. It is what it is. Live and learn."

"So I shouldn't give up yet?" I ask hopeful, despite my doubt.

"Just give him some time. Maybe he'll come around and maybe he won't, but isn't it worth waiting some to see?"

I close my eyes and nod. "It *is* worth it."

Chapter Twenty-Six

The next morning I wake up with a sick stomach, knowing today is the day of the show. I try to imagine Will watching it, and I only feel worse.

Miraculously, the copy of the show I requested never arrives. I roll my eyes after hanging up with the hotel's front desk manager. Thanks to my sarcastic and angry state, I'm sure this isn't a technical or delivery issue. The studio is making sure that I have to see it in real time with the rest of our viewers.

Just after lunch another wave of anxiety hits, and it gives me an idea. An old friend of mine, Erika, lives in Baltimore with her husband. We've remained friends and touch base once in a while. She and her husband always have the day after Thanksgiving off, and there are two broadcasts of the show today, one earlier while I'm still at work. Maybe she can watch the early broadcast and let me know if it's better than I fear, or if it really sucks. Luckily she picks up the phone on the second ring.

She gets a kick hearing that I've switched from cooking shows, and she's delighted that I worked on a Christmas show since she knows how much I love that holiday.

Unfortunately I have to share that the situation isn't as rosy as I'd hoped. I explain that I'm worried the studio took over the project and made the subject look like a fool, that we've become close and I'm worried what this will do to him.

She promises that she and her husband, Liam, will call with an honest assessment after they watch the show.

At five-twenty my phone rings.

"Hey, Erika," I say nervously.

"Hi, Sophia." I can't tell what to make of her tone.

There's a long pause.

"Well, we saw the show."

I hear laughter in the background and then a muffled "Stop it!" through the phone.

"So how was it?" I ask, trying to sound casual.

"Well, it was very clever, and I must say I was amazed to see it all. That guy, Will is it? His house is stunning—so creative. It's over the top. It's really... just wow! I can't imagine how much time it takes to set up."

"Yeah, it's a lot, I know, but he likes doing it." I feel strange, as if I'm justifying what Will does.

"He must."

"So?"

"Well... I'm not going to lie. It's really unflattering to your friend. He comes off as a bit unstable," she says.

"Like a lunatic!" Liam yells in the background.

My stomach plummets. "That bad?"

"If I were this guy, I'd be furious. You're going to hate it. If I were you, I'd discourage him from watching it. It will just enrage him and he can't do anything about it. It'll just be a bad memory in a few weeks."

"Until they run it over and over in reruns," her husband adds with a snicker.

"Would you shut up!" she yells back. "I'm sorry about him, Sophia. He's kind of punchy tonight."

I grit my teeth. Erika's expressive husband is the last of my worries.

"Hey, thanks for letting me know. I'm grateful to be forewarned from a friend rather than watching it cold."

"No problem. I just wish I had better news."

"I do too, Erika. Believe me, I do too."

After the shoot, a group of us stop for burgers and beer before heading back to the hotel. I'm not driving so I cut loose a bit with the booze in an attempt to numb my mind.

Later in my room I intend to just crash early, but the television calls to me in the most taunting way. I check my watch repeatedly as I flip through the channels, knowing that Will's show will be on again in a matter of minutes.

No way, I say to myself, trying to shake off the masochistic impulse.

Do it! my internal crazy woman screams.

I get under the covers and pull the blanket up under my chin, my eyes wide as I wait for the torture to begin.

Once the show starts my feeling of dread grows as each moment passes. I imagine that despite the time difference, Will would've watched the early broadcast and experienced the horror already.

In my tipsy state, the whole thing seems like a fuzzy, ridiculously bad dream—more like a nightmare. It's almost clever how just about everything Will says is followed by footage that makes him look like a bozo. Either Helene the so-called writer, who is now identified as a prominent psychologist, explains whatever affliction Will has makes him do such obsessive things, or there's a contrast shot that dispels the logic of whatever Will's just explained. If I wasn't so horrified about my involvement in this and what it will do to Will, I'd be impressed with the crafty editing.

My mouth gapes open after the front yard interview where Will proudly presents the different outdoor displays and talks about the people that come from near and far to see the house. The upbeat shots then cut to interviews with angry neighbors that I wasn't even aware had issues. They go on and on about what a nightmare Will's house has created for the neighborhood. I'm acutely reminded as I watch how during my first conversation with Will I assured him the show would help his cause getting neighborhood support. Instead it's blown it to hell and back.

The worst moment in the episode is where Will talks about the kids visiting the house and how much it means to them. The scene cuts to some snotty nose boy saying that he went to the house last year and the owner was a big show off and not even nice to them—that he was always telling everyone what to do. He insists that he didn't get his gift ornament when the house visit was over.

"My Dad said he's just a big goofy jerk that needs attention and should grow up."

Dr. Helene follows the expressive brat with comments that paint Will as an unfulfilled egomaniac. I want to reach through the television and punch her in the face.

I'm stunned and can only imagine how devastated Will was to see this. He must have been heartbroken to be trashed by one of the kids he thought he was helping.

When it's finished, I play the entire episode again in my head. My brain rewinds certain scenes over until I'm almost reciting the dialogue by heart. When I finally pass out, the moonlight is creeping in the window, casting silver shadows across the dark room. In the quiet darkness I face the fact that Will didn't call after the show aired, and I doubt he'll ever call again.

I wake only a few hours later, and despite the hangover and horrible sleep I feel as lucid as I ever have. I've made a decision. Now I just have to figure out the quickest, most efficient way to follow it through.

Chapter Twenty-Seven

I'm still making plans as I pack for my flight home. Positively flattened by my emotional and physical exhaustion, all I want is a world where non-bedazzled Easter eggs are sloppily dyed by little kids, a place where leprechauns don't leer at your breasts just because they're at eye level, and where Will is still in love with me.

On the plane ride, I stare out the window, trying to imagine my future. How will I feel about my career now? How will True Blue feel about me? I put all of my talent and effort into my work, and I feel completely duped by it. How will I drum up the same kind of motivation I'll need for future projects? Everything feels tainted, ruined like a special party dress with something unspeakable splashed across the front—an ugly stain that will linger even after the dress is cleaned.

When the plane lands at LAX, I send Rachel an e-mail asking for a meeting with her on Monday morning. In the terminal, I connect with the ride the studio arranged. While they collect my luggage, a sore throat hits me like a freight train. By the time the driver gets me home, my nose is running and my head's throbbing.

Awesome. On top of everything, now I'm sick.

Leaving my suitcase unopened in my living room, I pump myself full of Airborne and zinc lozenges, a bottle of water, and hot tea. With the tissue box on my bedside table, I put on my most comfortable jammies and get into bed. I don't get out of it again for anything but the most basic necessities until Sunday night.

On Monday my cold is under control enough for me to take care of what I need to at work. I'm not on the steadiest ground, but by the time I head into Rachel's office, I've played out the conversation I want to have in my mind so much I feel like an actress in a play, reciting her lines.

When I'm done presenting my resignation Rachel looks at me, dumbstruck. "You're seriously quitting your job over a Christmas special? Do you know how many people would kill for your position? Are you really going to throw it all away?"

"I know it seems crazy, but this whole experience has made me take a hard look at my career path and how far I've veered from my original plans."

Rachel looks at me skeptically. "You're a producer. Don't you realize how hard won that job is?"

"I do, but at what price, Rachel? This type of work is never what I had intended to do. I went to film school wanting to produce documentaries. I wanted to show people a side of the world, or other cultures, or even themselves that they may not have seen otherwise. I had big dreams."

"Didn't we all." Rachel arches her brow.

"Once out of school I got scared about paying the bills and not being able to get a job."

"Which is no small issue." Rachel points out.

"True. So I compromised in a small way on the first opportunity that came along. Then with each new opportunity I compromised a bit more and more. Somewhere along the line I convinced myself this genre of TV was sort of like documentaries and maybe, in the beginning, a few of them were."

I can tell from Rachel's expression that she's scanning her brain, trying to think of examples, but she remains silent.

"Then over time, the shows became more and more entertaining and began to manipulate the concepts and the subjects for the biggest shock value or sensationalism."

"So," Rachel says.

"So, now there's nothing real about them anymore," I say.

"Who cares as long as people like watching them?"

"I do." As soon as those two little words fall out of my mouth I realize that they're the fundamental truth to both the person that's been buried under the layers of a worker bee trying to hold onto a career, and the inspired person I aspire to be.

It's finally my time to turn off the GPS that was programmed into me and take a sharp right turn.

Rachel shakes her head. "Well, I'm sorry to lose you. I just hope you know what you're doing."

"I do. Frankly, I want to be proud of what I do, not embarrassed by it."

A hard look falls over Rachel's face as she squints and her mouth purses. "Well, I guess that's it then."

I get up, walk to the door, and pause before I turn around.

"I know now that you guys knew from the start what you were going to do with this show, didn't you. You used me to lure Will in. I overhead a conversation in Massachusetts about how you purposely kept me in the dark so I'd get Will fully on board for the shoot. The plan all along was to make him look like a freak. Wasn't it?" The fury fires in me as I wait for her answer.

"Is that the real reason you're quitting?" Rachel asks, folding her arms over her chest. She doesn't even dispute it.

I consider the question and then nod. "It's part of it. Why would I stay? I'm mad at myself for being so gullible. Believe me, it won't happen again."

I square my shoulders, and for the first time I feel taller than her. Rachel looks uneasy, and it makes me wonder how she lives with herself.

"What you guys did was unethical and despicable. You have no regard for the results of your actions or how it affected Will personally or professionally. You think I only care because of my feelings for him, but you're wrong. I care because it's the right thing, and you should care too."

As I walk down the hallway, out the front door of True Blue Entertainment and to my car, the layers of disappointment in myself peel off and drop away until I am light as air. One strong gust would surely toss me into the sky where I could finally test my wings and fly.

Maybe I'll soar, I say to myself, smiling. All I have to do now is figure out how.

When I get home, I flip open my laptop and book of contacts. I scoot in my chair and get right to work, starting from the very beginning all over again.

As I update my resume, and send out e-mails, I'm finally able to think of Will with a thought other than loss.

I bet he'd be proud of me. That very idea gives me hope and inspires me. Later that night I curl up on my couch with pen and paper and imagine what I would say if Will were sitting here next to me. A wave of emotion washes over me. As soon as I press the tip of the pen onto the paper, it takes off as my heart pours out across the pages.

Dear Will,

I'm writing this letter knowing you may never read it. I would understand if you set it on fire and let the ashes blow off into the wind. But if you read it or not, I need to put these words into the universe in the hopes that one day they will find their way into your heart.

If nothing else I can't live with the idea that your last memory of me is such a disappointing one. As I got to know the man that you are, my respect for you grew and took shape until you were larger than life to me. Now my greatest wish is that I can be a person that you'd respect with equal measure. Even if I never see you again, I want to be a woman that deserves a man like you.

With this in mind I'm starting over, starting from scratch with not just my job, but my dreams, and I'm willing to do whatever it takes to finally get on the right road. I've been blind, dazzled by a career that felt successful, yet had no soul. It took this experience with you to make me see that... to make me realize how far off my course I had wandered. My eyes are wide open now and I know what I have to do and the sacrifices I must make. Thank you for showing me the way.

You are an amazing man, Will. Thank you for loving me.

The time I spent with you, however short, made me believe in love again. I used to be seduced by the writing of Byron as he spun gold thread around words of love. I had romantic ideals of who the man would be that I would one day completely give my heart to. Yet every man I met fell short of my dreams. And then I met you....loving, generous, warm-hearted, insightful, creative, beautiful...you.

You were, and are, the real deal. You loved me whole, seeing beauty in even my bruises and imperfections. You accepted my flaws while nudging me toward a brighter light. It took only the most egregious emotional betrayal for you to finally walk away from us. You deserved more.

I may accept my penance for not protecting you, but know that I will never stop loving you. I ache for what I've lost. I dream at night of being in your arms. I have fantasies that one day we will talk again and I'll see that smile, and hear the joy in your voice that always lifted my spirits.

As long as my heart beats, I can't end this letter…I will keep writing it and sending it across the currents and winds that move between us. Know my love is always there.

Sophia

Chapter Twenty-Eight

The following Saturday I sit in my car, gripping the steering wheel. I debate turning over the ignition again and bailing, maybe coming back another day when I feel less raw and vulnerable.

All week I have been focused like a laser on starting over with everything, and it's given me a false sense of courage to face Will. Maybe quitting my job and giving notice on my apartment was enough for one week. I can always come back another time. But will I?

From this distance, even without the Christmas decorations, Will's house looks like a fantastical oversized dollhouse. I wonder how I'll feel if Will isn't home. I also wonder how I'll feel if he is. I reach over and run my fingers across the fine linen envelope and gift box sitting on the seat next to me.

Damn girl, just do it. I push open my car door, gather the package and letter, and step out.

I slowly walk across the street and up his walkway. I notice the burned patch of lawn where the gingerbread house once stood. Other than that, there's no trace of Christmas outside and it's the first week of December. I take a deep breath and press the doorbell. I can feel my blood pressure pulsating in my temples like my head's going to explode.

Please answer, please answer, I repeat like a prayer.

Unfortunately a girl, wearing provocatively form fitting clothes opens the door and stares for a moment before pointing at me like an accuser.

"Hey, you're that girl," she says.

"Sophia," I respond, squinting. Recognition finally hits me square in the forehead.

"And you're Liza from the sorority. What are you doing here?" I ask, not caring how ballsy I sound.

"Well, thanks to you and that stupid show, Will has us taking down all the Christmas stuff. He said he wants it to look like it was never here." She makes a pouty face. "Think of the kids that will miss out."

I have to stand silently for a minute to process everything. *Taking down all the Christmas stuff? There you go.* Of course, he's taking it all down. He probably hates Christmas now... all thanks to my fabulous efforts.

My brain sizzles, and I feel as if my hair is on fire. I almost turn and sprint down the walkway but really wouldn't want Liza to report it back to the rest of the nubile college co-eds in Will's house. I'm not going to make it any easier for them than I already have.

"Speaking of Will, can you go tell him I'm here and would like to speak to him?"

Liza locks her hip to one side and rests her fist on her jutting hip. "I don't think—"

"Did the doorbell ring?" Will says, pulling the door open. When he sees me, he freezes for a moment. He glances over at Liza. She's still engaged me in a silent standoff with me.

I'm on the verge of tears and swallow hard to keep them at bay. He may not be ready to see me but he has to give me credit for being brave enough to come.

He studies my face and then turns to Liza. "Hey, Steph's looking for you."

She doesn't move and keeps staring at me.

"Liza," he says firmly, getting her attention. "Please go see Steph."

She huffs and marches inside after glaring at me one last time.

Will nods in the direction Liza just exited in. "Sorry about that."

His apology flusters me. "Yeah, I wasn't really expecting her to open the door."

"And I wasn't expecting you to come by," he says, seeming more distant than I'd hoped.

"Yeah, I thought about calling first, but I wasn't sure you'd answer."

He lifts his eyebrows but doesn't dispute my comment.

"So how are you doing?" I ask.

He tilts his head to the side and looks down. "I was wrecked after I saw the show. It was so much worse than I thought it would be. After it aired things got so bad at work and people contacting me that I had to take time off and shut down. Since then, some days are better than others."

I wasn't expecting so much brutal honestly. For a moment I feel as if I can't breathe.

"And you?" He looks back up again and our eyes meet. His are the same blue as the sky.

"Same. Your young friend said you're taking down all of Christmas."

He shrugs. "Yeah, that's true."

"And she said it was thanks to me and the show." I bite my bottom lip to keep it from wobbling.

He lifts up one brow. "Did she now? She's a provocative one, isn't she?"

We study each other but the little doors behind our stares are still firmly closed.

"Well, it makes me sad to hear that," I finally say softly.

He scratches his head. "What did Gramps say? 'The only constant is change.'"

"So it was time for a really big change?"

"Guess so."

I'm still undecided about giving him what I brought, but then gather my courage and hold my hand out. I offer him the small box with the envelope taped to the top.

"Well, now knowing that, you may not want this but I hope you read the letter. I put a lot of thought into it."

"Okay," he says, hesitating for a moment, but taking the package anyway.

I stare at his strong arms while they're close to me. I'd give anything to have them wrapped around me again.

My heart is slowly sinking. It's now probably somewhere between my knees and my ankles. He hasn't been mean, so that's progress. But he hasn't given me a single reason to hold out hope.

I blink back a determined tear and study my feet as I try to pull myself together.

"Well, okay. It was good to see you. Maybe—"

"Yeah, I'm glad to know you're doing okay," he adds quickly.

I feel the sting of his cutoff acutely.

"Take care," I say and turn quickly on my heel. I exhale and rush down the stairs and fumble for my car keys as I briskly walk to my car. I feel like a soft cantaloupe that has had the fruit slowly scooped by dragging the sharp edge of the spoon too close to the skin.

I start my car and make it at least two blocks away before I pull over. I lean over my steering wheel while my shattered heart spills out. I realize that unlike Humpty Dumpty, the biggest loser in nursery rhyme history, I don't have all the king's horses and king's men to help with the fallout.

Besides, just like me, the egg was doomed from the start. I'm pretty sure on my own I'll never be able to put all the pieces back together again.

Chapter Twenty-Nine

"You're one brave girl," Steph says, taking a sip of her cappuccino. Thankfully the coffee shop is almost empty. I don't feel like being around that many people right now.

"Brave? Why do you say that?" I ask, stirring my iced tea absentmindedly as I search my mind for any examples of bravery.

"To just show up at his house and face Will like you did... I know how angry he's been."

"Yeah, he wasn't really happy to see me." The edges of my mouth quiver and that hollowed out feeling comes back.

"I'm not sure if you knew, but I was helping with the tear down that day. I didn't find out that you'd shown up until you were already gone."

"I didn't know you were there, but I honestly wasn't in the mood to chat after he was done talking with me. It's better we catch up here."

"When Will told me you had come by, I told him how shocked everyone was when you quit your job and walked out of the studio." Her face turns red and she bites the tip of her index finger. "I assumed you had told him. So when I found out he didn't know—that you hadn't told him—I felt horrible."

"Don't feel bad. I'm sure it didn't matter to him anyway." I shrug and look up to see her response, silently hoping I'm wrong about Will not caring.

"Oh, he cared. He asked me all about it. I told him that you'd found out they had lied and used you to get him on the show. I also told him that throughout the production, they kept you at arm's length so you'd have limited knowledge and power over how the shoot was supposed to go."

"I still can't believe that they did that to me." I shake my head in disgust.

"They're such assholes," Steph agrees. "I also told Will that I'd heard from Rachel's secretary that when you quit, you read Rachel the riot act before walking out."

I grin, remembering the satisfaction of finally telling Rachel what I really thought.

"That made Will smile."

"I'm glad. Did he say anything else?" I ask, still grinning as I picture a happy Will in my mind.

"He asked if you were looking for a job. I told him that I heard you were looking for real documentary work."

It makes me happy that he knows about my career change. "How did he react?"

"Surprised at first, but then he looked impressed or kind of proud or something. And before I forget, what was in that box you gave him?"

"Did he open it?" I ask, biting my bottom lip.

"No, but he said he was going to."

"I wrote him a letter, and there was a special snow globe in the box."

Steph gives me a sympathetic smile and reaches over to give my shoulder a squeeze.

"He'll come around, Sophia."

"I wish I could believe that Steph. I really do." I look down, running my fingertips along the grain in the wood of the tabletop before looking back up at her. "So enough about me. How are you? How's work?"

"Some old, same old. I'm going to try to follow in your footsteps and get out of this reality show racket. I heard there's a new health-related channel opening up, and they're looking for people." She folds her arms over her chest.

"Cool. Good luck with that."

She suddenly bops in her chair and grins. "I almost forgot to tell you! Guess what news made Lindsey dance around the studio and howl like a sick cat yesterday?"

"I have no idea," I say, cringing at the disturbing visual.

"She found out that Darrell, the crazy dude who hurt Romeo and tried to burn down Will's place, has been sentenced. You know the three strikes law? Well this was his third strike. He's out!" She grins and gestures, pointing her thumb over her shoulder. Meanwhile, the landlord of the house they were renting found out about the arson charge and evicted them. Will discovered that the house is on the market and some renovating flipper is looking at it."

"That's awesome news. First the charges against Will from that night got dropped, and now this. I'm so glad. I can't imagine still having to deal with them as neighbors after what they did to him."

"Me too. Now all we need to make things perfect is for you two to get back together."

I sigh and rest my chin on my hand. "If only it were that easy. I wonder if he ever read my letter."

"I don't know, but I'll find out. Meanwhile don't give up hope." She lifts up her cappuccino. "Here's to the power of love."

"The power of love," I whisper as I lift my glass to hers. I think about my letter and the fact that Will was happy to hear I've taken steps to improve my life.

Steph lifts her cup even higher. "May love win out over all."

Chapter Thirty

I jump every time my phone rings, hoping it's Will calling. So, when he finally does, I almost don't believe it's him.

"Hi, Sophia, I wanted to thank you for your letter," he says, and I close my eyes, enjoying the sound of his voice again.

"I wasn't sure you'd read it." I tighten my grip on the phone.

"Yes, I've read it… more than once, actually." His tone is warm and I soak it in. It's been a while since he's treated me so tenderly.

My heart skips. "How many times have you read it?" I ask quietly.

"I've lost count. I carry it around in my back pocket."

I love that he's brave enough to be so honest. "I hope you realize that I meant every word."

"I could tell. You've got really pretty handwriting, you know?"

"So that's it. You like my handwriting?" I laugh.

"Well, more than just that. I liked all of it, and I want to tell you in person what it meant to me. I need to see you and was thinking we could meet for coffee and talk."

I grab hold of the edge of the desk to steady myself and sit down. "I'd like that," I say softly, trying not to get emotional because he wants to see me.

"I get off work early tomorrow, so I was thinking we could meet at that café we first met at. Say at four tomorrow? That is, if you're free."

"I'm free," I say without any hesitation.

He lets out a deep breath. "Great. I can't wait to see you then."

I give myself a pep talk before walking through the café doors. Even though I'm trembling inside, I remember how encouraging he sounded on the phone. I scan the café, looking for Will. When I spot him, he's already looking at me, his eyes lighting up when we connect. For me he's a match struck in a dark room. I feel his flame burning as I approach him.

He stands and pulls my chair out for me.

"Thanks," I say, scooting mine closer to the table and hanging my purse over the chair back. I cross my legs and fold my hands nervously in my lap.

"It's good to see you. Well, you know… when you want to see me," I say, anxiously.

"I do," he says, leaning toward me with a charged energy. He smiles as he studies me.

I squirm like a kid waiting to get on a theme park ride. He's making my heart do loop de loops.

We stare at each other silently. It's as if now that we're finally here we don't know where to start.

"I got this for you," he finally says, pushing a passion fruit iced tea toward me.

"Thanks." I smile and take a sip, remembering that I ordered this the first time we met.

He looks down and stirs his coffee. "So, I heard you quit."

I nod. "I sure did. Steph told me she shared that with you."

"And you're giving up your apartment?"

"Yeah, that's kind of tough, but I'm being proactive since my salary is going to be much lower moving forward."

"Are you moving out of L.A.?" His eyebrows rise and his mouth twists like he's worried about me leaving.

"Not unless I have to. I'd rather stay." The meaning behind my words falls heavy between us.

He takes a deep breath and nods.

"Would *you* rather I stay?" I ask.

He scrutinizes me intently and his eyes look sad. I'm on pins and needles waiting for his reply.

"I'd much rather you stay."

My heart skips and I close my eyes as his words sink in. *He wants me to stay.*

He clears his throat and when he speaks his voice sounds strained. "What can I do to help so you don't have to leave? Whatever you need...."

I sit up straighter trying to compose myself. "Thank you. Actually I had a promising interview this week. The bad news is there's a lot of travel, but the good news is that it's L.A. based."

"Tell me about it," he says.

"It's with this guy, James Ray. He's a documentary filmmaker... amazing stuff. I'd be in heaven working with him."

Will's hands tighten over his coffee cup and a muscle in his jaw twitches. "Heaven? That's a pretty big word. I bet he was quite taken with you too."

I nod excitedly. "I think he was. Our talk went an hour over what we'd planned."

Will stares out the window with knitted brows and his hands curled into fists. I can't tell if he's angry or confused but I don't like that something has shifted.

I narrow my eyes as I watch him. His expression changes again and his shoulders slump just a little. *Is he jealous of James?* I clear my throat and he glances at me.

"Did I mention James is gay?" I ask demurely.

He tries to hold back the smile. "No, you neglected to mention that."

I take a deep breath and tighten my hands over my knees. "Will, don't you understand that I'm still completely in love with you?" I lean toward him.

He smiles and looks down. When he looks back up, his gaze is full of blinding intensity.

"Yes, the letter that I read over and over... the one I carry everywhere in my back pocket? That letter pretty much made your feelings clear."

I relax my hands and give him a brave smile. "Good. I need you to be sure. I don't want to waste time and muddle around anymore. I may never be able to make up for my dimwittedness in the face of something so precious that you trusted me with, but I'll never stop trying. If you give me another chance, even if we're just friends, I want the opportunity to show you the kind of woman I can be."

"Damn, Sophia," he says, dragging his fingers through his hair.

"What? Too much?" I ask, worried I've overwhelmed him.

He runs his tongue over his perfect lips. The lips I desperately want to kiss.

"No, not too much. Actually you're just right." He gazes at me wide-eyed and sincere.

"This is in your hands, Will… my heart, everything. If it were up to me, I'd be in your lap right now kissing you senseless. But I'm restraining myself because this is all up to you."

"I see." He leans forward and watches me with his chin cupped in his hand and his elbow squarely on the table. "First let me say that nothing would make me happier than you in my lap right now, but I'd be the one kissing you senseless."

I blink and lean back in my chair. I'm pretty sure he can hear my heart skipping. Just the way he's looking at me is making me swoon.

He straightens up. "I almost forgot." He reaches over to the chair next to him, sets a small bakery box on the table, and pushes it toward me.

"Is this what I think it is? You once told me you got turned on watching me eat one."

He smiles. "I did."

I feel encouraged and look up at him adoringly. Just the idea of being in his bed again causes a blush of watercolor pinks to move up my chest and across my cheeks.

He looks at my neck and then up to my lips, which part just enough to put a satisfied smile on his face.

I pull open the box and admire the macaroons nestled in the wax paper. I lift one out and run my tongue along its edge.

"Damn," he says darkly as he studies me.

"So good," I whisper.

He silently watches me nibble away at the delectable morsel, slowly licking my fingers when it's gone.

"So, I was thinking…" He pauses, watching me pull my index finger out from between my lips.

"Yes?"

He suddenly looks very serious like a cloud is moving over us. I realize I can't taste the macaroon's sweetness anymore.

"Well, I've been thinking about how selfish I've been. I was so blinded by my anger over the show that I couldn't see how devastated you also were by what happened. It took me a while to realize how you must have felt, knowing you'd made me promises with the production while not understanding that you were a pawn in their scheme. You're a proud woman, Sophia. It's horrible what they did to you."

"It is, and I am proud," I agree. "All of this has been so humiliating but I've learned a lot from it."

"As have I. We were both in over our heads and just couldn't see it. As a consequence we both made mistakes that can't be changed. But together we can take what we've learned and start over."

"Do you mean the two of us start over? Like a do-over?" I ask, my eyes wide with hope.

"We can't erase the past but we can start fresh and start over. I could take you on a date, and this time it would be about getting close again without all that junk from the show to deal with."

"Just us? Is that why you had us meet here?" I ask with a happy smile.

He grins. "Yeah. I'm so damn clever, aren't I?"

"So clever," I agree.

He slides his hand across the table and reaches for me. As I slide mine into his I look up, realizing this is a big moment, like the pause on an award show when the envelope is carefully peeled open. I get the sense that my name will be called as a winner after all.

I squeeze his hand and take a deep breath as he speaks up.

"Actually I don't want to be clever, Sophia. I want to be straight with you like you were with me. Your letter broke my heart and put it back together again. It was the bravest, most loving gesture anyone has ever given me. Every time I read it, another layer of anger or disappointment disappeared. All that's left is this great big love I have for you."

I gasp and look up at him. "Big?"

He nods with a sweet smile. "Huge. Gigantic. Earth shattering."

"Wow. You aren't just teasing me?"

"My heart is yours, Sophia. Like you said in your letter, let's just keep writing this story. Let's never let it end."

I press my fingers together to keep them from trembling as I wipe the happy tears off my cheeks. The biggest smile starts inside of me and works its way to my face.

"So with that in mind, are you free tomorrow night?" he asks.

I feel giddy like the sun is breaking through the clouds and bright flowers are popping open like popcorn kernels in a hot kettle. Meanwhile all the little creatures gather to celebrate new beginnings. I can almost hear their tiny, high voices blending in harmony.

"Sophia?"

"What?" I snap out of my happy dreamland.

"Can I take you on a date tomorrow night?"

"Yes, please," I say with a grin.

He lifts up our hands and pulls me out of my chair and onto his lap. Every emotion I have is a jumbled blend of joy, passion, thrill, and relief. I don't even know what to feel at first so I lean into him and brush my lips along his jaw.

"I've missed you so much," I whisper.

"Oh, Sophia." He sighs before cupping my face in his hands and gently brushing his thumbs over my cheeks. He gazes at me with a warm expression, leans closer, and kisses me. Each following kiss is more loving than the last, and soon I'm a swoony puddle barely able to keep from sliding off his lap. I rejoice knowing this is the first forever kiss, because I will never ever let this man go and, I suspect, he will never let me go either.

When we finally part to catch a breath, his cheeks are red and his eyes bright, the most thrilled I've ever seen him.

"I'm so happy, Will." My heart's so light I feel as if I'm floating. I finally allow myself to imagine what the future can be and I'm sure this time we can be a better version of what we were.

He smiles and pulls me closer. Taking my hand, he kisses it as if he's sealing the deal.

"Me too."

Chapter Thirty-One
One Year Later...

Will leans over the back of the truck and unties the rope keeping the large spruce tree from sliding out the truck bed. He rolls his eyes and grins as I pull on my heavy gardening gloves. I look at the new building painted in a sunny yellow. The sign reads Center City Family Shelter.

I lean my face into the spruce with my eyes closed. The sweet whiff of evergreen brings back memories from my childhood when the whole family would head to the lot to pick out our tree. "Ah, nothing better than the smell of a fresh Christmas tree."

He takes a whiff himself before pulling off the last of the rope. "You sure you don't want me to get Hank to help us carry this inside?" he asks.

"What, you don't think I'm macho enough?" I flex my arms and wink at him.

"There's nothing macho about you, which is fine by me." He winks back.

He steps to the entrance of the shelter and rings the buzzer. The person that mans the evening desk props the doors open for us as we struggle to get the monster of a tree inside. Hank meets up with us in the main hall.

"What are you doing, Sophia?" he asks, stepping up and taking my end of the tree. Even though I'm doing okay, I decide not to fight him. Hank is always such a gentleman. As he and Will proceed, he nods toward the large family room. "Everyone's so excited you're bringing this tree. The kids have been making decorations all week."

My heart is full as Hank and Will set the tree upright and several kids run over.

A little boy named Chris turns to his mother and yells excitedly, "Look, Momma, a real tree." She smiles and joins him to stroke the branches where the needles are still soft.

While the men string the lights, Judy, the director, shows me the various art projects that have been lovingly worked on in preparation for tonight. Popcorn has been strung on string and dusted with glitter, paper chains have been looped together, and the handmade ornaments using pipe cleaners, beads, and colored craft paper are proudly lined up and ready to be hung.

"Which ones did you guys make?" I ask Chris and Shauna, Chris's sister who's joined him. They each hold up one for me to examine.

"I made a bunch, but this one's my favorite," Chris says standing tall and pointing out all the special details he added to his dog wearing a Santa hat ornament.

I compliment them both on their great work.

"How's it working out having the village in here?" Will asks Hank.

"Much better. Remember last year we had to put it up high behind the check-in desk so the kids wouldn't keep playing with and breaking the little ceramic figures?" Hank asks.

"Yeah, this is so much nicer. I'm so glad I spotted that oversized Lucite display case at the studio. Now they can enjoy it and walk around it with no worries."

A little girl with red hair runs up to Hank and tugs on his jacket. "Can you please turn on the trains, Hank?"

"Sure, Angela. Would you like to be conductor and turn on the switch?" She claps her hands and runs over to the village display.

I step next to Will and take his hand. He squeezes mine and kisses me on the top of my head. A feeling of contentment washes over me, one of those amazing moments when everything feels perfectly right.

After decorating, cocoa and singing Christmas songs, we say good night to everyone and Hank walks us out to our truck.

"Hey, Sophia, I found another family for your documentary. It's a sad story, but if I ever meet a woman who's going to pull herself out of her situation, it's this woman, Theota. She has a will of iron."

"That's great, Hank. Please tell her I'll check in and see if there's a time we can meet next week. It looks like our grant is getting funded after all."

Will wraps his arm around my shoulder and pulls me closer. "Isn't she amazing, Hank?"

He grins. "She sure is. And he's your biggest fan, Sophia."

"I know." I look up at Will with a smile.

"Say, did I tell you guys that they moved me up to the room on the top floor? It's so quiet up there."

"You told us they'd talked to you about it. So you have your own kitchen now?" I ask, proud of Hank. After he helped Will move some of his Christmas stuff to the shelter last year, the director was so impressed with Hank that she gave him all kinds of odd jobs. Eventually she asked him to join the staff and as part of his pay, he got housing.

"My own kitchen and a bigger living space. But honestly I haven't used the kitchen much. I like eating with Lisa. She's such a good woman," he says, his eyes twinkling.

"And from what I hear a great cook." Will teases him.

We say our good-nights and head home, feeling the warm satisfaction of knowing we put some smiles on the kids' faces.

We let Romeo out in the yard and sit on the deck hand-in-hand.

"I'm happy to see Hank looking so settled," I say as Romeo runs off to chase some critter in the yard.

Will sighs. "I've never seen him this content. He's broken the cycle of being homeless and I'm really proud of him."

"You know it happened because of you."

"No. He may have met the group at the shelter when he helped me set up the village and train set I donated last year, but the rest is all Hank. He's a good man."

I reflect on the year we've had. There have been setbacks and disappointments but wonderful things, too. I look at Will, and my heart swells, knowing our love has grown deeper than I knew was possible. I trace the bottom of his tattoo on his arm, my fingertip outlining the roots of the oak tree.

He looks down. "The tree's roots keep me steady," he says, watching with a tender expression. "Like you, Sophia."

"As you do for me." I feel the goose bumps on his skin. "You must be getting cold. Let's go inside and do something Christmasy of our very own."

"Like what? The house is pretty low-key now as far as Christmas goes."

"Hey, I love our little tree and homemade stockings on the mantle."

He laughs and squeezes my hand. "I do too."

"I know—we could shake up our snow globe. The one I gave you to win you back last year." I smile remembering the first time I realized Will had placed the snow globe front and center on his mantle.

"Okay. And then let's head upstairs and find other ways to celebrate."

He calls Romeo, and we head into the house. "So, do you ever miss that I'm not your big deal Mr. Christmas anymore?"

I look at him with wide eyes before wrapping my arms around him. "You're so much more than that, Will. You're everything I ever wanted, wonderful in every way."

His smile shines bright, warming both of us in its glow. "That's right—I always wanted to be so much more than your Mr. Christmas, Sophia. I'm completely yours and always will be, three hundred sixty-five days a year."

Acknowledgements

Thanks to my daughter, Alex for both supporting and tolerating a mother who talks far too much about fictional characters. I've passed on to you my excessive tendencies when it comes to holidays, and you've given me quite the fodder with your reality show fascination. We make a fine pair.

Big love to my sister Cheri, and dear friends Lisa and Judy who read early drafts of this story and asked all the right questions for me to go back in and make it better.

Huge thanks and hallelujahs to Angela Borda, Aviva Layton and Janine Savage: editors, drill sergeants, and delightful cheerleaders. You pushed me hard and I loved every minute of it. Will and Sophia thank you too.

Unending gratitude and a few ironic eye-rolls to David Johnston whose cover photography elevated my crazy ideas into something I'm really proud of. Your amazing talent and kindness are appreciated, while your wacky YouTube links and emails keep me grounded.

Jada D'Lee: uber designer, goddess and supportive girlfriend de-luxe…I'm so lucky to have you in my life. Thank you for all that you do.

Every Skype emoticon of love to my Lost Girls, Erika, Susi and Dawn. You've put up with endless babbling from me about a boy who loves Christmas. Your support and love has helped get me through a very challenging year.

Thank you Flavia for loving my words and taking them to the Frankfurt Book Fair. (I got giddy just writing that.) You're classy, smart and kind—someone I'm proud to work with. The future looks bright.

A big hug to my virtual friends around the world who have become dear real life friends…Azu, Laura, Jenn, Suzie, Mary, Liv, Irene, Elli, Sonia, Roberta, Jack, Erik, Michael, Christina, Kathy….I'd keep listing names but I'm terrified to leave anyone out. You guys have colored this crazy fic world in the most brilliant hues for me. I'm so grateful for your support and I'm proud to know and admire each and every one of you.

Last but very far from least....to the readers, reviewers, bloggers, Tweeters, and fic promoters....I wouldn't be here without you. I'm honored that you've welcomed my characters into your busy lives, and held them in your hearts. You have my gratitude and unending devotion.

Thank you one and all.

About the Author

Ruth Clampett, daughter of legendary animation director, Bob Clampett, has spent a lifetime surrounded by art and animation. A graduate of Art Center College of Design, her careers have included graphic design, photography, VP of Design for WB Stores and teaching photography at UCLA. She now runs her own studio as the fine art publisher for Warner Bros. where she's had the opportunity to know and work with many of the greatest artists in the world of animation and comics.

Mr. 365 is Ruth's second novel and is inspired by her varied experiences in the television world from winning big on a game show, to guest hosting on the QVC shopping network, to sharing a studio with a production team that produced early reality television. Her first novel, *Animate Me*, is a contemporary romance set in the animation world. She lives in Los Angeles and is heavily supervised by her teenage daughter, lovingly referred to as Snarky, who helps her plan and execute their yearly Christmas extravaganza.

Connect with Ruth:
RuthClampettWrites.com
https://twitter.com/RuthyWrites
https://www.facebook.com/RuthClampettWrites
http://www.goodreads.com

Made in the USA
Middletown, DE
11 June 2016